BEST

Gay

LOVE
STORIES

New
York
City

BEST

Gay

LOVE
STORIES

New
York
City

edited by

BRAD NICHOLS

alyson books
NEW YORK

Printed in the United States of America.

This trade paperback original is published by Alyson Books,
P.O. Box 1253, Old Chelsea Station, New York, New York 10113-1251.
Distribution in the United Kingdom by Turnaround Publisher Services Ltd.,
Unit 3, Olympia Trading Estate, Coburg Road, Wood Green,
London N22 6TZ England.

ISBN-13: 978-0-7394-7255-2

CONTENTS

INTRODUCTION

THERE'S SOMETHING ABOUT New York City. The excitement you feel walking its bustling sidewalks. The adrenaline rush you get when you find that perfect apartment, or job, or meet a new friend. The memory of when you first arrived. The anticipation of achieving great success.

There's also something about falling in love. The excitement you feel when walking hand in hand with that someone special. The adrenaline rush you get when you lock eyes. The memory of that first kiss, urgent and hungry. The anticipation of that tender embrace at the end of the night.

So, what better combination could there be than falling in love in New York City? In this year's edition of *Best Gay Love Stories*, I wanted to showcase not just the many facets of a great city, but also the many facets of love. First love, lost love, unrequited love, lasting love. And in these 24 stories, you get all that and more. Join some of our favorite writers, like Simon Sheppard, Shane Allison, Jay Starre, and many others, as they take Manhattan…and sprinkle it with the power of love.

Take a journey to the Big Apple and see love take a big bite out of it.

Enjoy.

—*Brad Nichols*

GOOMBAH

GREGORY L. NORRIS

JOEY SOMETHING-ITALIAN WAS part of *that* crowd, the guys in high school who made playing sports and bullying any guy who didn't their reason for breathing. He never slammed me against a locker, never flattened the back of one of my sneakers with the toes of his after stalking right up to me and stepping on my heel, hard enough to crush leather and scrape layers of skin off the bony part of my ankle, like some of them did. But once, when our paths crossed in the English Hall our sophomore year, he earned his wings with the rest of the Goombahs by punching Old Vincent, my beat up leather valise, out of my hands while I struggled to fit papers and art supplies into its open mouth.

That well-traveled soul, first my grandfather's, then my ma's, finally passing to me when I turned fifteen—the same year I renounced doodling on stray scraps of paper for drawing in real composition books—shot out of my hands and across the crowded corridor. It had snowed that morning. A skin of slushy, muddy footprints covered the floor. I wasn't one of the popular kids, so of course just about everyone who witnessed my humiliation doubled over laughing.

I scurried through the hostile crowd to retrieve the valise and the papers and pens and the box of crayons that spilled

1

out of its gaping maw. Joey Something-Italian had punched Grampa Wally's artist's travel bag right in the soft spot of its guts, making it regurgitate most of its stomach's contents. The crowd transformed into one gray-skinned colony creature, an entity with multiple heads and dozens of legs, a cackling, malevolent hydra. I struggled to reclaim my fountain pen, my English homework, and several sketches unlucky enough to have pulled loose from a pad that was being stomped by a dozen marching centipede legs, the prints from muddy shoes permanently tattooing its clean, white hide.

I managed to get hold of most of it, all but the crayons, which I abandoned, too embarrassed to claim them as my own. The box spilled its dozen basic colors, each one worn halfway down its unraveling paper skin except for the copper crayon. Their spines crunched and snapped under heartless heels, and as I hunched on my knees, fuming, Joey Something-Italian strutted past me, a wide, white smile beaming above his square jaw.

Joey's photogenic face went on a parade. He'd never suffered acne to the extent most of us did, something I couldn't help noticing as he towered above me. He pumped his fist and hooted, as if he'd just scored a game-winning touchdown and my valise had been the football. One of the Goombahs clapped him on the back, and then they passed by.

My humiliation came to an end. I picked up my stuff, wiped off the grit and the slush the best that I could, and moved on.

That day, Grampa's well-traveled valise added a few new scratches to its patchwork of craters. Joey Something-Italian put them there.

. . . . .

BENJAMIN CARDOZO HIGH, three years behind me, might as well have never existed. I wasn't one of those students who toed the party line. I didn't attend either of my proms. I didn't buy the class yearbook, so I never passed it around for people to fill with empty promises like: *You and Me, Friends 4-Ever* or *Math Club Will Never Divide*! And the last thing I wanted from Benjy-C was an ugly class ring, though I thought about buying one just to wear it on my middle finger.

Some people think high school is the apex of their lives, a big sweeping life-or-death costume drama of Broadway proportions. But by college, it just seems like bad local community theater, and you barely remember what the big deal was.

That said, I hadn't forgotten the incident in the English Hall because something like that— when you're the Christian who's being tossed to the hungry lions—stays with you forever. I only recognized Joey Something-Italian that afternoon because he was the Roman taskmaster who'd once paraded me through a bloodthirsty crowd. But I couldn't remember his last name—I didn't have that Benjy-C yearbook to reference.

So while Tina balanced our lunch trays on her lap, I wheeled her over to our favorite table with its view of the Atrium courtyard, I had little to go on. Just one bad memory and a brief flash of guilt, in knowing that more than once in the past, I'd probably jerked off thinking about him.

Now, he was only Joey Something-Italian to me, and he was prowling around the cafeteria at Queensborough Community College the same way he'd caroused with his fellow Goombahs back at Benjamin Cardozo High, terrorizing outcasts like me.

"What's wrong?" Tina asked. "You look like you've seen a ghost."

"I have. The Spirit of Assholes Past."

She followed my line of sight to the leather jacket standing near a misty cauldron of cauliflower soup and steam trays filled with zucchini medley, macaroni and cheese, and

3

Lyonnaise potatoes.

"You know him?"

"I used to."

"Hot," she said, fixing her glasses on the bridge of her nose.

I huffed a sarcastic grunt. "That Goombah whaled on me and Old Vincent back in high school." I unhooked the valise from my shoulder, set it on the table beside my tray, and gave it a loving stroke. Whatever interest I'd had in the salad and vegetables on my plate ended in a jolt of stomach acid. I briefly fiddled with my salad before pushing it away.

She was right; he did look hot. My eyes, which had never wandered far off target after recognizing him, pinned him in their sites. Leather jacket. Old denim, a pale shade of blue, belted, and riding low on his ass. Hiking boots, laced tight on big feet. My ankles would never survive a run-in with those shit-kickers.

His hair was shorter now, very neat in that kind of classic cut you see on professional athletes. Dark scruff of a short, trimmed goatee, what Tina likes to refer to as "chin fungus."

But that cocky smirk I so clearly remembered from our collision in the English hall was gone. This wasn't high school anymore—knock somebody around in the halls of a CUNY campus and you'd face more than a trip to the principal's office.

Tina, I noticed with a tilt of my head, had forsaken the hot Italiano for her soup and a textbook. When I looked back, Joey had made it to the registers and was paying out of a black leather wallet attached to a chain on his belt. I reached into Old Vincent and pulled out the plastic case containing artist's markers, forty-four colors of crayons, and my present sketchpad. But before I could draw anything beyond an angry red line, another of our friends arrived, turning our little duet into a lunch club of three.

"Ladies," said Cathy Swinley.

"Gentleman," I fired back. She smacked a kiss onto the top of my head. The smell of drawn butter and fried potatoes wafted down into my senses.

"You're too kind." She took a seat beside me. Cathy wore the understated blue uniform of the cafeteria staff, her mane of blonde hair pulled neatly behind her and held in place by a pair of fake jade chignon combs. "I can make you a doggy bag of leftover zucchini. Nobody's touching it. Carnivores."

"Thanks, but I've lost my appetite." I tipped my chin toward the registers. "Remember him?"

Cathy followed my direction, narrowed her pale blue eyes. "Well, well, if it isn't Low-Piano himself."

"Huh?"

"Joey Lopiano. *Low-Piano*. You remember."

Of course I did.

"What's a big man on campus like him doing in our little community college?"

"Who knows." I sighed. "Who cares?"

I caught a quiet ripple of black from the corners of my eyes, saw that Joey Low-Piano was cutting across the cafeteria in a line that would lead him for a close pass by our table, and found that I did care. Holding his tray in one hand, a textbook under the arm of the other, he strutted to within ten feet, all alone. No posse. No audience. He was even mumbling something to himself under his breath, pursing his perfect, sensuous lips when he looked up and saw me.

A glancing pass at first, his eyes quickly registered something, widened. It was, I imagined, like he'd seen a ghost as well.

He sat alone, all by his onesies, two tables over from ours.

What a comedown, I thought, for one of the former land barons, a real king of the turf of Benjamin Cardozo High.

Twenty minutes later, our circle of creative thinkers had swelled to five in all, including Janey and her boyfriend TJ. Joey, abandoned by his wingmen and left to talking to himself, ate his meal. Every so often, I felt the phantom tickle of prying eyes and knew I was being studied.

Mostly, I ignored it. But a few times, I fired back harsh stares only to deflect my gaze to my friends, when Joey's and my glances crossed paths. I'm normally not a vengeful guy, but I was that afternoon.

The extent of my revenge, however, was metered out as I sketched with the barely used crayons instead of my expensive artist's markers. It seemed poetic, given this reunion. My usually steady hand shook slightly, just enough to remind me that the body never truly forgets past traumas, and that this was how my hands used to tremble throughout high school.

When the fire alarm wailed without warning, smothering all conversations and laughter, my grasp on the crayon slipped, shooting a deep red gouge across the page. The pressure snapped the crayon's tip. I collected my stuff, shoved all of it into Old Vincent's protective leather belly, and tossed his strap around my neck. I then took hold of Tina's wheelchair by its handlebars. We started toward the nearest exit.

Beyond those doors, we often gathered in the open-air atrium to sketch on warm, sunny days, which this day wasn't. It was cold. It was snowing, just like that ugly day in high school. The irony struck me clearly as we exited the science building's first-floor cafeteria—trailing several paces behind our little club walked Joey Lopiano.

A blast of brisk November air cooled the heat on my cheeks and teased my spine into surrendering a shiver. Focused on the incongruity of the courtyard's pavement—I would have lived through my humiliation in the high school English Hall a hundred more times before allowing Tina to spill from her wheelchair—I caught snippets of conversation around us.

"Think they burned something back there in that ptomaine-trap you call a kitchen?" asked TJ.

"More likely, some stupid prick pulled the fire alarm, bitch-o-potamus," Cathy countered. "It's so high school."

"It's probably just a test," said Tina, but I don't think anyone except me heard her, and I was trying not to jostle her out of her chair, aware of the eyes drilling into the back of my denim jacket and the cadence of big feet in hiking boots marching at a close distance behind us.

We reached the circle of concrete under the trees we call the grotto—as in, 'Yeah, grab your sketchbook and meet me at the grotto.' I turned Tina's wheelchair around to face the science building we'd just evacuated, and in so doing, found myself facing Joey Lopiano directly. He soldiered up to us, looking tough, blowing on his bare fingers, the textbook still tucked under one arm. This time, when our eyes collided, Joey smiled a wide, dopey smile.

"Hey," he said.

I shot him a tip of my chin, that universal safe gesture between two guys. But as he moved closer, I confused the rush of nerves as being only that fight-or-flight jolt you get from adrenalin. It was that, but woven throughout was also a flush of attraction. He was handsomer than I remembered or would have admitted.

"A hell of a way to end lunch," he offered.

"Indeed." I was cold.

More blowing on his hands, he assumed the position with our very cool creative club of luminaries, as though he'd earned the right to be there. I felt Tina's eyes on me, replacing his. But I couldn't face her or any of them. My focus was locked upon him, drinking in the way he shuffled nervously in place, how he licked his lips. It struck me—he was more nervous than I!

Well, you should be, pal. Even if TJ couldn't take you down, and I bet he could, there are five of us, and only one of you now! I wanted to launch it at him, smack him in his handsome face with words the way he'd once punched the valise out of my hands.

But before I could talk myself into it, Joey Something-

Italian Low-Piano stopped blowing on his hands and looked me in the eyes. His lips moved a few times, however no words came out. He shrugged, shuffled.

"You're—" he started. Then he clamped his eyelids shut, swore under his breath.

"I'm what?" I said loudly. Now, everybody was watching us.

"You're really something," he answered dumbly, adding that dopey, handsome smile.

And whatever rage I'd felt about an incident from another time, another place, evaporated.

"No, I mean it. I was watching you, drawing back in there."

I briefly tipped my eyes down at Tina.

"Well, he is enrolled in the fine arts program, Jo-Jo," snapped Cathy. "Yeah, that's right, I went to high school with *youze guyz*. But what we can't figure out is what a gym-bo like you is doing here. Shouldn't you be, I dunno, at Yale or Brown playing football right now?"

Joey shifted in place, his eyebrows knitted together. "I only played sports in high school."

"That's not all he did," Tina snickered.

My heart galloped in my chest. "I've had enough of this trip down memory lane. Ta, my lovelies. You, too, Joseph."

The others offered a round of laters. I made sure Tina would be okay, she assured me she would be, and I started to cross the Atrium. I didn't get far when the stomp of boots on pavement behind me reached my ears. I didn't need to turn around to know who it was.

"Slow down, dude."

I sucked in a deep breath of the cold November air and dug in my heels. A practiced smile on my face, I revolved to see the others were still watching us, mostly out of a sense of the need to protect me, but also out of curiosity.

"What? What do you want?" I said in a low, threatening

voice. "You want to kick my ass again, like you did that one time in school? That's not gonna happen, man."

"No, I don't want to kick your ass. I want to say I'm sorry. Really sorry. What I did was so wrong. I'm sorry."

Joey extended his right hand, intending for me to shake it. I studied his fingers for a few seconds before accepting. They looked big, strong, and wonderful. But it was his eyes that finally convinced me. I had grown enough since high school to recognize their sincerity.

"Accepted," I said.

My smaller, thinner artist's hand vanished into his. Joey shook and I held on longer than expected, but I didn't mind, not one bit.

. . . . .

THE NEXT DAY, we were back at our table and Joey was again sitting alone, this time one row closer. We traded hasty glances. I watched him eat his soup the way all modern cavemen do, by gripping the handle of his soupspoon like a club. I also sensed his loneliness, how he had shuffled a little closer to us as though craving the safety of our numbers.

"Someone's got a boyfriend," TJ teased.

"Shut up."

"Oh, that big puppy dog has it bad for you." This came from Cathy.

I denounced her accusation, too. "Can I ask him to join us?"

"Sure," Tina said.

I took a heavy swallow to find my mouth had gone completely dry, then rose from my seat and forced my legs into motion. As I neared, there was no mistaking the way Joey's eyes lit. I moved to within a few feet of him.

"You want to eat with our club?"

Joey smiled. "Naw, I'm good."

"Okay." I started back.

"But I'd love it if you'd sit over here with me."

"To me, it's like there's art everywhere," he said. "Like, over there—"

Joey pointed at a kiosk covered in want ads, the train schedule, and signs for Broadway shows.

"Why that?"

He shrugged. "Because most of those ads are expired. The plays are probably closed, long gone. But every time I see one of those boards covered in ads, it reminds me of papier mache."

I snorted a laugh.

Joey's eyes widened and I fell into their pull. "What?"

"Nothing," I answered. "I just never imagined a guy like you would even know what papier mache is, let alone reference it in conversation."

"A guy like me? What's that supposed to mean?"

My smirk half-died. "Jock. Tough guy. Goombah."

Joey drew in a deep breath and just as deeply let it fly. The cold night air filled with the clean scent of the mint he'd popped into his mouth on the Q-27 bus, a million miles behind us back on Main Street. My memories of everything between there and here were blurry, too fresh, and provocative to be focused upon. I knew we'd left the campus together, headed into Flushing, but had taken the voyage in something of a daze.

"Yeah, I used to play football, but it wasn't my life."

"And art is?"

"Is it to you?"

"It sure is, but—"

"So it can't be that important to me is what you're saying?"

"I never saw you with a paintbrush in your hand in high school."

"Dude, that was a long time ago. And just coz you didn't see me drawing doesn't mean I wasn't drawing, or dreaming, or—"

It hit me then, that I was the one who hadn't evolved since that final clang of the last period bell released us from the prison of high school.

"Truth is, I'm in awe of you."

I shrugged.

"Look at you with your sketchpads and your spiky hair. You look like an artist. You're living the life. Hell, you're drawing with crayons, for chrissakes! That's fuckin' brilliant."

A rush of butterflies took flight in my stomach. "It's not that impressive."

"I think it is. I only wish I'd been able to be open about it sooner, like you had. I wish I hadn't wasted so much time. Maybe part of me was resentful, and that's why I did it."

I unhooked Old Vincent, briefly considered showing Joey the dings he'd forever etched into the valise's hide, but then thought better of it. I pulled out the artist's box and handed it over along with my sketchpad. "Why don't you give the crayons a try?"

Joey hesitated. Eventually, he accepted the case, but not the book. "Turn around."

"Why?"

"Trust me."

I slowly pivoted, caught the rustle of crayons being lifted and fondled with the care of fine brushes. His shadow was a tall, dark presence at my back, and for a moment, I struggled with my promise to trust him.

My doubts vanished when the warmth of his minty exhale teased my neck and I felt his hands upon my back. Joey started to draw on the right shoulder of my denim jacket.

"What are you doing?"

"Making art. Stand still."

Joey's fingers…

I leaned into his touch, into the soft point of the crayon, and found the rest of my flesh was reacting in icy-hot waves of pins and needles. Unconsciously, I tipped my head closer to his face. Our new nearness put his mouth mere inches from my right ear. Joey growled an appeased sigh.

"That better not say 'kick me.' " I joked.

"Trust me," Joey repeated.

And for no clear reason, I did.

As he traced little circles against my skin and touched me, I realized how gentle his hands were, artist's hands. My entire body felt electric, alive with energy.

When the Number 7 train pulled into the station, driving us apart, I hastily whipped off my denim jacket to see what he had drawn. It was a red crayon heart, perfectly drawn and wonderfully luminous.

. . . . .

A COLD, SNOWY November night whipped around us, but I barely felt its chill on the walk from the station to my apartment. The anticipation had my heart working double-duty. The cadence of its beats pounded in my ears.

"This is me," I said, indicating the two-story brick house. "You coming in?"

"Sure," Joey said, not making eye contact.

I started up the steps, aware of the tick-tock of my erection and dying for a drink of water, my insides on fire at the prospect of what would happen in the next few hours. But at the top step, I realized I was standing alone. Turning around, I saw Joey waiting on the sidewalk. I retraced my path to him.

"What's wrong?"

"I said I wanted to come in, but I'm not gonna," he said. "Because I want to so badly."

I shot Joey a look.

He reached for me, pulled me into a tight embrace. My confused senses filled with the clean, male scent of him: his leather jacket, his breath, the skin of his neck, his deodorant all combining into one magnificent smell. Not so confused, though, that I didn't feel the mighty fullness of his trapped dick, as it tackled mine the same way he'd once shoved guys down on the high school's football field.

"I want to," he growled into my ear. "You don't know how much."

I did though, judging from the firmness of his boner.

"But I don't want to screw this up. I don't want it to be instant. Real love don't work that way."

"Fine," I said. I didn't know whether to be flattered, annoyed, disappointed, or impressed. So I kissed the side of his face, a playful, flirty peck on the cheek.

As I started to pull away, Joey planted another full on my lips.

It was a kiss that left no room to doubt his sincerity. When we parted, I found myself wanting more than mere lust. I wanted his love, and for him to have mine.

"But I'd really like it if you'd let me walk you to the train tomorrow, walk you to school."

"Deal," I said.

We kissed again, and Joey walked me up to the front door.

THE AFTERNOON I
BELIEVED

JAY STARRE

IT WAS A glorious September morning. I was surprised by
that, in fact I was surprised by nearly everything that day.

I was in New York City. Under a cloudless blue sky with
the sun shining and a warm sea breeze blowing, the day so
far had defied my preconceived idea of what this intriguing
metropolis was all about.

I sat in an open square eating my lunch, feeling minuscule
beneath the heaven-scraping Twin Towers that rose and rose
above me like glass and steel cubicle mountains. A continent
away on the coast of British Columbia in my hometown,
Vancouver boasted skyscrapers of its own, and a skyline. But
New York City!

I was exhilarated, and I was a little bewildered. My behavior
only half an hour earlier had been strange, to say the least. I
was questioning that odd anxiety attack as I munched down a
New York City deli sandwich and gawked open-mouthed up
at those monumental towers.

I happened to glance away from that dwarfing sight and
found myself eye-to-eye with Aiden.

"With that look on your face, buddy, you've got to be a
tourist!"

I was so startled to have a complete stranger speak to me out of the blue, and an undeniably cute one at that, I gaped open-mouthed for just a moment longer, exactly like a tourist, before bursting out laughing. Aiden joined me, his head thrown back, and both of us actually howling out loud.

Because of its immense size, the square wasn't all that crowded. No one was very close and in a city of millions it was as if I had this amazing guy all to myself.

A funny, fun guy. A very hot guy.

Blue eyes, which squinted as he laughed, a big mouth with generous lips, sandy-brown hair neatly trimmed. An unusual soul patch of fair hair just below his plump lower lip that seemed at odds with the dress slacks and tie he wore that afternoon. Short sleeves revealed blond-furred forearms that were exceptionally well proportioned.

I took all that in as I gasped for breath while laughing hysterically

I could fall in love with this man. Yeah, right.

We were definitely flirting with each other, and neither of us missed the other's appraising body checks. His butt beneath those khaki brown slacks was firm. His belly was flat. I imagined his cock might even be hard. Mine was, which amazed me because I hadn't realized it until that moment. His free hand came out and I reached up to shake it. Introductions took a moment; he was Aiden, from New York City, and I was Jay from Vancouver, Canada.

He abruptly sat down beside me on the concrete bench I inhabited. A coffee and sandwich in hand, it was obvious he was on lunch break.

His thigh brushed against my bare knee. I wore shorts, perhaps another giveaway that I was a tourist. My cock got even harder.

"What were you thinking about when I came up to you? You looked so serious, even though your mouth was hanging wide open. You were staring up at the Towers like they were the pyramids of Egypt or something."

I didn't even hesitate to bare my soul. Something about him reassured me. His direct gaze. His laughter. His knee against mine.

"It was kind of stupid, actually. Half an hour ago, I was inside the lobby of that Tower over there, and trying to buy a cheap ticket for a play tonight. Suddenly, I didn't want to be in the building anymore. I remembered there had been a terrorist attack back in 1996 or around then, and I just felt really uncomfortable. Really, really uncomfortable. I had to get out of there. I couldn't run out quick enough. Weird, eh?"

"It's not that weird. A lot of us who work in the Towers remember that bombing. In fact, I don't think I'm going back to work now. Too scary."

His smile was teasing, but I realized he was serious. "You can't just do that, can you?"

"I shouldn't. But I've been doing a lot lately that I shouldn't. Let me show you New York City."

"Are all you Americans so bold?"

"Are all you Canadians such hunks?"

We were laughing again, so hard and so ridiculously out of control we both knew, without a doubt, we couldn't pass up the chance to spend some time together. It was fate.

Aiden and I chattered away nonstop while gulping down our respective lunches. He called in to work on his cell phone and made up an excuse. He had the afternoon off. I'd explained what I was up to, which was fairly simple. My first novel had just been published, and I was in New York to promote it.

"I've already hit three bookstores, but I want to go to three more I've got on my list before the day is out. Do you mind?"

"You're the tourist; it's your show. I can promise you there's lots to see, and much more than one afternoon's worth. I can't believe you'd come to New York for just one day."

We both burst out laughing again. I'd explained that my

buddy was a flight attendant and I'd flown with him on a pass, which meant I had to return with him the next morning. One day in New York City. But it was a free trip, and it was a hell of a lot better than nothing.

We walked, and walked. I was in awe at every single street and corner, and couldn't conceive of taking a cab or the subway now that I was in lower Manhattan for real and there was so much to experience.

Aiden didn't complain, merely commenting with a smirk, "You've got the legs for walking. Your calves are huge. Is your dick big too?"

"Big enough," I replied, flushing at the comment.

"You are shy."

"You aren't."

Aiden offered a confession of his own as we leaned out over a railing in Battery Park and gazed into the distance at the Statue of Liberty. His side touched mine, while one of his fingers trailed an electric line across my forearm resting on the railing.

"I'd love to fuck you. But I have a partner. It's not going well, though. It's really fucked, actually."

I flushed again. The finger stroked my arm; the voice was low and intimate while crowds swirled around us. The Statue of Liberty floated in a sun-kissed harbor, while we floated in a kind of vacuum of our own making.

"You don't love him anymore?" I asked, breathlessly. I prayed for the right answer.

"I still love him, tragically. He doesn't love me. I'm sure he wants to end it but he's too chicken-shit to admit it. Enough about that. You want to see the Brooklyn Bridge now?"

It wasn't the right answer. He was in love with someone else. He wasn't free to fall passionately in love with me and run away to Canada to be my partner for the rest of our lives.

The magic of the afternoon did not falter, even with that admission. His merry eyes belied the dark confession. He pulled me away and we headed for more adventures.

Outside the New York Stock Exchange I asked him to take my picture. "It's famous! All that money and power." I laughed as he shook his head sadly at my tourist aspirations but took the picture anyway. There, before that famous building, I was acutely aware of being in the center of a financial empire that was world spanning. All that power. Seemingly unassailable. Seemingly.

With the Brooklyn Bridge as a backdrop he obliged my photo needs again, then we headed north. "Greenwich Village. Gay bookstores. Gay men, all handsome as models, crawling the streets," I claimed with a broad grin.

He laughed and draped an arm over my shoulder for a brief moment. "We'll take our time. It's quite a walk. Besides, you've already got a New York gay man as handsome as a model strolling at your side."

He was handsome, but not in a classic sense. Not perfect enough, but more than perfect. I wanted to have sex with him, right now and all day long, fuck the bookstores and the only day I had in New York City to see it. I just wanted him in my arms. But he had a partner, even if they were having troubles. I wasn't a homewrecker. At least I didn't think so.

We walked and talked, stopped for coffee, watched the passers-by and talked some more. His knee pressed into mine when we sat. His side continually brushed mine as we walked. He touched me all the time. I pretended it was all foreplay and that before the day was over, we would be naked. Sucking and fucking our brains out.

The sexual tension only added to the exhilaration of my one-day magical journey through Manhattan. It was a long walk to Greenwich Village from the southern end of the island, but nothing I wasn't used to. I walked back home all the time. Aiden acted as if he didn't have a care in the world as he led me on, but it was his idea to stop and rest every so often.

We were almost through Soho, and Aiden promised

Greenwich Village wasn't far. "Time for another coffee break."

I excused myself to use the bathroom after all that coffee, and before I could close the door behind me, Aiden squeezed in at my back.

He smirked as I took a shy piss, then before I could grab him he grabbed me. Our hands were all over each other. He shoved both hands up under my T-shirt and pinched my nipples. I gasped before he covered my mouth and stuck a tongue deep inside. I crammed one hand down the front of his slacks and one down the back.

I felt his stiff cock in my fist, his deep ass crack with my fingers. I shook from head to toe and snorted air in through my nose as he tongue-fucked my mouth. I felt crazed, pumping his cock with my hand in his underwear, probing his ass and then fingering his butt hole when I found it.

Aiden returned the favor, his hands on my nipples plunging south to descend under my waistband. It was a cramped, not-too-clean and unromantic coffee shop bathroom. Sordid? Not at all.

Magical.

He broke away first. His smile was brilliant as he gazed into my eyes. "Let's go. We've got more walking to do before the day is out. I wouldn't want you to miss anything."

The throbbing heat of his hard cock and the silky softness of his asshole were what I would miss if we stopped what we were doing! Reluctantly, I obliged and disengaged. He laughed at my look.

"That was just a tease," he promised enigmatically.

Soho merged into Greenwich Village and I was suddenly on the most famous gay stomping grounds on the planet. I hadn't known what to expect, so I wasn't disappointed. The streets were more or less like the other streets we'd passed, although the pedestrians seemed more gay, if that was possible to define. Still, I absolutely loved every moment of it.

Three bookstore managers politely accepted my promotion

sheet and a complimentary copy of my new novel. "It's a promotion tour on the quick," I admitted to Aiden even though he hadn't made any disparaging comments.

"I admire you for putting yourself out there. I need to do something like that. My life is in a rut. Dismal." His smirk, wink, and laughter again belied his dark confession.

The sun had moved west over the city skyline, and I suddenly realized my day in New York City was coming to an end. I felt a momentary panic, but Aiden beside me steered me ahead.

"Washington Square Park is next. We'll watch the evening crowds before we take a final stroll up Fifth Avenue. You said you just had to see Fifth Avenue, even if it's only a few blocks, didn't you?"

The walking respite was welcome. We sat on a small strip of grass, which had been scarce in lower Manhattan. "I'm used to grass and flowers and trees everywhere. Vancouver is pretty green," I admitted.

"What else is different?" Aiden asked, staring into my eyes as he leaned against me and slipped a hand between my thighs.

I twitched at the intimate contact, glancing around to see if anyone was watching. A strange little carnival occupied the square in front of the famous white arch, and all eyes seemed glued to the acrobats and street performers. No one cared that Aiden's hand pressed into my inner thigh, as the daylight became twilight.

"There's more Blacks walking around the streets here. In Vancouver, we have more Asians," I blurted out.

He laughed and leaned in closer. "Is your cock hard?" he whispered in my ear. His fingers slid up my thigh and against my crotch.

"Can't you tell?" I gasped back.

He snickered in my ear and briefly groped me before retreating. I was so far gone in love and lust that I almost would have gotten down on my knees and sucked him off right there in public. In the last six hours I had fallen rapturously in love with this stranger.

"I'm in love with you, Jay. Let's go to my place and fuck our brains out. It's only a few blocks away."

I wasn't sure I'd heard him right. And he hadn't told me he lived so close!

"What about Peter?"

Peter. Aiden had mentioned the man several times in our rambling marathon conversation. The lover. The partner. The one he loved, not me.

"He's out of town until late tonight. We have a few hours. Will you do this for me? You don't have to."

He smiled, but his eyes were unreadable in the growing gloom. It was suddenly dark.

I nodded wordlessly. The magic of the day was being transformed into the magic of the night. He led me to his apartment, tucked upstairs in a trendy townhouse five blocks from Washington Square Park. I tried not to imagine what the rent must be.

It was larger inside than what I expected, mostly tidy with a few scattered books and articles of clothing neither he nor Peter had bothered to put away. Hardwood floor and comfortable furniture, nice, but it seemed a little too neat and impersonal. Aiden didn't need to tell me Peter was the decorator of the pair.

Aiden let go of my hand after he closed the door behind us, then, with a smiling nod, began to walk toward the bedroom, discarding his clothing along the way. I followed, breathless to see bare legs, his naked ass, and then his broad back and shoulders. He was shorter than me, but powerfully built. He'd told me he was a regular in the gym, a trait we shared.

My heart pounded in my chest. My clothes fell on the floor just like his. My hard-on bobbed before me, a column of honesty. I shook with desire.

Aiden was entirely naked by the time we were in his bedroom. As he bent to put in some music, I drank in the sight of his strong thighs. A pair of mounded ass cheeks rose above them. His body was nearly hairless. The sandy hair on his head was only repeated twice, at his crotch and on his forearms in a fine down. He turned, and his cock was a mirror image of my stiff bone.

I abandoned questions and so did he. There was only that sweet smile, a comfortable chuckle, then he was on his knees in front of me, taking my cock in both hands and feeding himself throbbing male meat. Wanton slurps sent shockwaves up and down my naked body. I lurched into his face, groaning.

Love and lust, like oxygen and flame, roared up in us both. It was an irresistible collision. He looked up at me as he sucked, not shy about meeting my eyes and grinning around the cock in his mouth. Orbs so wide and blue and soft, like the sky had been that afternoon.

His hands moved around to my ass, cupping the naked cheeks with fierce need. I spread my legs and allowed his fingers to slide into the crack, shuddering as he stroked the depths and found the hole.

His lips slid from my cock. "I need to fuck you," he gasped out.

I nodded, still unable to speak intelligible words. Gasps and moans were all I could manage as he tumbled me backwards onto his bed. Still on his knees, he pushed my thighs back to my chest.

Vulnerable, wide open to his gaze, I tossed my head from side to side. I had never in my life wanted anyone to fuck me so bad as I did at that moment. I felt my asshole clench, open, beg for him to fill it.

"Hot ass. I knew it would be. I'll get a condom."

He whispered those words against my pulsing asshole. I groaned and squirmed at the feel of hot breath against me. I longed for his tongue, and as if he read my mind, the raspy appendage swept across my butt cheeks, up and down my crack and over my hole. He licked me gently, not at all like he had gulped up my cock. I squirmed and moaned, on fire inside. My cock leaked all over my belly, and I knew if I even touched it, I would blow a load in an instant.

Aiden teased me with his tongue for a few delicious moments, lingering with flickering strokes on the pulsing sphincter before he moved away to crawl the few feet to his bedside table. I felt air on my wet ass crack and hole, and shivered again.

He was back, crawling up to crouch between my spread thighs. I had thrown my arms wide in surrender, but now that he stood over me, I reached up and clutched at his sides, pulling him into me.

"Fuck me, Aiden," I begged.

He smiled, winking as he squirted a stream of clear lube all over his condom-wrapped cock. I raised my head to look at it, firm and purple and twitching. It was a nice size, the perfect size. I absolutely knew it would feel perfect inside me.

He crouched and aimed. I lifted my hips to meet his thrust. Cockhead slithered over crack and hole, found its mark, and began to sink past convulsing anal lips. He pushed with a sudden grunt, and I was impaled on half his rod.

I groaned. He shoved deeper, then fell on top of me, thrusting home and cradling me in his arms as he began to fuck me. I wrapped my arms around his broad back, feeling the sheen of sweat beading his muscles, pulling him back deeper inside every time he withdrew even slightly.

We rocked in a gentle rhythm at first, his cock feeling out my hole, the sphincter clamping and possessing, and the cock testing and searching. He stared down into my eyes, his smile gentle, then biting his lip as he began to fuck deeper, harder, and faster.

He ploughed into me, our bodies writhing on the bed.

Cock rubbed my innards, seared my soul. I met every lunge, my own cock aching between our bellies, on the verge of release every single exquisite moment.

"God! I need someone like you in my life," he moaned. With his cock up my ass at the moment, it wasn't clear if he needed someone like me in his life to fuck, or for something more.

That afternoon, I chose to believe something more.

The feel of his solid body covering mine, his stiff cock pounding deep, his hips slamming against my naked ass, his eyes boring into mine, it was too much. "I'm shooting!"

I rose up, my cock erupting into his sweaty abs. Orgasm flooded through me, the hard pounding of his dick deep into my guts urging more and more juice from my emptying balls. He fucked me dry, then pulled out.

His sweat dripped down onto me. He whipped off the condom covering his flushed cock, and with a groan shot his own load all over my belly.

We lay together, uncaring about the drying cum and sweat. We began talking after a few minutes of quiet, hands trailing over each other's naked bodies, and finally stimulating cocks back to firm need.

He fucked me one more time, on my hands and knees on his polished wood floor. It took longer for release, and we worked at it with grunts, thrusts, and wild gyrations that would have done any pair of sluts proud. It was nasty and it was wonderful.

I dressed and faced him. He remained naked, still sweaty from our bout of wild sex. He grinned as he handed me a slip of paper. "Here's my e-mail address at work. Shoot me a message in about a week if you want to hear from me again. I have a lot of shit to think about. Is that OK?"

"Of course. Thanks, Aiden. For everything."

"No worries. Thanks to you too."

His soft blue eyes watched me as I stood at his door. I

closed it behind me, and let out a huge sigh. I was elated. I had no room in my overflowing heart to question. No room for anything but the hugeness of emotion that flooded me with euphoria. It had been the best day of my life.

Our flight left early the next morning. I said nothing about Aiden to my buddy, or to anyone. It was my secret, my private possession I cradled to my heart for the next few days back at home on the west coast in Canada.

I'd promised to wait a week before contacting him, but disaster intervened.

I'd only been home a few days when I was woken by a call from a friend. "Turn on the news. One of the World Trade towers is on fire in New York City. They think it might be a terrorist attack."

I watched all that morning along with millions of others as New York City writhed under a pall of ash and smoke. All of lower Manhattan—the magical streets Aiden and I had walked—was buried under smoldering bits of paper blown from shattered windows and shattered offices.

I wept, for New York City, for Aiden, and for myself.

Of course I e-mailed Aiden immediately, one eye on the horrible images on the television screen. I never got a reply. It was his office e-mail. His office was in the Twin Towers. In front of my disbelieving eyes, the Twin Towers crumbled into smoldering ruins.

I didn't even know his last name. We hadn't shared last names, even though we'd shared so much else.

In the aftermath of that disaster, and the magical day that preceded it, I couldn't feel regret. It had been a different world, an innocent world.

In time, I healed. Now, years later, I think I may be ready to go back to New York City. I may find Aiden there, by magical accident, just like I did before.

I still believe.

SECOND ACT

TOM MENDICINO

AT LEAST HIS reviews were good.

"Archie Duncan, in a sweet-natured performance, makes a fine Herbie."

"As Herbie, Archie Duncan gets an opportunity to show the crack timing he perfected during his long run in television comedy."

"Archie Duncan is in fine voice and is a perfect foil for the formidable Madame Rose."

"The only reservation I have about the casting of Archie Duncan as Herbie is that he seems a shade young to be a romantic interest for this particular Madame Rose."

That last one has caused a few weeks of agita. Madame Rose's publicist had gotten wind of the review before the offending copy of *Newsweek* hit the stands. God knows he'd earned his fees when he had to break *that* news. The word on the street was she'd been reluctant to take the part, protesting she was far, far too young for the role. But the production needed a marquee name, someone with the stature of her predecessors in the role. Madame Rose had two Tonys, four Drama Desks, a couple of Theatre World Awards, two platinum, and five gold records, and, most importantly, a rabid cult of gay boys who panted after her whirlwind courtships and Mexican divorces, surgeries (elective and otherwise), and annual farewell tours. *Of course, Rose is a young woman,* her manager pleaded; *after all she is the mother of BABY June!* Archie never did figure out how that argument accounted for the second act when Madame Rose is the mother of the obviously nubile Gypsy Rose Lee. Cast and crew were forbidden to mention Ethel Merman, who had looked rather matronly when she created the role.

Madame Rose had coyly flirted with Archie through rehearsals and previews after the *Newsweek* debacle; he got the cold shoulder on a good day and outright hostility on a bad one. Everything was definitely not coming up roses despite the strong advance sales and the expectation of a long run. His agent consoled him, promising him she'd forget it in a few weeks and, even if she didn't, it was worth it since a Tony nomination was all but in the bag. The Academy of Television Arts and Sciences had nominated Archie six times for best lead actor in a television comedy series, but he'd never won. It would be nice to hear his name announced when they opened the envelope, even if it was only in a supporting category.

The plan had been to return to Broadway as a star. He'd started out in New York years ago and made a big splash with a show-stopping tap solo in a dance musical that was the hottest ticket of the season. That landed him the second lead in the movie of the hit musical about high school delinquents, and that got him the series—a smash that topped the ratings its second and third seasons and went on for a seven year run. But the big movie offers never came in, because the industry was reluctant to risk a multimillion dollar budget on a project with a romantic lead whose career had been plagued by "is he or isn't he" rumors. He and his agent decided New York would be more benign to an actor with his "handicap." After the series was cancelled, there were negotiations to cast him as Robert, the lead, in a revival of *Company*. But the financial bankers pulled out when the husband-and-wife producers became entangled in a tabloid-fodder divorce and the project was in limbo, postponed indefinitely. The only firm offer back in L.A. was a throwaway Disney feature, playing the father of a teenage star known to be a monstrosity, who made Madame Rose look like Mother Teresa. Then his agent got the phone call asking if he'd like to audition for *Gypsy*.

"For June or Louise?" he'd joked, not letting on he was dejected at needing to audition for a supporting role that didn't even have a solo. Jesus Christ, Jack Klugman had croaked his way through it. He was more relieved than thrilled when he got the part; at least he hadn't been rejected. But they weren't quite through humiliating him. His agent approached the matter gently.

They want you to go natural, Archie. They want a Silver Fox.

He'd never thought going prematurely gray (they'd started coloring his hair on the series when he was thirty) would be a career advantage. All in all, it wasn't a bad gig, with none of the pressure that comes from having to carry the show, even if it's not exactly how he'd planned to begin his Second Act.

He's in costume, waiting for his call. It's been a shitty day. Why the hell did the show's press agent book him on *Good Morning New York* on a Wednesday, with curtains at two and eight?

The driver he'd been promised for a 7:15 A.M. pickup had stood him up. Apparently Madame Rose had commandeered car and chauffeur for a personal errand and no one bothered to tell him. It took his doorman twenty minutes to hail a cab in the pouring rain. He didn't discover he only had three bucks in his wallet until they reached the studio. The damn cabbie almost started an international incident, squawking like a parrot and threatening him with what looked to be a sawed-off broom handle. Thankfully, the lady security guard recognized the star of her favorite television show and came to his rescue.

It was downhill from there. The show's preternaturally

perky hostess, an aging cheerleader with blindingly white teeth and chipmunk cheeks, barged into the green room during the commercial break, gushing that she had had *absolutely the biggest crush on him when she was, God, like, twelve or thirteen!* She had something *very, very special* planned and hoped he liked it. Waiting to walk on the set, he had an adrenaline rush as the studio audience started squealing and shouting when his name was announced. His fans weren't exactly "girls" anymore. They were a little thick in the waist and wide at the hips and, not to be unkind, a bit bridge-and-tunnel.

Three minutes later he was completely blindsided.

Please everyone, welcome to Good Morning New York, Archie Duncan's mom!

He would never have agreed to do the goddamn show if he'd known they were going to sabotage him with a "This Is Your Life" stroll down memory lane. He could have used a couple of belts to fortify himself, and all they had to offer was a cup of lukewarm coffee. He'd smiled under torture, grinning until his face ached. The chipmunk bubbled and babbled, mistaking the murderous intent in his eyes for misty nostalgia. Only the fact that homicide might be career suicide kept him from strangling her with an eighteen-share audience as witnesses. What the hell was he even doing there? When he was on top, he'd earned more in a week than his old man made in ten years. He had residuals from a sweet syndication deal for a show that will run in perpetuity. He had plenty of fuck-you money. He didn't have to be up at that hour, suffering like that, to promote a show where he wasn't billed above the title. His name wasn't even on the fucking lobby card. It was God punishing him.

His mother chattered happily, enjoying the attention, as comfortable in the spotlight as if she spent every morning of her life with a studio audience of two hundred New Jersey and Long Island housewives and several thousand New York metropolitan area couch potatoes hanging on her every word. A tension headache drilled through his skull as he sat on the edge of his seat, ready to pounce if she started telling the chipmunk how cute he was at seven, lip-synching to Barbra and the *Funny Girl* soundtrack.

Good Morning New York wasn't finished with him yet.

Archie, you'll never guess who is waiting in the wings to come out and say hello.

Never in a million years would Archie have expected to find himself face-to-face with Angela Coladonato and Charlie Reeves, neither of whom had he seen since he left Northeast Philadelphia in the rear-view mirror, destined for fame and fortune.

His first co-stars! They knew him back then!

Someone, dear sweet Mom most likely, had provided the producer with the Archbishop Ryan High School yearbooks that recorded for posterity the earnest awkwardness and gravity-defying hair of Charlie as Sky Masterson, Archie as Nathan Detroit, and Angela as Miss Adelaide, then, in their senior year, Angela as Maria with Archie as her Tony, and Charlie as Bernardo.

Angela, that wasn't exactly acting you were doing there was it? The Chipmunk teased.

Archie smiled indulgently as Angela recounted their ancient history as high school sweethearts, confiding that Archie was her first kiss. The bridge-and-tunnel gals cooed when he and Angela hugged.

I think we really surprised him! The Chipmunk crowed.

Yep, he was surprised all right. Surprised how deeply he blushed when Charlie Reeves, still lean and lanky if a little thinner on the scalp, smiled at him. The chipmunk, not knowing when to leave well enough alone, begged them to treat the viewers to a reunion performance of *West Side Story*, something "easy" like "Tonight" (Christ, she must be clueless), but Charlie demurred, saying his singing days were behind him. Greater New York had to settle for Archie mangling a few verses of "Luck Be a Lady" from *Guys and Dolls*, accompanied by a barely tuned piano.

Archie took the three of them to breakfast before the *Good Morning New York* limousine drove them back to Philly. His mother was disappointed it wasn't Sardi's, but Angela and Charlie seemed happy to settle into the booth of an Eighth Avenue delicatessen and order omelets and bagels. They reminisced about Archbishop Ryan, drama club, the polyester costumes, and sweet old Brother Clement, the drama teacher who'd been a chorus boy before he'd taken the vows and who claimed to have saved Mary Martin's life when she almost choked in the flying harness during a matinee of *Peter Pan*. He and Angela shared a side of fries smothered in gravy, a Philly diner tradition, for old time's sake. He asked what they'd been up to since high school. Angela was married to a lawyer, had three girls, and had moved on to the leafy suburbs of the Main Line where she'd established a pastry shop that had won *Best in Philly* three years running. Charlie taught AP math at Archbishop Ryan and coached ice hockey.

"Kids?" Archie asked tentatively.

"No. Just the ones in my classes at Ryan."

"Married?"

"Divorced."

"Sorry."

"That's okay. Guess I'm not the marrying kind."

Archie choked on a soggy french fry. One of the drawbacks to fame is having the eyes of the entire restaurant on you when you're spewing cud all over the table. If you were a nobody, they would forget the entire incident in five minutes. But an encounter with a Television Personality becomes a Treasured Moment to be taken out and dusted off at family gatherings over the years. He recovered quickly enough and, embarrassed, apologized to the couple at the next table for disturbing their meal. Diners, feigning concern, drifted over to Archie's table to casually ask if he was all right, and, as soon as they were acknowledged, thrust whatever happened to be in reach—a napkin, the menu, the check—in his face, asking for his autograph. He was self-conscious the entire time, worrying that someone, Charlie, might detect a trace of sprayed food clinging to his black sweater. His mother announced to anyone within earshot that she was always warning Archie about eating too fast, that one of these days he was going to choke to death.

A catnap after the matinee and six aspirin haven't put a dent in his splitting headache. He just wants to get through this performance and put this miserable day behind him. The stage manager calls five minutes and he jumps to his feet. He needs to stop berating himself for getting caught up in the moment, at least until the curtain call. Angela and his mother were waiting in the limo and he and Charlie were standing on Eighth Avenue, saying their good-byes. The impulse overwhelmed Archie and he grabbed a pen from his jacket and scribbled his number, inviting Charlie to New York to see the show, orchestra seats, a visit backstage, an audience with Madame Rose in all her splendor. Worse yet, he threw his arms around Charlie and gave him a friendly hug. What an idiot! What made him think a high school hockey coach would want to meet Madame Rose? Christ, he'd really humiliated himself. What is he so fucking upset about anyway? It's not like he's ever going to see the guy again. He needs to forget about it, put it out of his mind. Besides, he'd only imagined that he felt something stirring in the crotch of Charlie's pants during their brief and awkward embrace. It's over and done and right now. It's showtime folks!

. . . . Six months later, the company is in a state of agitation. They're still playing near capacity on Saturday night and both weekend matinees, but the house is half-empty during the week and the producers have sent out the

chorus boys to woo the long lines of tourists at the TKTS booth. The stage manager is on edge, blaming it on the August doldrums. Madame Rose has been a bitch-on-wheels since losing the Tony to the twenty-three-year old ingénue in the new Lloyd Webber whose face is featured in an Estée Lauder ad campaign. Archie was nominated after all, only to be the bridesmaid once again. The sentimental favorite, an overweight old veteran making his swan song in a flop that closed after fifty-six perfor-mances including previews, got the Tony and a standing ovation. Why the fuck did he ever leave California? The teenage monster on the Disney picture had to withdraw when she was hospitalized for "exhaustion," publicist-speak for bulimia, and was replaced with one of the kid actors from his old series. He would have collected more money for six weeks of work than he'll collect over his year-long contract to bust his ass doing eight shows a week—that is if the fucking show doesn't close come fall. This afternoon's matinee was the pits. Tulsa called out, probably to catch the early ferry to the Pines; Louise called June a fucking cunt for upstaging her during "If Momma Was Married." Madame Rose, if nothing else, a professional, unfairly accused him of getting lazy and disparaged him as a sitcom actor. Even the curtain call was sloppy. And today was the show he'd wanted to be as perfect as if the house was filled with critics and Tony voters. Because today Charlie Reeves and date were seated Center Orchestra, Row E, Seats 15 and 16.

After he'd made an ass out of himself on Eighth Avenue on that cold, wet March afternoon, Archie was convinced he'd never see Charlie again. The month went out like a lamb, the Easter bonnets promenaded down Fifth Avenue, mothers (his own included) were feted and Tonys awarded, independence was celebrated and the phone call never came. But instead of forgetting about Charlie, Archie started to obsess over him, running the gamut of emotions from A to B as Miss Parker once wrote, from being pissed to being completely pissed, that a goddamned high school teacher had blown him off. After all, Archie was still a fucking star with the pick of the litter waiting at the stage door every night. Charlie Fucking Reeves probably had a hard time getting laid and when he did it was either because the poor woman—assuming that it was, in fact, a woman—felt sorry for him or was overweight and desperate. Thoughts of revenge and waves of dejection ambushed Archie at unexpected times. He'd rehearsed his response, trying to find just the right words to casually dismiss and embarrass the asshole if he tried to call at this late date. This irrational agitation over a balding teacher who probably lives in a row house and drives a car with a hundred thousand miles on the odometer could only mean Archie's edging into a mid-life crisis, premature of course, despite the gray hair. Maybe he needed Prozac or Ativan or Wellbutrin or, maybe, all three.

Charlie Fucking Reeves. *Guys and Dolls* was a long time ago, another life. Back at Archbishop Ryan, Charlie was tall, nearly six feet, and Archie, a year away from his hormonal growth spurt, short. Charlie, his muscles hardened by countless hours on the ice, had the developed, sinewy body of a man; Archie still looked the twelve-year-old with rheumatic fever who'd spent six months flat on his back in bed. Charlie had a trail of hair that crept around his navel and thick tufts under his arms; Archie had barely sprouted any growth on his upper lip. Charlie was his first crush and his myth had only grown over the years, nurtured by hindsight and unblemished by any brutal present realities. Archie always was more comfortable with the quixotic pursuit of romantic perfection than with real life, and all of his partners eventually disappointed him. Even the Golden Boy, twice nominated as Best Actor by the only academy that really mattered, was dumped after thirteen months, a record, when Archie, a mere sitcom star, declared a fatal lack of chemistry. Every time Archie found himself alone again, nostalgia would lead him back to the memory of Charlie, the gold standard who was safely sealed in the past and beyond the reach of disenchantment. Once a few years back he even thought about tracking Charlie down on the Internet. Something had stopped him; an instinct for self-preservation, and his good sense would have spared him the mortification of rejection if he had never agreed to appear on *Good Morning New York.*

And then, one oppressively humid morning last week, Archie was dodging a reckless taxi on West Seventy-sixth Street when the phone in his pocket rang with an incoming call from the 215 area code. Charlie Reeves was going to be in New York. Great, Archie said, attributing the nervous grip on his vocal chords that reduced his speaking voice to an adolescent squeak to his near miss with the grim reaper. Are you bringing a date? he asked, dreading the inevitable answer. Pause. Sure, Charlie'd said. I'll get you a pair of great seats. He wonders what she'll look like. There's a knock at his dressing room door. He'll know soon enough.

"Just a minute," he says, not wanting Charlie to see him in makeup.

Sure he was mildly disappointed, okay very disappointed, about the girlfriend, but it's a relief. The pressure's off. All he needs to do is be charming, take them to Angus McIndoe's joint, treat them to dinner and the house wine, impress the lady, probably an English teacher or hospital administrator, give them a story to share with their friends. What had he thought was going to happen anyway? That Charlie would come to New York to seduce him? Clean-faced, he opens the door and Charlie is standing there alone.

"Hey," he says.

"Hey."

"Where's your date?"

"Ah—couldn't make it."

The scheduled audience with Madame Rose was clearly a mistake now that Charlie's come stag. He probably doesn't even know who she is. Madame Rose is in a benevolent mood and Charlie, much to Archie's surprise, seems genuinely excited. They talk about her role in a Sondheim classic, something Archie knew only from the original cast recording but which Charlie appears to have seen three times. The nervous tic in Charlie's voice lingers even after they've left The Presence and Charlie's startled, but not unpleased, when the small crowd rushes them, pens and *Playbills* in hand, as they exit the stage door.

It's Sunday evening in the armpit of August and Matthew and Nathan and Bernadette have better places to be than midtown so Archie Duncan, star of a long-running television show, is the biggest attraction in this name-dropping, head-turning watering hole in the heart of the theater district. Angus is his usual effusive, democratic self, making sure to inquire after Charlie's name, occupation, and hometown. He buys the first round when Archie introduces Charlie as an old high-school buddy.

Mistake number two. Charlie looks a little uncomfortable, probably worried that Angus McIndoe assumed, incorrectly, that he and Archie used to diddle each other in the locker room. He hasn't touched his beer and probably wants to bolt back to Philadelphia. Archie drains his glass and squirms, trying to get the waiter's attention. Charlie slides his glass across the table.

"Here, take mine."

"You want something else? Vodka martini? Scotch?" Archie asks.

"Just a ginger ale."

"Sure?"

"Please, go ahead. I like to watch other people drink. I've been sober for eleven years."

Charlie, the high school teacher from northeast Philadelphia has a few deep, dark secrets of his own.

"Sorry," Archie says. "I mean, I'm not sorry you're sober. I mean sorry about the beer. I mean…I…sorry."

Charlie laughs.

"Nothing to be sorry about. I drank too much and then I stopped."

They study their menus, Archie, at least, painfully conscious of the minutes slipping away. This isn't a Hollywood movie and it ain't a Broadway musical, and it's apparent there isn't going to be a moment, an epiphany, a revelation, a catharsis, a showstopping Eleven o'clock Number. He orders a steak, rare, and Charlie orders the same, medium.

"You know, "Luck Be a Lady" was my song," Charlie finally says.

"Huh?"

"It's Sky's song, not Nathan Detroit's."

The conversation starts gaining momentum.

"Well, you had your opportunity. *Good Morning New York* would have loved to hear you sing."

They stay in the comfortable zone, not straying beyond their shared past, as if life had ended at graduation. They remember names Archie had long forgotten, Charlie updating Archie on the fates of those who, like himself, never strayed far and who now send their own kids to Archbishop Ryan. They speculate about others, creating outlandish destinies like prison and brothels and the seminary for some of the odder characters in their class. At one point, Charlie's shoe slides across the floor and rests against Archie's sneaker. Archie abruptly pulls his foot back, not wanting Charlie to think he was taking advantage of an innocent need to stretch a cramped leg.

Archie insists on picking up the tab.

"What time is your train?" he asks.

"I drove," Charlie says.

Archie walks with him to the garage and when Charlie, self-conscious, asks if he minds if he smokes, Archie asks to bum one. Charlie's hand is shaking when Archie leans forward for a light.

"It was good to see you man," Charlie says.

"It was good to see you too."

"Stay in touch."

"You too."

"You want a ride?"

Archie's an actor, but he doesn't pick up the cue.

"I'll catch a cab."

"Naw, I'll give you a ride."

It's been a great evening, better than he'd expected. Why not extend it another ten minutes? The garage attendant delivers a Honda Accord that had obviously left the showroom when Charlie still had a full head of hair.

"How many miles you got on this?" Archie asks.

"A little over a hundred. Figure it's good for at least thirty thousand more."

Archie had at least got that much right. The shabby car feels strangely comfortable to someone who's grown accustomed to trading-in every year to navigate the mean streets of Brentwood. The radio station is tuned to a Classic Rock station. Charlie drives slowly, maybe to delay the inevitable, more likely because he's intimidated by the NASCAR-qualifying traffic. Archie calls out directions and for a minute, just a minute, he's tempted to steer them on to the West Side highway, north to the bridges, onto the Thruway, and into the endless night.

"This is it," he says, as they approach his building.

"Okay," Charlie says, as he shifts down to neutral and stops the car on the street. He turns, extends his hand for one final farewell and hesitates, his palm hovering for a brief moment before it tentatively settles on Archie's knee.

· · · · ·

WHAT TIME DO you need me to set the alarm?" Archie asks.

"I'm an old maid schoolteacher," Charlie laughs. "It's August. Whenever you need to get up. Unless you're kicking me out."

Their bodies spoon and Charlie drifts into sleep. Ten minutes later he's snoring, one more item in the litany of flaws Archie's learned in the course of a few hours. He's balding. He's a recovering drunk. His abstinence makes Archie feel like an alcoholic. He smokes. He drives a car with a hundred thousand miles on it. He listens to Classic Rock. God only knows what Archie would discover if they actually spent twenty-fours together. Tomorrow's Monday, no performance, and he has no intention of getting up early. He burrows into Charlie's body, content, ready to fall asleep. He needs his rest because, when he wakes, he has an opportunity to begin his Second Act again and do it right this time, and he's going to need all his energy to prepare for all the things about Charlie he's going to learn to live with.

WORLD'S FAIR

TED CORNWELL

THE COURTS ON the edge of Jackie Robinson Park in
Harlem were a mess, but at least there was no wait to get one.
Adrian Kellogg stood in the center of one of the end courts,
kicking acorns toward the fence, in order to minimize the
risk of ankle injuries. Even as he worked to clean the tennis
court, some winged seeds, like small helicopters, spun down
onto the green asphalt. With these, Adrian could not be bothered, since they were thin and stubbornly resistant to kicks.
They might occasionally distort a bounce, but it was hardly
likely that someone would twist an ankle on a maple seed.
Through the fence, with a monochrome beige school and a
sea of concrete in the background, the trees of the thin park
between the courts and 145th Street looked like anxious refu-
gees awaiting word from some distant country, where they
might be allowed to emigrate and start a new life. Through
these trees Adrian first caught sight of an unfamiliar figure,
with tennis rackets sticking out of a canvas backpack, walking
briskly toward the courts and returning his stare.

Adrian, who had fastidiously arrived early knowing that
the courts would require some tidying, watched as a young
man with black, curly hair and an indiscernible ethnic makeup
entered the gait and marched toward him. Adrian felt like

the captain of a lone ship, watching another vessel approach, wondering if friend or foe manned it. The newcomer had an orange bandana tied around his forehead and wore cut-off jeans and a tank top, not a positive omen for a tennis player, even by the loose standards of dress that prevailed in New York City's public parks. He was slightly pudgy, but this blemish put Adrian at ease and distracted him from the beauty of his new challenger's face. Even with the baby fat, Adrian, who was recalcitrant with strangers, though not painfully shy, imagined licking the man's soft brown legs.

"Do you want to play?" the young man said, apparently by way of introduction.

"Yes, we can play until my friend comes," Adrian said.

With businesslike economy, they retreated to opposite sides of the net (tennis isn't designed for courtship). Adrian pulled some old balls out of his bag and they began to rally. Surprisingly, for Adrian was quick to assume the worst, his opponent was at least as skilled as he was, and knew to start warming up with soft shots and slowly add pace to the ball. The mysterious arriviste hit two-handed forehands as well as backhands, like Monica Seles. Adrian himself hit with one hand on both sides, a la Steffi Graf. They were still testing each other, neither hitting at full strength, when Terry Auerbach arrived. It took Terry's insouciance to raise the level of etiquette and unveil the newcomer's identity and backstory. After warming up and watching them for a moment, Terry approached Adrian on the court.

"Where did you find that hottie?" he asked.

"I didn't. He found me actually, right here just a few minutes ago."

"Who is he," Terry asked.

"I don't know. He didn't say."

Shocked that they hadn't exchanged names, Terry convened a get acquainted conference at the net. Manabu was from Brazil, where he'd studied dentistry. He hoped to study dentistry in the U.S. eventually, but for the moment he was working for his uncle, who managed a recycling contractor in the Bronx. He was thirty-one years old. (Adrian was thirty-eight—or thirty-nine if you counted the eighth grade, a year he'd banished from memory and erased from the record.) Manabu's eyes widened when Terry described Adrian as an art curator who worked at the Whitney, the occupation perhaps falsely suggesting some high level of affluence or intellect. Terry graciously insisted, with Adrian's full support, that Manabu stay. They played Canadian doubles. In the end, it was Terry who compensated for Adrian's shyness by insisting that they all exchange numbers. Adrian was glad to think that Manabu would not disappear back into the forest of buildings, never to be seen again, as so many men had done in the past.

That Manabu was different from Adrian's many earlier paramours only became apparent in stages. In those earlier days, Adrian had always felt like the young and insouciant one, who doled out his love in finite portions and was always on the lookout for a promotion.

The first indication of this change came several weeks later, after the two had played tennis several more times and gone to dinner, and eventually courted their way back to Adrian's Garment District apartment on three or four occasions. Manabu suggested, rather bluntly, that it might make sense for him to more or less move in with Adrian. Adrian's apartment, an "L" shaped studio of generous enough proportions for one person, would be problematic for any couple, even when one traveled as lightly as Manabu did. Normally, the first hint of unstable tenancy, the first whiff of residential neediness, sent Adrian into a fast retreat. A boyfriend from the Bronx eager to move out of an overbearing uncle's house? That news in itself might have led Adrian to stop his mail, disconnect the phone, and arrange for a friend in Miami to drop a postcard in the mail, in which Adrian would maintain that family emergencies had taken him out of town, perhaps permanently. This time, Adrian did not flinch. He did not try to reason with Manabu. Rather, he thought of creative ways curtains might be used to divide space and make the apartment seem bigger. How an armoire might augment the two small closets. He noticed bulky furniture that might be removed to open up space. Moving was out of the question, of course—the apartment was rent stabilized.

"Maybe just on days when I'm not working the next day, I could stay here with you," Manabu said.

Adrian found himself agreeing, even apologizing that he had so little to offer by way of hospitality.

"It's not as small as it seems," he said. "Once I get it organized better, it will almost seem like a one bedroom apartment."

Manabu laughed. "In Brazil, many large families live in apartments smaller than this. My family even, though we were not poor, had only a small house. Two kids in each bedroom, and my parents had a bedroom. But in Brazil you are outside so much, it seems OK."

They were sitting on the futon bed, which they'd folded up into a couch, watching Harrison Ford attempt to save Michelle Pfeifer from mysterious perils in a haunted house while she pursued a murderer next door. Adrian had been nuzzling his face into Manabu's hair and had paid little attention to the plot. He wondered, is this really what Manabu wants? To be here, with me, permanently? Or is this just a stage, one layover on a long journey, like the many I went through? He thought that perhaps this arrangement was just a convenient outpost, a way of escaping the Bronx on weekend nights and enjoying the frisson of the city. As the months went by, there were nights when Adrian would say he was tired after dinner, when Manabu wanted to stay out later. He knew not to try to keep Manabu on a tight leash, even if he didn't fancy the idea of seeing him wander off toward the clubs of Chelsea all by himself. Still, Manabu always came home, alone, even if it was sometimes in the wee hours of the morning. Adrian hadn't denied himself the city's temptations, why should he try to bottle up Manabu? If he lost a little sleep with worry, then that was a price he had to pay, he knew.

Unlike the courts in Harlem, where they'd met, the courts in Flushing Meadows Park were full of peril, as far as Adrian was concerned. Which is to say Manabu had plenty of opportunity to meet other gay tennis players in the biggest park in the aptly named borough of Queens. Just about every member of the gay tennis league played out there. At times, the courts were so queer that you might have thought you'd wandered into the Gay Games. Adrian knew many of the players here were every bit as outgoing and flirtatious as Terry Auerbach, but not nearly so virtuous (Terry and his partner recently celebrated their eleventh anniversary). Manabu, naturally, was very popular. Many men invited him onto their courts. Everyone sought him out as a doubles partner. Adrian began to understand why Nate Florio, who didn't play tennis, was always there reading a book in the grass, keeping an eye on his boyfriend Victor, who was a rated 4.5 USTA player who had once worked as a go-go boy at the Monster. Keeping tabs on Victor seemed a full time job for Nate.

By contrast, Adrian could only shrug as Manabu stuffed scraps of paper with phone numbers into his pockets. Adrian found himself appraising himself against the competition. Were they wealthy? Were they younger than he? In better shape? Whenever he saw Manabu talking with someone he didn't know well, he couldn't help imagining the two of them driving off together in a convertible Mercedes toward the shore towns, where Adrian couldn't even afford to rent a weekend home. What was Manabu's level of commitment? What was his temptation threshold?

And this proved yet another stage in the realization that Manabu meant more to Adrian than anyone had in a long time: the depth of jealousy he felt whenever he saw someone like Anthony Gelson, who was only thirty-six and owned a place in East Hampton, tussle Manabu's hair during a change-over between games on the court. Adrian resolved to lose ten pounds and wash out the gray at his temples. If he couldn't cordon Manabu off from the crowd, he could at least hope to be the one holding Manabu's hand when the music stopped.

. . . . .

ONE DAY, IN early August, after they'd been together for almost five months, and at a time when Manabu had started spending three or four nights a week at Adrian's apartment, rather than just one or two, Adrian couldn't stop himself from broaching a question that had been on his mind, though he didn't know if he wanted to know the answer.

"Are we going steady?" he asked. "I mean, are we boyfriends?"

"Yes, yes, of course, we are boyfriends. We are steady," Manabu answered.

A brief thunderstorm had driven them from the courts. They had hidden under the canopy of elm trees, with the other players, until the storm passed. To pass the time while the wind and sun dried them off again, Adrian and Manabu had walked over the heart of the old World's Fair grounds, where they sat on the rim of the giant Unisphere that punctuated Flushing Meadows Park like a relic from some era of rabid utopianism. The site of the Unisphere always made Adrian think of old science fiction movies, really bad ones, with their comically off-balance visions of the future. They sat on the edge of the pool beneath the giant globe, which, looming over them, seemed ominously totalitarian. Adrian imagined it was crafted by proponents of one world government, who expected a future when all racial and ethnic differences would be blanched out of existence. Instead, it presided over a cornucopia of distinct racial and ethnic groups sharing one park in America's biggest city. As the weather cleared, Adrian watched the Latinos marching back into the park from Crotona, toward the soccer fields where they'd been when the rain broke out. He imagined on the other side of the park, Asians were streaming in from Flushing. A whole stew of humanity had probably taken shelter under the subway station, which was elevated this far out of Manhattan, and they too would be making their way back into the park, which seemed a sort of world congress of recreation where each continent was well represented, even four decades after the World's Fair had been here.

To emphasize his affection, Adrian grasped Manabu's hand. Manabu did not pull away, though in general Manabu wasn't fond of too much public affection. Adrian and Manabu eventually got up and walked back toward the tennis courts. They held hands part of the way, and Manabu began suddenly to speak of the future.

"I want someday to have a house in the country, a place where the dogs can run free," he told Adrian. "Maybe near a lake. Someplace with no other houses nearby. At least a one hour drive away from the city."

Adrian did not bother explaining that such a place would have to be much farther away.

"We could have this house, and also your apartment," Manabu added, as if suddenly remembering to include Adrian. "During the week we could live in the city, and go to the house for the weekends. Does your apartment building allow dogs? Or will we have to leave them in the country with someone to take care of them? Either way, we must have at least two dogs."

They returned to the courts, and it was sunny the whole rest of the afternoon as far as Adrian was concerned.

. . . . .

IF WATCHING MANABU sharing an intimate laugh with another player during a changeover sparked a little flare of jealousy, you can imagine how Adrian felt when Toronto suddenly arose in their path, or at least in the path of Manabu. Suddenly, New York and the plan to study dentistry seemed like a manuscript about to be abandoned. Toronto loomed ahead like a new book, ready to be populated with new characters and story lines. Adrian, whose vacation time had been depleted with a trip to France with friends to see the French Open in May, had little choice but to bless Manabu's temporary decampment, even as he feared Toronto—a city which he'd never visited—might replace New York in Manabu's affections, just as he feared other tennis players might snatch Manabu from his grasp. He imagined Toronto as a glimmering city on a great lake, where all the homosexual men had prestigious jobs in downtown office skyscrapers and lived in fabulous penthouses that would make his studio apartment in a walk-up building look like an urban trailer park. How long before Manabu met someone with such an apartment? Someone with a car for trips to suburban tennis parks with manicured lawns and courts kept to country club standards? (He'd always envied the Canadian civic spirit that he occasionally read about in papers, and imagined the country characterized by a sort of genteel egalitarianism and widespread affluence.)

There were complications, or at least conditions, imposed upon Manabu's plan to stay in the United States. Immigration rules required that he spend a certain period of time out of the country before he could come back. A month or two, maybe three—the number seemed to change every time Adrian asked about it. Manabu was not one to keep track of details, and resented being asked too much. Adrian suggested he might come to visit on weekends, or at least one or two weekends, but Manabu reminded Adrian that he'd be staying in a boarding house, with other immigrants, some of whom might keep live chickens in the hallways.

Adrian got the hint. He remembered being thirty-one himself and didn't want to push his luck. If Manabu wants a solo experience, he should have it, he thought. Manabu was grateful at least that Adrian's friend Sarah would drive them both to the airport. Though he traveled light, the duration of this trip required more than could be comfortably stuffed into the back of a cab and carried into the terminal on one's own. At the gate, Adrian squeezed his hand tightly for a moment. Manabu squeezed back and kissed him on the cheek. Then he was on his way.

. . . . .

THE FIRST WEEK, they talked nightly on the phone. The second, Adrian only managed to reach Manabu twice, but he seemed jovial when they finally spoke. The third week, as a test of his own self-sufficiency as well as of Manabu's devotion, Adrian decided to wait for a call. When Manabu did ring, it was to ask if Adrian could send some spare golf shirts. It turned out to be unseasonably warm in Toronto for October. He'd been surprised to hear Manabu blurt out, "Love you," at the end of the call. He'd been imagining Manabu in the back seat of a cab, holding hands with a new acquaintance he'd just met at a local gay bar. Two days later, Adrian received a letter—never a good sign, as far as he was concerned. Once, in his twenties, he'd broken up with a drama teacher by post, fearing a maniacal scene if he did it in person. When the man, several years older than Adrian, had arrived at his doorstep in tears, Adrian couldn't think of what to say. "You could have at least said it to my face," the teacher had uttered, as Adrian closed the door on him. Though as far as he knew no curse had been uttered, ever since, Adrian had lived in fear of recriminations. He believed he might be under a spell that required him to receive equally boorish treatment. He hoped the statute of limitations might have passed.

He stood in the foyer, looking at the envelope with its neat, almost impeccable handwriting. It was as if Manabu had used a tracer while addressing the envelope. The cursive letters were of equal size, the capitals proportionately larger than the lower case letters by just the right amount. The slant of the letters was sensitive and consistent. The "i" dotted crisply, not with an affected circle. The flourish beneath letters just this side of garishness, suggesting creativity and spirit. The closed "o" suggestive of a dependability, especially with secrets.

He dreaded opening it. The fates, if they had been on guard, wouldn't have allowed such good fortune to fall into his hands. Manabu was doomed to be tasted, appreciated, and whisked away from him. What talisman had Adrian to bring him back? He didn't believe in sorcery, except as a sort of superstitious belief in poetic justice. It wasn't just once in his twenties, after all. There had been others who'd been mistreated. Many times, Adrian had simply stopped returning their calls.

But he wasn't a toxic bachelor, at least not anymore. Couldn't even he have at least one more chance with love? After all, who in New York's gay social swirl had never been caught down on his knees in the Eagle by an ex-lover? (Adrian, the sort of person who swarmed an airport gate when attendants were trying to load a plane by row, was fond of thinking his peccadilloes were not unique but were typical rights of passage.)

He turned over the envelope. Manabu had drawn, with his elegant penmanship, a simple heart across the seal. Adrian's own heart fluttered, as they say. It could mean nothing, of course. He still hesitated to unseal the envelope. A heart sent out of pity, or as an apology? A heart to signify some sort of intimate affection for an ex-lover, such as a lesbian might send? Or an I love you, I'll be back soon sort of heart, like the guitar Richard Dreyfus leaves behind in *The Goodbye Girl* when he must travel out of town for a spell? Sooner or later, Adrian knew he had to open the envelope, and could only accept whatever classification the heart fell into. But for the moment he enjoyed just beholding it. If nothing else, it must mean Manabu felt, even if only in the past tense, something very real.

COINCIDENCE

D. E. LEFEVER

PAOLI, PENNSYLVANIA. IT seemed to me a *zillion* miles from New York City—a measure of distance from childhood that had no concept of geography. Even now as an adult, the City felt distant although little more than a two-hour train ride from Paoli. But the day was special. It was the second weekend of December 2005. I arrived at the Amtrak station early, almost as though doing so would accelerate my arrival in New York.

This trip was an annual event. One weekend each December I got lost among the crowd of shoppers on Fifth Avenue, skaters at Rockefeller Center, the patrons of MoMA, and the nighttime crush of theatergoers. But today my timing was, at least in part, to catch the release of *Brokeback Mountain*.

The early morning train was crowded. Taking a window seat, I picked a dog-eared, discarded issue of *People* from the floor, and fixed my eyes on the magazine, feigning interest to avoid any interruption. As the train sped past the rundown neighborhoods and industrial yards, and through the urban centers, I gazed out the window barely seeing anything. My thoughts drifted between eager anticipation of the city and earlier memories of the magic of Manhattan.

I recalled my initiation into "the City." It was, as I learned from attending school in upstate New York, a place that required no further identification. "The City" simply was, and is, New York. As part of the final leg of my return to school from holiday break, changing trains and terminals from Penn Station to Grand Central allowed time in the City before final departure. Tradition required meeting friends "under the clock" at the Biltmore where getting served without being carded was an almost certainty in spite of our obvious youth. I considered myself fortunate to be a part of a generation that had experienced the elegance and glamour of that destination. It was a place filled with well-dressed, good-looking men and fashionable, ageless women.

Seated at small, circular tables among massive marble columns in an enormous room, people quickly moved on to greet others or catch a departing train. The room echoed with laughter and the buzz of inaudible conversation as the tables filled and emptied. Dressed in coats and ties, a drink in hand, it was about as grown-up as one could ever expect to be. It was the seed of my annual return to the City, as predictable as migrating wildfowl. Now in my early forties, I quickly turned my thoughts from the demise of the Biltmore to the excitement of my arrival in Penn Station.

I deposited my suitcase with the baggage-check room, uncomfortably reminded of the pre—September 11 conveniences of storage lockers. I exited onto Thirty-first Street. It was 10:56 A.M. according to the station clock. In the bitter cold morning I avoided the taxi stand and found an idling cab for the short ride to Lowe's on Thirty-fourth Street. My ticket purchase on Fandango avoided a long wait in line. I handed it to the attendant and followed his finger with my eyes as he pointed me in the direction of the theater marked "*Brokeback*." Momentarily stopped in line, I felt someone tug lightly on my jacket sleeve: "Excuse me," I heard from behind as I turned, half expecting to recognize a familiar face.

"I saw you get on the train at Paoli, didn't I?"

It was no one I recognized.

"I don't mean to be rude, but the coincidence—New York's a big city—I just had to ask." He paused. "Philly would seem a more logical place to see *Brokeback*. Don't you think?" He said with a knowing smile.

Briefly I felt a bit awkward with the somewhat strange question. But I liked the smile, the admixture of confidence and timidity.

"Sure. I remember seeing you," I said somewhat jokingly. "That red turtleneck and ski cap would be hard not to remember." I returned the smile as we were moved forward by the ushers who were attempting to get the growing crowd into more orderly lines. But timing abruptly ended any chance for further conversation.

Once inside the theater I took a seat mid-row some twenty plus rows from the screen. Glancing along the row I saw the red sweater separated from me by more than a dozen other patrons. As later arrivals found seats, and I watched the assorted messages and previews flash across the screen, my mind was occupied by the all too brief exchange with someone whose name I didn't even know. I'd already lost any clear image of his face, unsure if I actually knew the color of his eyes or hair. The sweater and ski cap were what I remembered most, but from my seat there was no way of taking another look. I just knew that I liked his smile, the way the corners of his mouth turned up slightly, suggesting a hint of dimples. We were, I judged, nearly the same height and build, maybe he was a year or two younger. But my preoccupation quickly faded with the soundtrack of *Brokeback Mountain*.

It was my first ever experience where silence, of the "you could hear a pin drop" kind, filled the room and was followed by applause as the houselights came up. I stood to exit, noticing the figure in the red sweater linger to allow others to leave. Aware that I was in step behind him, he began moving toward the door. When we separated from the thick of the others, out of the darkness, he hesitatingly turned in my direction.

"You in a hurry to get somewhere, or do you have time to grab a cup of coffee? I saw a Starbucks a couple blocks up the street."

"Sure. Sounds good," I said. "You lead the way."

Once out in the early afternoon sunlight, conversation turned to *Brokeback Mountain*. The sidewalks were busy with shoppers darting in all directions, elbow to elbow. People were eager to get quickly out of the cold; it was not the place for more than fragmented questions and answers that were available for all to hear in disjointed bites.

Starbucks was packed with shoppers on break. Even meaningless conversation was impossible with the chaos of customers weaving with drinks, elbowing their way past the endless line. Conversational tones escalated, and then briefly faded, as people moved in and out, while others with one finger lodged in their ear shouted into cell phones. I had that unpleasant feeling I sometimes get at cocktail parties—the sense of being trapped, unable to thread my way across the room, impatient with the inability to talk to the person at my side. I have to focus to know which of multiple conversations I am a part. After minutes of standing in line, I noticed the couple whose table we were crowded against stand up, as if they were getting ready to leave.

"There's a seat. Tell me what you want," I said. "There won't be another chance at a table anytime soon."

I returned with two Grande Lattes. Placing the cups on the table, I extended my hand to the outstretched arm across from me. "My name's Jonathan Collier," I said.

"Brad Mason."

"I need thirty seconds to catch my breath." I paused. "Waiting for that movie to come to Paoli in January may have made more sense. But now that we have a seat, I'm glad to be here. Besides *Brokeback*, what brings you to the City?"

"My sister and brother-in-law live in Brooklyn. My plan was to see the movie and then go spend the weekend with them."

"'Plan was?'" I asked.

"My sister called just after we left the station. She was hoping I wasn't on the train yet. Jim, that's her husband, his father was in an accident in Boston. They're leaving to be with his mother."

"You don't have a bag?" I asked.

"I checked it at the terminal," Brad answered.

"That's where mine is too," I said.

Sitting across the table at Starbucks was my first real chance to see Brad. Jockeying the sidewalks pre-Christmas in New York required a degree of defensive maneuvering that didn't allow for intimate conversation, and certainly provided no safety for distraction. He was tall, at least six feet, give or take an inch, with black hair beneath that red ski cap. His eyes were hazel, maybe green. They were clearly the most noticeable things about him. When engaged in conversation, they communicated along with his words. He was more than just good-looking. His face was quite handsome with a square, masculine jawline, and that lingering evidence of a dark beard even after shaving. But his appearance was almost secondary to his changing facial expressions that revealed warmth and confidence that shifted with ease to unmask a gentle side.

"What brings you to New York?" Brad asked.

"I come in around this time every year. I have for years. It's just a fun, vibrant place to be after Thanksgiving. I love the Christmas atmosphere of this place—the fantasy of the window displays, the excitement of the shoppers, even the City noise. I just made *Brokeback* part of the package. I would probably be here anyhow."

"So what do you do, now that you've seen the movie?" Brad asked.

"No set agenda. You're more than welcome to join me, if

you like. Sounds like your plans fell apart."

"You sure you don't mind?" Brad asked.

"No, no. Over the years I've always done it on my own. It'll be fun to do it with someone else. Anything in particular you'd like to do?"

"I'm the intruder. You call the shots," Brad said. "If I really don't want to do something, I'll let you know."

"You like museums? There's MoMA. I read something about a contemporary design exhibit, innovative things that supposedly protect against injury and stress, like sports gear, special tents, stuff like bug netting. It'll be crowded I would guess, but that's probably what we expected coming here this time of year. At least it will be quieter than this place."

"You live in Paoli?" I asked once we were in the quiet of MoMA.

"About twenty-five minutes from there. It's a rural area. I live on a farm."

"And you? "Brad asked.

"Same." I smiled. "Mine's in the country, too. What do you do there?" I hesitated. "You don't exactly fit the image of a farmer."

"I'm part of a small, internal medicine practice right in Paoli. And you?"

"I'm a lawyer, in-house with a real estate development company over in Malvern."

The next two hours were spent browsing the gallery, mostly getting acquainted—college, graduate school, family, siblings, travel—the sort of random things that are the stuff of getting to know someone. Conversation came easily. We peppered each other with questions; neither of us seemed much into any of the exhibits. Here and there we paused for a superficial exchange of opinion about an odd-looking prototype or strange gadget. It was just enough to satisfy some unspoken recognition that we were in a museum, not aimlessly drifting through a shopping mall.

"I don't mean to be too personal, but are you in a relationship?" I asked as we were back out on the street.

"No. You?"

"No."

We laughed.

"Thanks for getting that out of the way," Brad said.

"You noticed. Lawyers do ask a lot of questions. Sorry if you thought you were in a deposition back there. I really don't intend to be prying."

"That's ok," Brad said. "I didn't want to spend the whole day together just knowing that you're someone who got on the same train in Paoli to see a movie in New York." He grinned. "If you hit the tender spots, I can always change the subject."

"What's next?" I asked. "Anyplace you want to go?"

"No. Not really," Brad said. "But if we're making a day of it, any chance we might get *Rent* tickets for later, that is if you'd be interested? I've wanted to see it for years."

"Sure. One of our senior vice-presidents gets last minute tickets for clients all the time. He heads up our New York projects so it goes with the territory. I'll give him a call. But in the meantime, I'd like to go to Brooks. It's my last Christmas purchase; my dad wants a scarf. I could use a couple new ties, too. It's on Madison. We can just grab a cab. Then it's your call. Must be something you'd like to do."

. . . . .

"SHIP THE SCARF and ties, Mr. Collier?" The salesperson asked.

"Please," I said. "We through here, Brad? Anything you want to look for?"

"No, thanks. But maybe now I could pick up my bag. I'd like to try to find a room near the terminal for the night. I could stay at my sister's even though she's gone, but I don't want to go all the way to Brooklyn after the theater gets out."

"Sure, that's fine. I don't want to be presumptuous, and maybe you want your privacy, but you can stay at my hotel. I'm a little embarrassed to admit that my reservation is at the Ritz on Battery Park. It's got a separate living room. I know it's excessive, but I like to splurge. I only do this once a year. It's my Christmas gift to myself."

"You sure?" Brad asked. "Sounds like I'm disrupting tradition."

"You're not. The day has been a nice break from tradition. Let's get our bags, check-in, relax a bit. Maybe we can find someplace for dinner if we have time before *Rent*."

"Sounds good," Brad said.

. . . . .

"NEED HELP WITH those bags?" The bellhop asked.

"No. Thanks. But we do have theater tickets for eight o'clock. Can you add a rollaway in the living room after we've gone?" I asked the desk clerk as we headed to the elevators.

"What a view," Brad said as he followed me into the room. "I'd say you splurged. I sure didn't expect to see the Statue of Liberty today."

We stretched out on the king-size bed, turned to CNN, and fell asleep. I awoke with Brad still in a sound sleep. His face was turned in my direction. His black hair fell across his forehead, its blackness accentuated by the black, fitted T-shirt. He was not muscular, but his body was well defined. I listened to his quiet breathing and inhaled the lingering hint of his aftershave lotion woven with his masculine scent. I remained only a minute or two, got up, showered, and was nearly dressed before Brad heard me moving about the room.

"Got time for a quick shower?" he asked.

"Sure," I said.

"Hotel restaurants sound good," Brad called from the bathroom. "OK by you? It's on me."

"Sure. What's your choice?"

"I'd like the one that overlooks the harbor. We can't get that in Paoli."

The hostess at Rise led us to a tall, round table with side-by-side bar stools pushed tightly against the window in the far corner. Once seated there was time to unwind with little need for more serious conversation. The day was already almost nonstop with questions, from the simple exchange of information to the more intimate ones that go deeper inside.

The view beyond the harbor was an endless stretch of lights, like an animated postcard with barges and tour boats seemingly in slow motion. We leaned on the glass top table with our elbows touching as we identified familiar landmarks—the lighted skeleton of the Verrazano Narrows Bridge—Ellis Island—the Statue of Liberty silhouetted against the night with the lights of New Jersey behind. In the exchange of a glance or smile was the realization that we had crossed a threshold to something more than just becoming friends, more than physical attraction.

"We need to get a cab," I said, although I wanted to linger longer. The thought of *Rent* was suddenly an intrusion.

"OK." Brad hesitated. "By the way, I enjoyed the day . . . a lot . . . but I think you already know that."

"Thanks." I hesitated. "I've got a bit of a confession myself. I wasn't joking this morning when I told you I saw the red sweater and ski cap in the train station. I really did. But I noticed the handsome guy wearing them, too. I owe you one for persistence."

We laughed as we descended the steps from the hotel to a waiting cab.

"West Forty-first Street. It's the Nederlander Theatre, I believe." I told the taxi driver as I slid into the rear seat with Brad behind me.

The temperature had dropped since checking into the hotel; the evening was gusty and icy cold. Brad slid tightly

against me, encircled me with his left arm, and pulled me
against him. He put his right hand in my coat under my chin,
complaining loudly of the cold. I clasped his hand in my
hands and pressed it against my mouth for warmth. On the
sidewalk outside the theater, waiting for the doors to open,
we stood together huddled in the midst of the biggest crowd
we could penetrate. Once inside, we took our seats almost
within arms reach of the stage, in the space ordinarily occupied by an orchestra. The theater was tired looking and the set
sparse, but the performance was energetic and the music, at
times, ear numbing. Brad took my hand in his, lifted it across
the armrest, and, squeezing it, lowered our entwined hands
above his knee. It was a terrific show, but one I was anxious to
applaud at final curtain call.

Back in the room, Brad threw his coat across a chair and
turned off the lights, enveloping us in the muted glow of the
City after dark. Momentarily we stared across the lighted
skyline. Simultaneously we reached toward each other, our
hands coming together, pulling upward against our chests.
Brad touched my face with the palm of his hand, running
his fingers up the back of my neck with his other hand. I
methodically unbuttoned his shirt, pulling it free of his pants.
It hung open, exposing the hair across his upper chest that
trailed to below his navel where it was terminated by the top
of his shorts. His stomach was hard. I undressed to my boxer
shorts as Brad unbuckled his belt, dropping his pants to his
ankles.

We leaned against the window jam, pushing tightly into
each other. I ran my fingers down his chest, through the hair
above his navel, feeling his stomach ripple at the touch of my
cold fingers. He stepped out of his pants and moved to the
bed. He pulled me onto the bed beside him. I ran my hand
along the inside of his muscular leg as he circled his fingers in
my groin. He turned, abruptly rolling to the side and came to
rest sitting on the edge of the bed.

"Sorry," He said. "I just need to say something before we go any frther."

"You OK?" I asked.

"I know my timing's bad." He said. "But I've got to tell you . . . this is not one night for me. It's you . . . not the day . . . the time . . . not the place . . . not *Brokeback Mountain* or *Rent*. Just needed you to know what I'm feeling."

I could see his taut face in the light of the urban sky, his nakedness clothed in a shadow cast from a chair by the window. Silence settled in the room. I did not respond. With passion faded in time, I crouched behind him, my hands on his shoulders, pulling him against my chest.

"I don't want to leave Paoli Station next year without you, either, Brad." I paused. "Before today, I thought this kind of thing happening 'at first sight' could only be a myth."

"Me, too." Brad said, his tense facial muscles relaxing.

We fell back on the bed, holding each other in stillness, allowing our simmering longing to reignite the passion.

ROUNDING THIRD

NEIL PLAKCY

A LITTLE WHILE after I started going out with Holly, I met her brother Jeff. He worked for a law firm with offices on Wall Street, proofreading on the night shift, and played third base on their softball team. One Saturday Holly and I met at the Columbus Circle entrance to Central Park and walked together to the softball field for the final round of the city championships. We brought a picnic lunch and a big old bedspread, which we set out on the grass beyond third base.

"Jeff played in the minor league for two years after college," Holly said as we chewed on cold chicken legs and watched the warm-ups. "He was really good but he didn't care about it enough to make it to the majors."

Jeff was clearly the best player on the field. His team won the championship, and there was a lot of celebrating and spraying of champagne. He was on a high when he came up to us afterward, hugging and kissing Holly, then hugging me, even though we'd just met.

I was thinking I might be bisexual then, though I hadn't had much experience with guys. After being gripped in Jeff's strong arms, my interest in him popped way up.

The law firm was only a few blocks from South Street Seaport, and he knew the shop I managed there. "Yeah, I've been past there a few times," he said. "You have all those old maps, don't you?"

I nodded. The store sold nautical memorabilia, old maps, antique whaling tools, and other related merchandise. It was a little on the quiet, stuffy side, not much business except for dedicated collectors, but that made my job easy. I was surprised he knew of it, because we're tucked away down an alley and most casual tourists never find us.

"I know my way around the city," Jeff said. Then he was dragged away by one of the partners who wanted to brag about him.

"They're trying to convince him to go to law school," Holly said as we packed up our picnic. "All the partners think he'd be a great attorney. He's so smart. I swear he's the smartest person I've ever met."

"You're just saying that because he's your brother," I said. "I bet everybody thinks their older brothers are brilliant."

Holly shook her head. "I mean it. When we were kids, he used to read the dictionary, for fun. He was always coming up to me and using these words I'd never even heard of. He could have been a Rhodes Scholar, too. He was offered the scholarship, but he said there just wasn't anything in England he really wanted to study, so he went to play ball instead."

"I'm sure your parents loved that."

"Jeff has a very strong personality," she said. "That's why we fight so much. When he wants to do something, there's no arguing with him. My mother wanted him to take the scholarship, but she couldn't do anything about it."

The next Tuesday, Jeff came past the bookstore just around closing time, on his way to the law firm for a night of spell checking and fact research. He had an hour to kill, so we walked down the street to an Irish bar with a neon harp above the door. We drank Killian red ale on tap and talked about our fathers.

"Mine was a pilot, in World War II and then the Korean

War, and he got married late," I said. "My mother was a lot younger than he was, almost fifteen years, and they never planned to have kids at all. He was a pilot for the airlines by then, and she was going to keep flying around the world with him."

"Sounds nice," Jeff said.

"Then I came along. My mother settled down to do the happy homemaker Donna Reed routine, and my father kept flying off to exotic places. I was the only eight-year-old on the block to have a zebra skin rug, and I carried my books to school in a genuine alpine climber's knapsack."

I paused to take a long swig of my beer. "I knew my father couldn't hang out and do kid stuff with me. Most of the time he was thirty thousand feet in the air, and when he wasn't he was firmly rooted in his Naugahyde recliner, stretched out in front of the TV set in the living room. So I never really had much of a dad, growing up."

"My dad was too much," Jeff said. "All the time I was growing up, he was crazy for baseball, and he made me that way, at least for a while. All during the season it was Yankees this, Dodgers that, and who's going to win the pennant. Every day after he came home from work, he'd go out and throw the ball around with me. It was his dream for me to play in the majors, and when I didn't want to it nearly made him crazy."

"So are you going to law school?" I asked. "Holly said you were thinking about it."

"I might," Jeff said. "But just for the experience. I don't think I'd ever want to be a practicing attorney. There's so much crap you have to take, so much you have to do that's false. I won't compromise my principles for a dollar."

I was impressed. I admit, I was naive, and I was already a little in awe of him from what Holly had said and from watching him play ball, so it was easy for me to get carried away. We talked about the Mets, and he knew the stats on every player since the fifties. He remembered every game he'd ever seen in detail and analyzed plays in a way that seemed to open up the game to me, as I had never seen it. When we left the bar, he asked if Holly and I would like to have dinner with him on Saturday night.

I agreed readily, but Holly was less than enthusiastic when I told her. "Your brother's a great guy," I said. "What's the matter?"

"He's a little pompous, don't you think?" she asked. "I mean, I know he's smart, like I've always said he's the smartest person I've ever met, but it just wears on me after a while. And we just saw him last week. That's enough."

"Come on, please?" I asked. "I really had a good time with him tonight."

"All right," Holly said. "But this is it."

I couldn't understand what Holly was complaining about. We had a great time at dinner, and Jeff and I made plans to play racquetball the next week. After playing, we went out for a beer. "So why'd you stop playing ball professionally?" I asked. "Holly says you were really good."

"Let me tell you a story," he said. "This was when I was playing in Arizona, in the triple A league. I had hit this beautiful grounder, straight past the pitcher, deep into center field. The sky was this absolutely perfect light blue, only a few puffy clouds floating up high. I was running really well, it was like the ground was helping me along. I rounded third, headed for home, and I suddenly thought, I can do this. There's no challenge left in it. A couple of weeks later they offered to move me up to the majors, but it was too late. I wasn't into it anymore."

"Wow," I said.

We started to hang out together a couple times a week, playing racquetball or having beers or sometimes going to an old movie that Holly had already seen ten million times. Jeff had seen them all ten million times too, but he was always willing to go again.

Holly started to get a little jealous of all the time I was spending with her brother, and I could sense we were drifting apart. It was a matter of time before one of us got fed up, or met someone new. I had the feeling I was hanging on to her because I was afraid I'd lose my friendship with Jeff if Holly and I broke up.

Jeff and I talked a lot. He was always giving me advice, from how to grip my racquet to what stuff I ought to feature in the window of the store. One night, after we'd shared a couple of beers, he decided he had to show me exactly how the displays at the front could be rearranged, and we walked back to the store together.

Once we got away from the hustle and bustle of the Seaport, the narrow streets of downtown were mostly deserted. In a few hours, the Fulton Fish Market would come to life, and the cobblestones would be sloppy with fish guts. But in those few hours between the departure of the Wall Street workers and the arrival of the trucks bearing fresh and frozen fish, the area was quiet and almost spooky. Jeff had the night off, and both of us had probably had more than we usually did to drink. I remember laughing and stumbling against each other on the cobblestone street in front of the bookstore.

We lowered the old-fashioned window shades so that no one would think we were open, and started moving around displays. I got a little giddy, dancing with one of the manne-quins, and I spun around and would have fallen to the floor if Jeff hadn't caught me.

There I was, in his arms again, just like I'd been the first time we met. Only this time, he did just what I wanted—he kissed me. And I kissed him back.

All that brotherly camaraderie we'd been developing slipped away as our lips locked. He grabbed the back of my head and pressed my face to his, and I wrapped my arms around his back and pressed my body against him. The next few minutes were a mad rush of discarded clothes and naked bodies.

When we were both spent, we found ourselves lying on the floor in the middle of chaos—a tipped-over display of maps, a nest around us of his stuff and mine. The sex had been wilder and more passionate than anything I'd had with Holly—or any other girl, for that matter. The topic of bisexuality was shelved for me; I was gay.

"Well, this is awkward," Jeff finally said, when I'd become embarrassed by my nudity and pulled my legs up to my chest. "I've never stolen away one of Holly's boyfriends before."

"Have you wanted to?"

He shrugged. "She's dated a couple of cute guys, but you're the first one I've really been interested in."

The store was lit by big, hanging incandescent lights with bulbs that were meant to look like candles, and it was like a spotlight shining on the events of the past few weeks. "I am?"

"I figure we've been dating since that first time I asked you out for a beer," he said. "I was just waiting for you to see it that way, too."

"So you knew that I was—"

"Hoped is probably a better word." He reached out and took my hand. "Was I wrong?"

I shook my head. I was playing over all those beers, those movies, those racquetball games. Being in the shower at the health club with him, I'd stolen the occasional glance at his perfect body, then looked away before my interest gave me away. And all that time he'd been pursuing me, so subtly I hadn't noticed until he dragged me back to the shop after hours, and finally kissed me.

"So," I said. My mouth was dry. "Um, Holly."

"You're going to have to decide between us," he said. "My sister doesn't share well." He grinned and scooted his body over next to mine again. "Neither do I."

I let him know, by kissing him, that I chose him.

. . . . .

THE NEXT DAY, Friday, I had plans to meet with Holly after work. She came down to the Seaport, and we walked over to this Peruvian seafood place that had just opened. We were just finishing our ceviche when she said, "Look, I know what's going on."

My heart rate zoomed. "Um, ok," I said.

"Our relationship isn't going anywhere, but you've been hanging on because you and my brother are friends now."

"He's a great guy," I said.

"In your opinion. Most of the time I think he's a pompous blowhard. You do know he's gay, don't you?"

"Um, I got that idea," I said.

"Usually he doesn't like to tell people. He's afraid they'll judge him. 'My private life is my private business,' he always says. I don't really care one way or the other, but I hope he finds a boyfriend who can put up with him."

I nodded. "I hope so, too."

She reached across the table and took my hand. "So no hard feelings?"

I would have burst out laughing if I could have. I sure had hard feelings for Jeff. But I said, "Nope. These things happen." I paused. "So you wouldn't mind if I kept in touch with him?"

She shrugged. "It's your life."

My body was electrified as Holly and I left the restaurant. I couldn't wait to tell Jeff what had happened. But then, on my way home, I started coming up with doubts. I remembered Jeff's explanation about why he'd quit baseball—that the challenge had gone out of it for him. What if I'd just been a challenge he'd set for himself: could he steal his sister's boyfriend?

I kept thinking about it, in bed watching the late news. Even when I finally fell asleep, I had vague ephemeral dreams about Jeff parachuting down from a plane to the front yard of my parents' house, telling me that my father had confessed we weren't really brothers at all.

I woke up at five-fifteen, looked at the clock, and then sank back into the pillows and sighed. Saturday morning, my day off, and I couldn't sleep late. I wondered what Jeff would be doing.

His shift ended at 6:00 A.M., and I knew he usually stopped at the coffee shop across the street for a cup of coffee and a doughnut, before walking back across the bridge to his apartment in Brooklyn.

I got up, got dressed, and took the subway down to Wall Street. I walked to the coffee shop across from Jeff's office and sat at the counter. I stared at the classical designs on the paper coffee cup and thought about what I wanted to say.

He walked in a few minutes after six. "Hey, this is a nice surprise," he said. He sat down next to me and ordered coffee and a donut. I told him about my conversation with Holly, that she'd said she didn't mind if Jeff and I stayed friends.

He didn't say anything for a long minute, and I felt all my disastrous premonitions coming true. Jeff couldn't stick to anything—as soon as the challenge was out of it, he was gone.

Finally he said, "I'm looking for more than friendship," and it was so different from what I'd expected that it took me a while to process.

"I keep walking away from stuff because I'm scared of what people will think of me when they find out who I really am," he continued. "I mean, that business about why I stopped playing ball. Bullshit. I had a crush on another player, a straight guy, and it was tearing me up." He paused. "Did Holly tell you I've been thinking about quitting the law firm?"

I shook my head, still digesting the meaning behind the words. The waitress was at the far end of the counter, talking to the fry cook. The nearest patron was an older guy in a suit three stools down. We were in the middle of the city but it was like we were all alone.

"But you, you're still here for me, even after we—you know. And that's making me think that maybe other people will stick around too." He looked at me. "You are going to stick around, aren't you?"

I reached below the counter and squeezed his hand. "You'll have to chase me away," I said.

We sat there for a while, drinking coffee, and not talking much. Finally Jeff yawned and said he really needed to get some sleep. We made plans to meet up that evening, and he headed off to Brooklyn.

I started walking back uptown, and when I came to Gramercy Park, where I had a tiny studio apartment, I was still really stoking, so I decided to keep going. By eight o'clock I was at Central Park, at the softball field. I sat back on the lowest of the bleachers and looked up at the sky. It was a beautiful light blue, just like the sky Jeff had described on the day he decided to quit baseball. I closed my eyes and dozed for a while. No restless dreams of parachutists, just a nice, peaceful sleep.

When I woke up my muscles felt funny, from stretching out over the uncomfortable bleachers. I jumped up, did some warm-up exercises, and then started to jog around the bases of the softball field.

I decided it was time I forgave my father for not being there for me, and for making me an only child. I had met Jeff, and I thought maybe he could fill some of those empty spaces in my life. It felt good. I went hard around second, running sure and strong, as if the ground was leaping up to meet me. I heard an imaginary crowd roaring, cheering me on. Then I rounded third, heading for home, feeling great, knowing that Jeff would be there waiting for me.

THE SUBWAY KISS

MICHAEL T. LUONGO

HE AND I met late at night, in a small theater on the Lower East Side. That might sound like the start to an erotic story, and while what was on screen was certainly sensual, our meeting turned out to be the beginning of a quickly stunted romance.

The film was an art house revival of *Pink Narcissus*, the dreamy, pink 1971 work of James Bidgood. The images on screen were weird, misty, psychedelic, full of men dressed as harem boys dancing with flailing penises, and stage sets of giant cocks in a satanic Times Square. Almost thirty years after their creation, the images still remained shocking.

While I was mesmerized by what I saw on screen, it was what walked in late to the theater that kept my interest all the more: a well-built man had plodded down the center aisle, blocking everyone's view as he decided where to sit. I could not tell yet if he was handsome, I could only imagine. And he had upset no one in the crowded theater—all eyes were instead drawn to this mysterious figure. He found a seat against the wall in the front and stood up as he pulled off layer after layer, a jacket, a sweatshirt, a button-down—his muscular shoulders, and narrowing waist silhouetted against the vivid images on the screen. For just a moment, his last layer of clothes, a

T-shirt, was caught in the rapid pulling, lifting at the moment the screen grew a bright white, revealing a well-toned chest and a chiseled face under thick wavy hair. Italian, Latino, Greek, maybe even Sephardic, something Mediterranean for sure. The image of him remained imprinted in my mind as the movie continued, competing with what I paid to see on screen.

I had come alone to the theater but when the film ended and the lights brightened, I noticed a friend and his lover in the audience, and so I went up to chat. The handsome mysterious man remained in his corner against the wall, his eyes focused on the screen as the credits rolled. Quite a few other men stayed in their seats, pretending to be interested in the credits too, but their eyes were transfixed on this man, anxiously awaiting when he would stand up to leave, giving us all a better view of what he looked like, to see if what we imagined lived up to reality.

Even to my friend, it was obvious I was not so interested in talking with him as much as I was on keeping an eye on this intriguer. It was when I asked, perhaps even a little too loud, if he and his lover too had noticed the man, that the object of my attention stood up and glanced in my direction as he hovered over his chair. He put back on the layers he had so quickly removed before, and, once tightly bundled, he plodded heavily back up the aisle, not looking at me or a single other person. All of us who remained, and there were many, giving each other glances as if assuring each other what we saw was real, not simply a hallucination like the beautiful men on the screen had seemed to be only moments before. But now that the handsome man had left the building, there was no reason for any of us to stay and feign interest in the details of the making of the film. We all filtered quickly out of the theatre, the blackened screen, and the last of the white lettered credits rolling behind us.

Out front, I lit a cigarette and bid my friend and his lover good-bye with quick pecks on their cheeks. At the corner of my eye, I don't need to tell you who I caught sight of. He had moved slowly away from the theater, and so I proceeded rapidly but quietly in his direction, even if it was the opposite of where I really needed to go. He was not hard to catch up with. Looking back to this moment in time, nearly seven years ago, I think he wanted to be caught by someone in the theater. That someone turned out to be me.

I came up from behind and paced next to him, looking at him now and then to try to get his attention. He tried to look as if he wasn't noticing me, and I tried to look as if I were giving my cigarette, an accessory in my show, more attention than him.

"What'd you think of the movie? You were just at the movie, right?" I finally asked him after a few blocks, the most obvious thing I could say and far from an easily escapable yes or no question.

He smiled broadly and pulled his head back, aware he had finally been caught. "It was OK," he said, seeming like a question. His pace had slowed, and then we looked at each other and smiled.

To see him up close was to take in a vision of strong masculinity, a roughly handsome man whose looks gave away a tough past, but who knew how to polish himself to throw someone off, to keep them guessing about him. I felt myself shudder in the kind of surprise when the cable guy, the UPS man, or some kind of blue collar worker shows up to do repair work and he is unexpectedly handsome and sensual, yet out of place in his element. He had a cleft chin, and his cheeks were high and angled, like a 1980s cartoon superhero. His nose was Roman, almost broken, with somewhat of a sneer, and the pores of his skin, giving away a life in the sun too long, or of harsh smoking, were clearly visible. His hair was black, curly, and thick, unkempt, but he pulled it back as I looked at him, running his fingers through it slowly, trying to appear nonchalant about meeting me. He was immensely striking, his handsomeness overpowering its rough base.

In the midst of taking him in, I asked him where he hailed from. I almost thought he answered that he was from out of town, and since it was shortly after Christmas, a time when the city floods with tourists, it seemed to make sense. It was only when I used it as a way to continue the conversation that he clarified he lived uptown, not out of town. I couldn't exactly place his accent, even if it seemed a variation of something local. It wasn't Queens, it wasn't Brooklyn, and it wasn't New Jersey where I'm from. I knew he was not a transplant who had moved here from some other part of the country. Long Island was where he had grown up, he finally explained when I asked, but now he lived in Harlem, settling there only very recently, just one more of an increasing number of white gay men moving to the world's most famous black neighborhood.

All I wanted was a one-night stand, but it was obvious that even if I tried to add heat and immediacy to the conversation, he wasn't going to take it there. I have no use for relationships, they get in the way of travel, and of writing, and the two things I prefer to do with my time. I knew as we continued chatting that he was leaning toward a date, a commitment beyond the here and now, an act to prolong the time until I got what I wanted, what to me is the inevitable outcome of two gay men meeting each other. Sex. Still, a date. I liked the concept. He had been the most handsome man in the theater, the one everyone wanted, and here I was talking to him, setting a date. I had the giddy feeling of a 14-year-old as I shook his hand and said good night before we walked away in two different directions. We had exchanged numbers, not deciding though who would call whom first. I knew though, that I wanted to consummate this relationship. I wanted to sleep with him, which had been my intention when I followed him the long blocks from the movie theatre.

He wound up calling me first though, leaving a message on my voice mail early the next day. I picked the restaurant, Taza de Oro, an inexpensive Cuban spot in Chelsea, authentic, with character, one there long before the neighborhood had become gay. Here, and in only a few places, did these ancient neighborhood eateries still remain amidst the new and polished places that seem to catch everyone else's attention. I relished these spots, showing them to out-of-towners and friends new to the city like a vanishing native species that had to be seen before it disappeared from the face of the earth in a New York gone cold and corporate, safe for mall-bred Midwesterners whose vocabulary only contained chain restaurants.

Jason was his name, and when we sat across from each other at the restaurant, I said, "Could be Jewish, could be Greek?" He answered maybe it could be either. He was actually adopted, raised by a Long Island family who never really knew what he was. The only thing he carried from his true mother's family was that first name, Jason, and his ambiguously Mediterranean good looks. Could be Jewish, could be Greek, he said, by name alone. The features though like all of my guesses when I first saw him at the theater could have placed him as Italian or Puerto Rican too, anything within the spectrum of New York's swarthy ethnic elements. We argued these fine genetic points as his large hands played with mine under the table, bringing home the reality that such things really don't matter when you find someone attractive.

He was an artist, a painter, and a perfect complement to my writing. At the time, I was barely published, and I too had only recently made that leap across the river from suburb to city in the hopes of furthering what little record my ambition had so far revealed to the world. We had done it from opposite ends of the region—him from where the sun rises over the sea heading up the LIE, myself from where the sun finally passes after it has radiated over Manhattan's aspiring souls on its way down the turnpike to Philadelphia. Cheap housing was our mutual drive. I lived at the top of Manhattan Island, in Washington Heights, and he had settled into Harlem. I thought my rent was phenomenally cheap, but even his surprised me.

He lived in a slum building though, one full of poor crack addicts, but with huge, almost cavernous spaces that he could use for his studio. Cheap plentiful space untouched by Corcoran Realty. It was an artist's dream, save for the problems of living among addicts.

"Lightbulbs," he said. "Lightbulbs are a problem." He intrigued me with this story of the dark hallways in his building, a walk-up. Every few days, he said he was replacing them, never understanding what was happening to them, until, like a lightbulb in a cartoon, it dawned on him. His neighbors were stealing them and selling them for whatever they could, at most a quarter on the streets, or to stores around the corner.

"Who would go to such lengths for twenty-five cents?" I asked. "Drug addicts in need of a fix," he coolly responded, the answer was so clear and logical. I lived in a bad building, full of roaches and mice, but the building was all families who looked out for one another, even caring to welcome and protect ambitious suburbanites like myself. It was safe. No one, as far as I knew, stole anything, least of all a stupid lightbulb.

But it was a funny story, a way to get to know him better. Finally he explained the solution was a portable light—one that couldn't be stolen in the hallway because he always had it on him. He pulled a flashlight out of his bag and said he never left without it, how else would he climb the dark staircases at four in the morning? Besides, it made a good weapon just in case, still a concern at the turn of the millennium, especially for suburban boys our age raised on the horror stories of family and neighbors who commuted in during the 70s and

80s. That aspect of the city was long gone, but pervaded our thoughts everywhere we went, even if once dangerous areas were becoming untouchably overpriced living spaces.

Jason told me he spent a lot of his time painting in the studio, but he had yet to sell a single piece, or have a show, any of the things expected of successful artists. It was then that we got to the topic of money and what he did to really earn it. I had a part time job, that was how I really made my living at the time, until the writing and the dreams paid their dividends. What was his part time job, how did he pay the rent?

He was strangely mute and fidgety when I asked this question. To think back, he could have simply lied, making up something, but instead, he refused to answer the question, and his eyes no longer met mine. "Jason, how do you make a living then?" I asked again, feeling that a simple date had become an interview, an interrogation.

"I just make a living, I know people. I survive somehow." This and a crooked smile were as detailed an answer as I was going to get.

In New York, the anonymous city, there are a lot of ways people who don't have jobs can make a living. Being Italian, I've had a lifetime of experiences meeting men who had no real job, save for the kind that become plots of movies and cable TV series. Jason didn't seem to be that. That he might have even sold drugs came to my mind but really, maybe he would have made a better living if that were the case. And if he were selling, he certainly didn't act like he was using, even if people can put on a good show.

But really, there was only one thing I could think of as for how he made his living, someone as handsome as he was, and that wasn't the kind of man with whom I would want to be in a relationship. I wasn't judging what he did, if that is what he did, but how would I know anyway? I had had enough lies in the supposedly serious relationships I had left behind. Those lies revealed themselves over time, I didn't need to start a new relationship, which began with a lie, and one I felt I already knew the answer to.

The conversation didn't go very far after this, breaking into little bits and feigned smiles between the both of us. When the bill came, he didn't even reach for it. I knew I would have to pay. "Can you get it?" he asked, seemingly well practiced. "You picked the restaurant tonight." "Sure," I said, "you'll get it the next time, and I'll let you pick where we go." But I knew there would be no next time.

We left the restaurant, and ever the guide, I pointed out a few things irresistible to me, like how the Port Authority office building, that huge art deco monstrosity across the street from the restaurant on Eighth Avenue, had more usable space than the much taller Empire State Building, finished at the same time, but all elevators. He seemed fascinated, but after a few moments of meaningless conversation, I didn't want to play tour guide anymore. I just wanted to head home. I had already resolved in the restaurant that this would go nowhere. I could barely afford myself, and to date someone, paying for everything, my time not my own, would never do. I had a resume waiting for lists of publications to round it out. I would never have the time if I gave myself over to him, to the idea of a strange love, a love that might never give me what I wanted and who would always have me foot the bills. And just how did he make his living, kept rolling through my head. Who would I be sharing him with?

We both lived off the A Line and descended together down the Fourteenth Street entrance. We caught ourselves checking out all the other men waiting for their rides home on the platform, until the familiar steel train appeared before us. It was crowded and we huddled together around one of the poles, our hands purposely touching, overlapping, entwining around it. We had less than twenty minutes left together on our date in this very public space. I still wanted to make the most of it. Looking into each other's eyes, we talked again about the Bidgood movie and what we would see together for our next date. It was strange to make plans I knew I had no desire to carry through on.

After the long run between Columbus Circle and Harlem, the car door opened at 125th and Jason said it was his stop. He didn't ask me to come with him. I knew that was not how the night would end. But here on the subway, I was for the here and now. I knew he wanted to kiss me good night. I felt, I should let myself go. I would never date Jason, and it was obvious now I would never sleep with him. But I had never before given myself over to the movie-scene feeling of being swept away in a kiss on the New York subway. I let his token of a tongue slip into the slot of my mouth. Even this fantasy was shattered, if only slightly, by the betrayal of a reality—I tasted the garlic from the palomilla at the Cuban restaurant on his breath. Still, I kept him in, letting his tongue probe, feeling the smile on my face, delighting in the subversive thought of stealing kisses so deep underground in this steel shaft that hurtled through the city's granite bedrock at sixty miles an hour. This was what I would get from him, this would be my memory of him, my fond final memory.

It was a long, deep kiss; he nearly missed getting off the train, running out just as the doors snapped into place, waving through the glass at me with a huge smile, one hand against his ear, imitating a telephone. "Call me," I knew he was mouthing. Little Dominican girls, who were surely my neighbors a few more stops up in Washington Heights, looked up from their orange fiberglass seats staring silently at me. I am sure they had been doing so from the very moment my lips had touched Jason's, but I had simply never noticed them until now. I held onto the pole for balance, dizzy and self-conscious from the kiss.

· · · · ·

I NEVER CALLED Jason, and he never called me. For months, I felt sort of guilty, wondering, even if I knew from the get-go that he was bad news, what it would have been like to date him. And, never once again did I see him; never once again did our paths cross. New York is a city of eight million souls, but it's really a small town, and circles close into each other. I've fucked men anonymously in lurid places, or in their own homes after a late night clubbing, hoping never to see them again, only to run into them again and again all over the subway system when I am making connections of another sort. But as for Jason, the last time I saw him was after our first kiss waving at me through the glass at the end of that first and only date. He still remains a part of me though, my first and only romantic subway kiss. He comes to mind as what never was, each time the A train opens up on 125th Street on my long subway ride home.

DANCING ON AIR

ROB ROSEN

THE CAB PULLED up to the Chelsea brownstone just as the sun sat its fat ass behind a row of five story buildings to the west. A rosy, warm glow turned the blue sky a brilliant pink. It was a perfectly apt greeting.

"Special, just for me," Loni said to himself as he exited the cigarette-infused cab, and took his first deep breath of New York City air. The cab pulled away and left a cloud of exhaust fumes in its wake. Loni coughed once, but otherwise retained his upbeat disposition. "One big queen. One Big Apple. One big—" he stopped mid-sentence and bent down to retrieve a sullied flyer off the sidewalk. "...party. One big party. They must've heard I was coming."

He grabbed his suitcase, climbed the stairs that led to the front door of the building, and used the key that the landlord had mailed him. He rented the apartment sight unseen after spotting the ad on Craigslist. First month's, last month's, and a security deposit of a thousand bucks. In total, twenty-five hundred dollars—his entire life savings, almost. It was a risky undertaking, considering his financial situation, which was bleak, at best.

Still, his job as a window designer at Bloomingdale's would start in a week, and he'd be back on his feet in no time flat. He'd just have to stretch out his remaining two hundred dollars until then. Minus the thirty for the cab ride, that left one seventy.

"Plenty," he said, "if I stick to Ramen noodles and instant coffee until my first paycheck."

He opened the door to the building and walked inside the miniscule lobby, setting his suitcase down and then closing the door behind him. "Now, where's the elevator?" He scanned left, then right, and finally forward, but all he saw were dingy, cobwebbed walls. "Well fuck me," he said with a tired groan.

The ad stated that the apartment was on the sixth floor with a park view. It failed to mention anything about being a walk-up. "Fuck, fuck, fuck," Loni said as he heaved his heavy luggage up and around the first flight of creaking stairs, pausing as he reached the second to catch his breath. This he repeated five more times, until his back was nearly broken and his arm felt like it was ready to fall off. When he at last reached number 602, he dropped his belongings heavily in front of the door, sat down for a quick rest, and uttered, "Home, sweet home."

Only home wasn't so sweet.

"Goddamn," he said, once he found the strength to open the apartment door. "Maybe I should've had him email me a picture."

It was, as the ad described, cozy, if you were into sleeping in a glorified closet. And it was newly painted, albeit in a snazzy prison gray. Hardwood floors? Sure, though the wood was from two centuries ago. And the view of the park? "Three trees and one homeless man do not a park make," he nearly cried. "Oh look, two homeless men. Great, I won't be lacking for company."

Loni closed his eyes and counted to ten. "New York, New York, it's a hell of a town," he sang, and then opened his eyes. "Oh well, it could be worse." Though, in all honesty, he couldn't figure out how. And then he unpacked. Luckily, the apartment came furnished. Furnished-ish, that is. One mattress. One dresser. One garbage can. Two plates, a fork, a spoon, a mug with I ♥ NY painted in faded letters, and a bag of Fritos of indeterminate age.

"What was the security deposit for? In case I ate the Fritos?"

When he was done, and he put two sets of sheets on the aged, stained mattress, he flopped down on his new bed and stared at the cracked ceiling above. "I think this is how Barbra got her start. No, wait, it was Madonna."

He suddenly remembered the flyer and pulled it from his back pocket. "White Party at Roseland Ballroom," he read. A picture of two hunky, shirtless men in white shorty-shorts was printed beneath the wording. "My kind of party. And Roseland. Sounds like Disneyland, only for queers." Then he read the bottom of the flyer, "thirty-five dollars at the door." He grimaced and threw in a "fuck" for good measure.

"Okay," he said, after he'd given it some thought. "No coffee. Just Ramen. And I already have an outfit. Besides, it's the first night of the rest of my life. And *Roseland*. It sounds so, so, enchanting."

Once the rust ran through the pipes, which only took ten minutes, Loni showered and slipped into a pair of white slacks, a white vest, and some white sneakers. "Perfect," he said, admiring his lean torso in the cracked mirror, above the cracked basin, that rested on the cracked tile floor. He was, of course, referring to his outfit.

And then he was off. It took a couple of short bus rides to make it to West Fifty-second Street, plus a couple of blocks of walking, which was only slightly terrifying, but he made it. It was still somewhat early, so the line outside was a mere fifty or so guys in length—fifty stunning gay guys all in white. Loni imagined that this must be what the queue to heaven looked like.

Minutes later, he was walking into the turn of the century

building, through a beautiful white, satin lobby, and right into the ballroom.

"Holy cow," was all he could manage as his eyes adjusted to the dark interior. "It really is a ballroom." He assumed that they weren't being literal when they called it that; but looking at the memorabilia they had hanging on the walls, he found that Roseland had been a ballroom since the twenties. People had been coming to dance there for eighty years. And no wonder, he thought, the place truly was spectacular. He'd never in his whole life seen anything like it. And it was chock full of young, handsome, gay men.

Who needs Ramen noodles, he thought. He could survive on this. The sheer energy of it could sustain him.

He found himself at a stairwell and climbed to the next level, which was a balcony that circled the ballroom. He leaned over and stared at the scene below. The space itself was a giant rectangle, with the dance floor smack-dab in the center—the most massive, most dazzling dance floor he'd ever seen—and to the side of this was a curtained, raised stage. But it was the lights above, the lights that swirled and rotated and bounced and shed their rays across the room, which mesmerized Loni. He'd never seen lights like this before. They bathed the mostly shirtless dancers in every conceivable color, turning the spectacle into a living, breathing kaleidoscope. And the music was crystal clear, deep, beating house, which caused his body to vibrate and his soul to soar. It had never felt so good to be young and alive.

"First time at Roseland, huh?' came a voice to his right.

Loni jumped, shocked out of his reverie. He turned to the voice. Inches away from him were a pair of the most shockingly blue eyes he'd ever seen. "Yeah, how did you know?"

"You had the look. I had the same look the first time I saw it, too."

"It's pretty amazing." He paused and grinned sheepishly at the stranger. "Name's Loni, by the way." He stuck his hand out. The guy shook it with a good, strong grip.

"Doug," the guy said, and smiled a wide, glorious smile. "Nice to meet you, Loni. I've never met a guy named Loni before."

Loni blushed. "Um, yeah. Well, my mom had a big crush on Burt Reynolds, and she thought she was having a girl, so—"

"You're named after Loni Anderson?" The guy laughed and then quickly stopped himself. "Sorry," he said, with his hand covering his mouth.

"No, it is sort of funny. Luckily, most people don't even remember who she is anymore."

He smiled at Doug and stared into his deep, blue eyes. He quickly noticed that the rest of him was just as nice to look at. He had dark, short-cropped hair, long sideburns, and a cute, little pointy goatee. Both men were the same height and body type, and both had on white vests and white slacks.

"I like your outfit," Loni said.

"Who needs a mirror when I have you," Doug said, and inched in closer. The two were now shoulder to shoulder and looking down at the crowd, which was growing by the second. They stood that way through a couple of songs. Loni's heart beat rhythmically to the music. His body tingled in anticipation at what was to come next.

"Loni?" Doug said, breaking the silence, as he turned his face to look at him.

"Yeah, Doug?" Loni turned too. The lights swirled over Doug's face, splashing him in color after color, but the sapphire eyes always remained intense and constant.

"Wanna dance?"

"Uh huh."

He paused and grinned. "Wanna kiss me first?"

"Uh huh."

Oh, it was a beautiful kiss. A perfect kiss. Soft and warm and tender and eager. Their bodies fit snuggly against each other as they held hands and kissed and swayed to the pulsating music. Loni quickly forgot his lack of money and wretched apartment, and concentrated solely on the handsome stranger with the stunning eyes.

Eventually, Doug led him back down the stairs to the dance floor. "Have you danced yet?" he asked Loni.

"Nope, not yet. I only just got here."

"Oh man, are you in for a treat. There's nothing like dancing at Roseland."

Loni hadn't a clue what he could mean by that. He'd danced on plenty of dance floors before. They were all alike.

He was wrong, of course.

Roseland was indeed a ballroom. You didn't just dance on the floor. You glided over it. It was something you noticed as soon as you stepped onto it. Loni smiled as he faced Doug.

"Oh my God," he yelled over the music.

"Yep. Told you so. It's like dancing on air."

Like a cloud, Loni thought, with an angel.

The crowd swelled as the beat picked up. The lights overhead pulsed and strobed. The Venus was dropped, a massive circular array of lights that spun like a merry-go-round. The crowd raised their arms in the air and shouted their delight. Their hands moved side to side, as if they were magically helping the Venus to spin faster and faster, which it inevitably did, drenching the revelers in a flood of light.

Doug reached out and held Loni close to him. Their vests were now open, and their toned, thin bodies, dripping with sweat, were pressed hard against each other. Their lips once again met. Their tongues swirled. Their eyes stayed locked— brown on blue, blue on brown. The music and the lights faded into the background. There were only the two of them, gliding on a stream of air. The vests came off. Hands found nipples. Lips pressed harder, as did bodies. The eyes stayed opened and locked. It was pure, unadulterated bliss on West 52nd Street on the greatest dance floor ever made in the greatest city in the world—Loni's city, to be precise. His home.

They stayed that way for hours, dancing and kissing, and enjoying the new, lustful feel of each other's bodies. Until, by the end of the night, they felt like they'd been together forever. Sadly, however, before they knew it, the staff was shouting last call and raising the lights.

"Loni?" Doug whispered in his ear.

"Yeah, Doug?" Loni said, nuzzling his neck.

"I gotta go home." It didn't sound right to Loni. He didn't say he had to go home and would Loni like to go with him. It was more final than that. More sad than glad. He added, "I only meant to stay for an hour or two. I have to go to work in the morning." He looked down at his watch. "Actually, I have to go to work in a few hours."

"Oh," was all Loni could say as he struggled to keep his smile.

"Sorry, Loni. I'd love to invite you over, you know. It's just that I don't want to have to rush you out. Here you go, though." He produced a business card from his wallet. "I'm off tomorrow. Call me and we'll get together. Okay?"

Loni's heart filled with joy. He held on tight to Doug and gave him a long, deep kiss. "Yep. Count on it," he replied.

"Promise?" Doug asked, expectantly. Longingly.

"Promise," Loni promised, grabbing Doug's goatee and pulling him to his lips one final time. "I'll see you tomorrow."

"I'm off the next two days, Loni." The wide, beautiful smile returned, and the eyes sparkled a fierce blue.

"Okay, Doug. Then I'll see you tomorrow and the day after that."

"*Mhm,*" came the happy response.

The two walked out into the warm, morning air, hand in hand. Loni's heart only slightly broke as they parted. Both waved and turned around repeatedly as the other faded into the distance. Then Loni headed for a corner vendor, where he bought his first New York knish and a Coke. He wolfed it down in two seconds flat, and smiled as he remembered his first evening, and morning, in the big city. And then he headed home, still dancing on air, even if only figuratively.

He came back to earth suddenly and harshly when he entered his apartment and got undressed.

The card had vanished.

He searched every pocket, twice, and then a third time. But it was nowhere to be found. He'd obviously dropped it somewhere, maybe when he was paying for his meal. He quickly got re-dressed and ran outside and retraced his steps back to the bus stop, but he couldn't find the card. It was gone.

He walked dispiritedly back home and collapsed on his front stoop. His head fell in his hands, and he cried. He cried long and hard. He knew it was silly. He'd only just met the guy, only knew him for five, six hours. But the thought of never seeing those dazzling blue eyes again, of never feeling those soft, full lips again, was as painful as a knife plunged deep into his very heart. And worse yet, he had looked at the card, briefly, when it was handed to him. All he could remember of it was Doug's last name: Smith.

"Great," he lamented. "Doug Smith. How many Doug Smith's can there be in the Manhattan area."

When he found a phone book later in the day, there were fifty-two Doug Smiths, twenty-nine Douglas Smith's, and seventy D. Smith's. It was hopeless.

Doug spent the rest of the week acclimating himself to his new surroundings. He strolled through Central Park. Rode the elevator up to the top of the Empire State Building. Took the ferry to the Statue of Liberty. And hopped on train after train, uptown and down, traversing the city he now called his own.

On each trip, he'd glance here and there in hopes of somehow catching a glimpse of his dream man, of his Roseland romance. But there were seemingly millions of people in the city, and none of them were Doug.

He was, therefore, relieved when his first day of work finally arrived. He could, at last, concentrate on something else and forget the misery of a love surprisingly found and then promptly lost. He was also down to his last fifty bucks, so a looming paycheck was gladly looked forward to.

He'd already planned the window display at Bloomie's. It had come to him on his very first night in the city. He was going to bathe the large displays in beams of colored lights, which would dazzlingly bounce off the all-white dresses and gowns the store sold. It was sure to catch the eyes of the passersby. He was eager to make his vision into a reality, excited to be creative at last, so he got started right away.

When the last of the displays were completed, when all the mannequins were dressed, and all the lights plugged in, he stood in the last window and flicked a switch. It was glorious to behold, even from his up close vantage point. He then turned and faced the street. The crowds were already gathering to admire his work.

He smiled and waved.

And that's when he spotted them: the eyes—the startling blue eyes in the crowd—staring intently at him.

"Doug," he shouted, with his hands and his face pressed against the window.

Doug scowled at him and flipped him the bird. "You promised," he mouthed.

Loni's heart nearly stopped beating and his stomach dropped. Doug turned to leave. Terrified, Loni screamed, "Wait!" and pounded his fists on the window. Doug waited.

Loni hopped out of the window and back inside the store. He found a piece of paper and a magic marker. He wrote his message and jumped back inside the window. Thankfully, Doug was still outside, and the crowd had grown, hopeful for a spectacle.

Loni held the paper up to the glass. He watched as Doug

squinted. He was too far away, too buried in the crowd, to read it. Loni waved him closer. Doug pushed through and up to the window. Loni sank to his knees and pointed to the paper.

"You lost my card?" Doug shouted up at him, still looking angry and upset.

Loni nodded and continued to point at the paper. He mouthed a "sorry."

"You're an idiot," Doug shouted.

Again Loni nodded.

A smile reappeared on Doug's adorable face. The glint in his magnificent blue eyes had returned. "Did you miss me?" he shouted.

Again Loni nodded, even more vigorously.

"How much?" Doug shouted, putting a hand up to the glass.

Loni simply pointed to the display as he put his hand to the same spot on the opposite side of the glass. Doug understood. Loni made sure to stand the mannequins on clouds of cotton.

They were dancing on air.

And, again, so was Loni.

CHOCOLATE HEART

SHANE ALLISON

I SEEK OUT the perfect card 'cause I care enough for Chris
to give him the very best. There are rows of greetings written
in sweet script, decorated with flowers, hearts, and teddy bears
most adorable. But no one ever keeps cards. They just sit on the
coffee table losing their meaning, collecting dust. I decide to
forego on the card cliché. The original idea was to compose my
love in the form of a poem and glue it in the cover surrounded
with red and pink glitter. There's nothing like Valentine's Day
in New York. I love it more than Thanksgiving and Christmas
combined. It's right up there with Halloween with me. I'm not
too fond of turkeys and a jelly-bellied man dressed in a red
suit. Just as I start for the door of the drugstore, I notice an
assortment of candy on the end cap. I'm mesmerized by chocolate-covered coconut, chocolate chocked full of almonds, along
with chocolate with mint and caramel centers all in the shape of
sweet, delicious hearts. At least two aisles are strewn with red,
pink, and white teddy bears and heart-shaped boxes wrapped
in cellophane. Cute, stuffed things surely aren't Chris's thing.
You really can't get anymore straight-acting than him. He's a
card carrying, football-watching, baseball obsessed type of
homo. We like to neck in the back seats of taxis like private
schoolboys behind the gymnasium.

The candy I have my eye on is all but sixty-five cents each, which is well within my budget considering I only have a buck and some change rattling around in deep denim pockets. It's rough in this big apple of a city. "Don't worry, baby," Chris says. "You'll find something." I love it when he calls me baby. My friends can't stand him, think he's got acid for blood, but they don't know him. "He's a playa," they tell me, but I ain't tryin' to hear that. Chris is actually very sweet. He's a manager at Thirty-fourth Street Bowl. It'll be ten years this May we met on a sweaty dance floor at Stonewall.

I had called in advance like usual to find out if there was a cover charge. I almost didn't go out that night. I had spent my last twenty bucks getting drunk off three-dollar margaritas at Pieces. I was bored sitting around in my crappy apartment, and wanted to go out for a little bit of this and a little bit of that. It was only midnight, and the bar was filling up fast with the usual suspects: femme fags, glamorized drag queens, and straighties out to see the freaks in frocks. I broke past sweaty bodies and conversation, making my way upstairs to a packed dance floor. Chris was a shy, slip of a thing sitting off in the corner of the upstairs bar. I hated the bar, really. The drinks were watered down and overpriced, and the bartenders were more like gangsters practically threatening to whack you if you didn't buy six-dollar vodka tonics served in juice glasses. Chris was adorable, standing beautifully beneath searchlights and gleaming disco balls. I was shy myself and never talked to anyone. I went for the music mostly. I couldn't keep my eyes off him. I'd watch as he turned down club boy after club boy. After watching him for what seemed like an hour, I grew a pair, and went over to introduce myself. Good thing, too, cause he was about to disappear from me forever into a haze of cigarette smoke. I told him how I couldn't help but notice him standing off in the corner alone. Fed him this line of how he was the most adorable thing in the joint, and that it was a shame he wasn't dancing. Chris laughed as if he had heard different versions before. I didn't ask him to dance. We got acquainted over boisterous techno. He had just moved to New York from Denver where he worked as a manager at some five-star hotel I had never heard of or read about. Chris and I grew weary of the crowds of people and the annoying remixes of Madonna songs. We accompanied each other downstairs into a quieter comfort zone. I hung on his every slurred word, watched his sweet lips move as he spoke of wanting to live in Europe someday. Said he really can't stand the taste of alcohol that he only drinks to take away his inhibitions. We spoke of old eighties TV shows like *Alf*, the *A-Team*, and *Knight Rider*, realizing we were die-hard fans. I couldn't believe he was giving a loser like me the time of day. I was sure the free Jell-O shots had something to do with it. By the time we started making out, it was last call, but we didn't care as we groped flesh, caressing cologned chests, and tugging at waists as we kissed in a cranberry-colored booth seat. Once the bar was closed, the beefy Puerto Rican bouncers pulled us apart, forcing us to *take it outside* as one so delightfully put it.

I sucked Chris's alcoholic tongue as we French-kissed beneath a Greenwich Village moon, running my fingers through Chris's black, feathered hair. His hothouse chest heaved to my touch beneath his vintage sleeved, woven shirt. He kept pulling me hard to him, forcing things most private to touch in our jeans. Chris begged me to take him right there that night on Christopher Street. Pedestrians sauntered by and whistled as we put on a show. I remember one guy walking past and saying, "Ah, true love." Chris asked me if I had a place. I didn't want to take him back to my crappy, mouse infested pad that was really right across the street from the bar. My place was across, or down the street from everything, which is why I loved the area so. It was simply convenient. But the rents were getting outrageous, forcing most Manhattanites into the belly of the burroughs, me being one of them.

I lied, and told Chris that I lived in Queens, but it seemed like every time we kissed, little hearts began to tumble out of my eyes, stars started to dance around our sultry bodies. So much so, I couldn't help but come clean with the boy.

"You liar," he said smiling. Chris held onto me in his drunken haze as we made our way across the street. I prayed that my roommate was asleep as I turned the key in the lock of the battered door. Last thing I needed was for Chris to see my roomie dressed in a pink bathrobe, walking around in those damnable fuzzy green Oscar the Grouch slippers he liked to prance around in. We made our way up a spiral of stairs. Luckily, I lived on the first floor. As we entered, the hall was dimly lit. My roommate's door was closed. I could hear the music from the play *Hairspray* seeping from beneath the slit of his door.

My room was an embarrassing mess. I hoped that Chris was too drunk to notice the shadeless windows and walls chipping with paint. He sat in an old, green desk chair I had found in Union Square, and wheeled all the way back to my place. Chris didn't seem to care, considering he was four sheets to the wind. "You want something to drink?" I asked. "I got water." "Water's cool." I dismissed myself to the kitchen I was hesitant to enter after stumbling upon a mouse the week before. I spent two weeks in my room with a butcher knife under my pillow. My roommate, Matty, set a few glue traps, but the only thing they caught were roaches and food crumbs. There was no deceased rodent in sight.

I poured Chris some water in a glass decorated with little pink flowers. Glasses I purchased from one of those corner 99-cent stores. Chris smiled up at me as I handed him the glass of ice water. He was sweating a little, so I turned on the table fan that was sitting on my metal, orange desk an ex-roommate had given me before he moved out to go live with his boyfriend in Hell's Kitchen. He drank it all. The boy was one thirsty twink. He needed something to surge through his system other than cheap bar booze. We started to kiss again, tugging and groping beneath the hot light fixture above us. Our body temperatures soared, chest pressed against chest, fingers fidgeting in sweaty, black hair. We breathed heavy in unison. After we made love, we held each other like a warm-blooded cliché. Chris wanted more that morning, but I was running terribly late for work, so we exchanged numbers on torn slips of legal pad paper. I called his number from the computer lab where I worked to make sure it was legit. He hadn't made it back to Williamsburg, but I recognized his voice on his machine. We went on two dates plus four brunches and a dinner before we fell for each other like star-crossed lovers. We turned into one of those couples that started finishing each other sentences, holding hands as we walked past azaleas through Tompkins Square Park. I can't believe it. Ten years. Chris and I have been through the worst of it. We've seen friends' break up over things most petty and miniscule, but we're still kickin' it, still going strong.

Perfect, I think, as I examine the candy. I decide on the heart filled with chocolate-covered caramel. I walk to the counter with my gift in tow. A rush of excitement flushes over me. It's the same feeling I always get when I do something nice for Chris. The smile on my mug starts to sweeten, much like the foiled treat I was about to purchase, imagining the look on his face when I give him my heart, so to speak. I place the candy on the counter. "Aww, that's nice," the cashier says, wearing a tight, light blue knit top, sporting a hot-pink hairdo. "Yeah, it's for someone special." She asks if I have a CVS card, and like always, I tell her no. I think about getting one just so they can stop asking. I only come in the joint everyday to buy some gum. She runs the chocolate heart beneath the scanner. "That'll be one-forty-two," she says. I reach within the pocket of my jeans, and fork out a crumpled up dollar bill and shovel out a handful of loose change, picking out the exact amount of quarters, dimes and pennies. I hand the money to Melanie, which is her name sketched in black permanent ink on a plastic tag pinned on the left side above her breast. "Do ya need a bag?" she asks. "No thanks." She hands me the heart and my receipt.

I exit the automatic, double glass doors. I have a good hour to spare before my baby's shift is up at the bowling alley. I saunter over to Virgin's where it's packed to the rim. I sift through the same books, and CD's I want to buy, but never have the money for. I fish out my pocket-sized notebook jotting down the titles of new albums by my favorite bands. A list of all the things I plan to purchase once I find work. I thought of going to beg for my job back at the computer lab, but Chris doesn't think I should. "You could do better," he tells me.

My mind is preoccupied with thoughts of Chris. I get so wound up in him, it's like I can't take another breath until he's with me. Color me obsessive. I spend whole nights tossing and turning as he dances in my head like sugarplums.

I look at my watch that's four minutes behind. I frantically seek out a clock on the walls of the megastore. One hangs behind customer service. It says 12:30. I sit the new PJ Harvey CD back in its rightful place and head for the door. I didn't want to risk running late, or missing my Chris by only a few measly minutes. I walk out of the store post haste, sprinting past two brawny Hispanic brutes that look at me like they want to tackle me to the floor. I don't want the chocolate in my hand to start melting. I wouldn't want Chris to unwrap the candy only to find a melted lump of milk chocolate and caramel. I take he Brooklyn Bridge; it is ridden with cars. I become angry and short-tempered every time the traffic slows, swearing and cursing like a comedian from *Def Comedy Jam*. Coldplay plays from the CD player, as I bang on the steering wheel in frustration. I holler at the blaring cars before me. *Green means go, stupid!* Just when I think I'm gonna make it, the light turns yellow. Normally, I would run it, but I already have one hundred and seventeen bucks in traffic tickets.

I stare at the chocolate symbol of love resting on the car seat as I wait for the longest traffic light in the world to change. *He's gonna like this*, I think to myself. Things turn green, and I'm well on my way. The next three lights down Tennessee Boulevard all remain green, allowing me to barrel straight through.

To my surprise, the bowling alley lot is thick with business. It's freezing cold, and I have to piss to a degree of racehorse proportions. I stand outside turning and looking indecisively to both sides of me where two stores stand. I saunter past the Dollar Tree where the windows are plagued with pink and yellow Easter bunnies. I take a leak at the foot of a maroon-colored dumpster at the end of the building. The warm urine puddles at my GBX boots. The weather's been up and down for the past week, and tonight it was colder than a dead man's dick. I jump in my car, folding my arms in an attempt to keep warm. I look at the chocolate heart wrapped in colorful red and pink foil shadowed beneath streetlights of peach. The bulb of ideas in the attic of my brain flickers on. I tear a blank piece of paper from my notebook and begin to inscribe. *Do you love me? Check box yes, no, or maybe.* I laugh thinking of those days of passing these very notes in class during my years of grade school innocence. I know Chris'll get a kick out of it. I take the candy and wrap it in the wide-ruled note scribbling *with love* between its blue lines. I notice they're beginning to turn off the neon beer signs. I sit patiently in the cold car awaiting his arrival. I don't care how cold this night is. I'd wait in an Alaskan blizzard for my baby. I can hear a commotion of conversation beneath shadows. *It's him.* My own heart starts to beat frantically within me. I crack the automatic window watching Chris saunter out with his back-pack of heavy things. "Hey," I say. Chris throws his bag in the backseat. "How was your day?" I ask. "It was okay." I take the chocolate and stuff it in the pocket of my leather jacket. He doesn't say much on the way home. "Am I in trouble?" Chris doesn't answer. It's as if he's in his own world. *I must be in trouble*, I keep thinking. *He wants to break up. That's it. He's going to leave me.* His pad isn't far from where he works. A light is on, and the blinds are closed. Chris always likes to leave on a lamp in the living room to ward off burglars.

I tail behind him with my head held down to the sun-bleached asphalt as if I was a boy in trouble waiting for his punishment, desperate to know what was wrong, wanting to know if he wanted to call it quits after ten years of loving. I'm a monstrous thing towering over his short, thin frame. He unlocks the door, leaving it agape for my invitation. I love his apartment because he doesn't clutter it up with furniture: Just two sofas and a coffee table strewn with new DVD's and junk mail. It smells of TV dinners. I sit on the couch facing the kitchen with my hands tucked nervously in my pockets. "Chris, will you say something," I say, staring down at his stack of flicks. "You barely said a word in the car. What's up?" "Nothing, baby. Just had a bad day at work." I ask him if he wants to talk about it. "Nah, forget it. I missed you. I apologize for giving you the silent treatment," he says, as he nests between my legs, resting his head against my chest, oblivious to the fact that he's making me hard. Chris grabs the remote and turns on the tube. "You sure you don't want to talk about it?" I ask. "Same old shit, really. Just people being assholes." I hand Chris the chocolate heart cocooned in the wide-ruled notebook paper. "What's this?" he asks. "Something silly," I reply. I rope my arms lovingly around his belly as he unfurls the note's corners, taking out the hunk of chocolate love sealed in Valentine-colored foil. "Happy Valentine's Day," I say, running my fingers through feathered hair. He grabs a pen, and checks the yes box to my question then turns and kisses me. The hair from his new 'stache pricks my upper lip, but I don't mind because it's him. He unwraps the red and pink foil from the chocolate heart, and breaks it in half. The caramel center oozes forth, sticking to Chris's fingers. He hands me half. "Cheers," he says, as our chocolate touches. The caramel sticks to the roof of my mouth. We hunker down, cuddling in the rent-to-own sofa watching an episode of the *A-Team*. "Love you," Chris says before he kisses me again. "Love you more," I reply.

IN A CITY OF EIGHT MILLION PEOPLE

BRAD NICHOLS

THERE WAS EVERY reason in the book why we should not have fallen in love. There was every reason why we never even should have seen each other again. But we did, and we did. In a city of eight million people, all of whom seem concerned only with the phone call they're on and the phone call they're waiting for (often at the same time), how two people managed to lock eyes and make contact, not just once but twice, is all the more remarkable.

But the story isn't really about that initial contact; no, it's the serendipitous way the second encounter occurred. To understand just how random it was, though, you really have to back up and tell the story from the start. So I will. And it begins quite simply, the way many a young gay man's night starts, with hope, with promise, and sometimes with the idea of ending it with a good screwing. But something a little bit different would happen this night. A connection would be made, but an opportunity would also slip away as quietly as the night.

. . . . .

IT WAS A Sunday evening in Manhattan, and usually that just meant I paced my one-bedroom apartment in nervous anticipation of the coming workweek. But it's a holiday weekend, Monday is President's Day, and I'm pacing not because I'm anxious but because I'm torn about how the evening might shake out. The eternal question begs at me: should I go out?

I'd been out late Friday night drinking with friends, and all day Saturday I'd stayed in as a snowstorm blanketed the city, keeping all New Yorkers inside except those with kids or those making deliveries. Now, the snow had been reasonably cleared, the cabs were swishing through the slushy streets and the raucous laughter of people drifted up to my fourth floor windows, open a bit to let out some of the excess heat from my apartment. I stole a glance outside, then back at the clock. There was life outdoors on this extra weekend night, and indoors there was nothing but reality television and a ticking clock. A decision seemed to be looming.

Before I knew it, I'd tossed on blue jeans and a sweater. I grabbed my leather jacket and a wool scarf and made my way down the stairs. I live on the West Side in the 50s, what the rich folks call Clinton, what the locals call Hell's Kitchen, and what the gay boys now call "Hellsea." There are any number of gay bars in the neighborhood, with more popping up seemingly every day. I had my usual hangout, but tonight I decided to pick Barrage, a sleek, casual place with little pretension and lots of cute guys.

That includes me. Not to sound conceited, because I'm far from that. But vanity is a gay man's enemy, and we like to be told that we're cute or hot, or "doable." I'd been told all three on various occasions, but it had been awhile. My boyfriend Steve and I had been broken up a good seven months and the prospects since then had been about as thin as a supermodel.

So, here I was, thirty-one-year-old Jake Davis, opening the glass door to Barrage on West Forty-seventh Street and being welcomed by a hunky bartender with a smile, the sound of Madonna on the sound system, and the curious looks of about a dozen guys. It's our nature, you see, to check out the new arrivals, and at this moment that new arrival was me. Steve and I used to play a game at our local joint called "hot or not hot," and depending upon what we chose and who walked in decided who bought the next round. Shallow, sure, but doesn't shallowness live close to vanity in our world? I received a couple lingering glances, but mostly the crowd returned to what had previously occupied them: themselves. That was fine, the night was young. I took an empty bar stool and ordered a Bass.

For the next hour, I drank my beer and listened to the music and smiled at some guys as I read through the latest editions of *HX* and *Next*. Occasionally I would turn to see who was sitting beside me and we'd nod or say hi or comment on the music. The jukebox seemed stuck on a rotation of classic eighties: lots of Madonna, some Duran Duran, OMD's "If You Leave." I was debating whether to do just that—leave—or to order a second beer when someone new took up the bar stool next to me. He looked about my age, had dark wavy hair that grew out over his shirt collar. He also had really nice eyes; maybe green, but the lighting in here was low. Still, it wasn't the color that I had focused on; it was something else in his eyes, a wide-eyed openness, almost a piercing nature. I felt like he could look right through me…or into me.

"Hey," I said, suddenly compelled to talk with someone. Okay, with him.

"Hi."

"I'm Jake," I said, deciding he would have been in the "hot" category of my game.

"Sean."

We shook hands; his touch was strong and confident. I

liked that. Heck, I liked him. Instantly. Definitely attractive, seemingly friendly, and apparently alone. And nicely dressed, as well, in a dark suit and blue dress shirt, sans tie; his face had a day's dark stubble. Interesting look for a Sunday night, I thought, wondering what his story was. I decided to find out.

"Can I get you a drink?" I asked him.

"Oh, uh, sure. Thanks. What are you drinking?"

"Bass."

"Make it two."

I did. Or rather, the bartender did. I slid a twenty onto the bar. Ignored the change, and really, ignored the scene that was enveloping the bar. Because as the night's action swirled around us, the music growing louder, the crowd expanding, the atmosphere heightening with a certain sexual energy, Sean and I became more insulated. We had a second drink together—his treat—and we talked about our lives, our jobs, recent dates, movies, music. He'd had to work today—he worked in the fashion industry—and they were prepping a photo spread and he was required to meet with the client, even though it was a Sunday.

"I just got off work, that's why I'm so, uh, dressed," he'd said.

I told him he looked nice. He told me I was nice.

Another Madonna song came on. Everyone began striking a pose.

"My God, what's next, Bette?"

"Maybe Barbra," I said.

"That's when we leave."

Perhaps for the first time in my life I had an urge to play some Streisand.

As our second beers got low, I began to sense a shift in the air. His eyes grew even more focused on me, if that was possible. His knee touched mine, and our eyes locked again. I reached out, my fingers grazing against his free hand. Contact had been made: first with our eyes, then knee to knee; finally, actual skin to skin, and the feeling between us was suddenly, enticingly electric. We both knew what was happening, what was going to happen, and even if we wanted to, we were powerless to stop it.

As I drained my glass, the bartender came by and said, "Another, guys?"

Sean took charge. "Uh, no, thanks."

And when he said those words, he wasn't even looking at the bartender. Sean only had eyes for me.

I'd already learned he lived in Queens, and he knew my apartment was only a few short blocks away on Tenth Avenue.

"So," I said, as my heart pounded. "My place?"

"Not unless you want to give some cab driver a show."

"I'd rather keep you to myself."

"Good plan."

And so we left, and so we walked on wet, snowy sidewalks, down Forty-seventh Street and turned up once we'd reached Tenth Avenue. Traffic was light on this late Sunday night, both on foot and on the streets, and in a city of eight million people it seemed that we were the only two people around. Sean had taken hold of my hand, and he held it tight, squeezing it even more when we would make eye contact.

Five minutes was all it took to get back to my apartment. I escorted him in, closing the door behind me. I felt his arms encircle me from behind, felt his body press against mine. There was a noticeable bulge in his pants; I could feel it against my ass. His hand drifted down to my crotch, where a similar reaction was taking place. And then I felt his lips— on my neck, on my ear. Soon I turned around and his lips met mine, and the kiss was sweet and tender at first, before taking on a more urgent sense of need...of want. He pressed me against the wall of my apartment, and the kissing grew more intense, to the point where our knees simultaneously buckled. We needed to sit down...or better, lie down. My bed was closer than my sofa.

"I'll be right back," I said, trying to regain some semblance of myself. Because I felt like I'd been living outside my body, watching as this fantasy played itself out. And it was a fantasy and not just one about sex, but about a connection that seemed to be growing between us, an expression of something more than your standard weekend horniness. I excused myself to the bathroom, stupidly telling him to make himself comfortable. Like a line out of a bad date movie.

But when I emerged two minutes later, Sean had done just that, made himself as comfortable as possible. Pillows from my bed had been scattered to the carpet, along with his clothing. Overdressed, I shed myself of my jeans and sweater, and slid in next to my newfound lover. He kissed me, and I kissed him, and I drew my hand down his chest, toying with the light covering of dark hair. I told him he was sexy, and he told me the same, and then he told me how much he liked me and that this wasn't just sex and I said the same, and as our passions consumed us we said other things in the moment that were either fueled by desire or beer or some such emotion that creeps up only on those loneliest of nights.

We proved to be a compatible couple, sexually speaking. We each liked to kiss and lick, to suck and screw, and we did all of that and more, and even though the clock inevitably turned night to early morning and dark began to give way to light, we were lost in our own moment in time. When at last we agreed to give up our bodies to sleep, I looked back at him and there was that look again in his eyes, that connection I'd first seen at the bar, the one I'd seen again when I first entered him, the one I'd last seen when he'd climaxed—power in them, a power that drew me to him.

I decided to take a chance, and I spoke the words I'd thought. "I love when you look at me that way," I said.

But Sean had already fallen asleep. Those eyes had closed.

. . . . .

I AWOKE THE next morning to an empty bed, and as a result, a surprisingly empty heart. Sean was not in the bathroom, or in the living room, or making coffee in the kitchen. His suit no longer decorated the floor, and the pillows he'd tossed there only hours earlier appeared as neglected as me. Sean was gone, and after a diligent search, I found no sign that he'd ever been here, save for the torn condom packets in the trash. Not even a tiny slip of paper, saying he'd had a good time, here's my number, call me, I want you again, again.

Those eyes, so wonderful, so sweet, had belied an inner truth. They had hidden a streak of betrayal.

I slept most of the day, and the next day the long weekend was over. The snow had been mostly plowed away, or it had melted in the heat of a new day. I knew the feeling. And so I went to work, my routine finding its way back to me like a lost lover, until a week had gone by and then another had. I went out, I saw friends, I watched TV on my TiVo, and I thought, more than once, about Sean, about the way we'd connected, and about those eyes and about the way he'd left me.

But that wasn't the end of the story, you already know that much. You know we found each other again, and you know we fell in love. But like all good stories, even when the ending is known to you there's still the thrill of discovering how it came to be, how we got from Point A to Point C. What was Point B?

I'll tell you, it was fortuitous that Sean and I ever saw each other again. And of course that was the key, seeing each other. Our eyes locking, two people randomly finding each other in a city of eight million. It was a moment where nothing else but fate could have been playing, an instant spark of recognition and desire that erupted in a glance so quick that time would have had a difficult time recording it.

. . . . .

WORK KEPT ME late one Thursday, a couple weeks after I'd met Sean. He'd been on my mind, mostly because of the missed opportunity—or was that a lost opportunity?—between us. Part of me wondered why he left, and part of me said just move on, cute guys in New York are like the *Post*: a new one every day, and easy to read. So, I was heading out the door at just after seven-thirty and the snow had started to fall again. We were still locked in a cold, snowy winter, and not unlike that holiday weekend when I went out to Barrage, the snow had a twinkling, romantic quality to it. It hadn't all turned to slush yet.

Still, I hadn't worn my boots, and so I headed toward the subway. (Many nights I just walked home, work being on the east side, home on the west.) Down the stairs I went to Fifty-ninth and Lex, I joined the throngs of New Yorkers as we escaped the wet snow and retreated to our subterranean city. The narrow platform wasn't crowded, and I imagined the snowy weather was delaying certain trains, notably the N, which came from Queens via elevated tracks. So I wasn't surprised to see an R train come first, but that didn't matter to me, as either the N or R would take me to Times Square, where I would get off. So I hopped aboard, finding a small area near the doors in which to stand. The doors closed, and the train jostled forward. A familiar rhythm set in, and despite the fact that I was surrounded by strangers, I could feel my whole body relax; I'd be home in fifteen minutes.

Fate had another plan, though, and given its result, how could I object?

As we pulled into the station at Fifth Avenue, my eyes were directed to the Queens-bound side of the station, and I looked on as dozens of anxious, tired, and impatient New Yorkers waited for a train to whisk them home. I caught sight of a man with dark wavy hair, dressed in a dark suit somewhat hidden by a long overcoat. There was something familiar about him, and my eyes actually did a double-take, and that's when they found themselves being stared back at. It was Sean, waiting on the other side of the platform, and he'd somehow seen me and I'd somehow seen him. My initial reaction was that simple: this wasn't possible, not in a city of eight million people. But on that second glance, there was no denying it. He was my lost Sean. The train was coming to a stop and just then I noticed another train barreling into the station from the other side. With my view suddenly obscured, I lost sight of Sean—I had no idea which train he needed or whether he truly had seen me, and all at once I found myself saddled with a case of indecision. What to do? Here I'd just seen the man I wished had never left my bed that morning, but the opportunity to see him and talk to him and ask him why he left was quickly disappearing. My train had stopped, the doors had opened, and people were getting on and people were getting off, both at the same time, and I stood like a frozen statue, unsure what to do. What if I got off and Sean was gone? What if he got on the train and disappeared down the subway's dark tunnels? Looking at the subway doors like they were a portal to another time, another adventure, I steeled my legs for a last minute call to action.

Pushing people to the side, apologizing as I did so, I ran for the open space between the doors—just as they were closing. Subway doors are not like elevator doors; they do not spare your body, they do not give you a chance to push them back. But somehow I managed to squeeze through, and, with a slight bruise to my leg, stumbled onto the platform. Once again the doors closed, and the train pulled out of the station. This time I wasn't on the train, I was on the platform, seemingly alone—most everyone had hopped aboard the train.

The same was true, I noticed, on the other side. The Queens-bound train had already left, taking with it most of the waiting passengers. I found myself walking down the platform, trying to determine whether Sean had gotten on that train. I didn't see him, and as a result I began to question my own eyesight—did I really see him, or were my eyes deceiving me. It was not unlike when Sean and I had made love that one night and I'd detected something in his eyes that went beyond the night, beyond the moment.

Okay, so Sean was not to be seen, and what had I achieved in the process? Delaying my trip home was all. I stared down the tunnel and did not see an oncoming train. Yet, I did hear a rumble in the distance, and quickly I determined that the train was once again coming toward the opposite side platform—Queens-bound. A stupid impulse took over—or maybe it was my hormones?—and I raced up the stairs, crossed over and bounded my way down the stairs on the other side just as the train was pulling into the station. The doors opened and I hopped aboard and I urged the doors to close and wished the train forward, as though it could catch up to the previous train, even though I knew that was unlikely; or better yet, impossible. One had been an N, this one was an R. After Fifty-ninth & Lex, they went into separate sections of Queens. I told myself to just get off at the next stop, and then catch the next train back downtown and forget about this ridiculous pursuit. It was a flight of fancy, based on a one-night stand that had little chance of moving forward, especially given the fact I had no idea where to find the man whose eyes, whose heart, had seemingly pierced me.

The conductor's voice broke me from my thoughts. "Next stop, Fifty-ninth Street, Lexington Avenue, final stop in Manhattan. This is a Queens-bound R train to Seventy-first Continental."

So, when the train came to a stop, I did the rational thing (for the first time since boarding the subway). I got off and walked to the other side of the platform. All this back-and-forth on subway platforms might have gotten any number of tourists turned around, but thankfully I'd been in New York long enough that I had the tricks of the trains down pat. I stood on the downtown side, feeling foolish but anonymous, too—such was the joy of New York. No one was paying attention to you.

Except, someone was.

Someone by the name of Sean.

He was leaning against one of the metal support columns, about a hundred feet away. His arms were crossed, and he was staring directly at me. A smile lit his face, and truth be told, that smile seemed to travel across the platform and find its way to mine, because I was grinning uncontrollably. At last I moved forward, and so did he, and before long we'd met in the middle of the platform.

"Hi," I said.

"Hi," he said back.

It wasn't awkward, our reunion, but it wasn't perfect either. I think neither of us knew what to say after the easy greeting; the next words were always the hardest, because they determined the course of the conversation, the flow of the relationship.

"I can't believe I actually saw you—on a subway of all things," I said.

"Yeah, but you know, perhaps—"

Whatever else he said was drowned out by the thrum of an approaching train. No, make that two trains, one on each side of the platform. Our eyes locked, and then as quickly parted, as we both watched the two trains barrel their way into the station. One waited for me, the other for him. Doors were opened, people got off and got on, announcements were made, and neither of us made any move to, well, move. We waited out the noise, the activity, the departure of both trains, and finally we were alone on the platform, and finally Sean finished what he was saying.

"—our meeting means I shouldn't have left you that

night."

On a night of closing doors, suddenly one had opened.

"Why did you?" I asked.

"Come on, neither of us wants to go home. Let's get a drink."

And so we left the subway, and found our way to the closest bar we knew, another laid-back bar with a cute clientele, O.W. (once named Oscar Wilde) on 58th Street. We settled onto stools at the bar, we ordered a couple beers, and suddenly our night from a couple weeks ago had drifted back to us as easily as the snow fell on Manhattan's streets, and for the first time since our serendipitous meeting on the subway our shoulders relaxed and our bodies reacted to each other. I leaned over and I kissed Sean, and he kissed me back, and then suddenly he said, "I'm sorry, Jake."

"Why?"

"For leaving you."

"Hey, there was no obligation to anything beyond that night," I said, not really believing it but wanting to give him a chance to save face.

"That's sweet of you to say, but we both know it's not true."

"So then tell me," I said, taking a sip of beer as a delaying measure to the question I truly wanted to ask, the one he hadn't answered when I'd first asked it on the subway platform. "Why did you leave?"

"Because, I heard what you said—that you loved me."

"I…I never said…oh, Sean. Do you mean as you fell asleep? Oh, but what I said was that I loved when you looked at me. Your eyes, they have a power all their own, and I found them looking into me, and maybe what they saw was love and maybe what you felt was a kind of transference, that maybe I was showing my love even though I didn't even realize it. I know, it's all too much, and all too soon, who could believe it when you just meet someone in a bar, that's not how it's supposed to go, you're not supposed to fall in love in a bar. And I don't know that I did, but I think I did later, in my apartment, in my bed, with you. But then you left, and I had no way to reach you, no way to find you."

"And then New York took care of the rest; It made sure to connect two people who knew what they wanted but were afraid, too, of what they wanted."

I leaned forward and kissed Sean again. He opened his mouth, receptive to my lips, my tongue, my touch.

"Shall we try again?"

"Yes, but not tonight."

"No, no, that's not what I want. A second-night stand would hurt me that much more."

"So," Sean said, "how about you give me your number, how about we go on a date, and how about we take it from there?"

I agreed, and I gave him my number and he gave me his, and then we finished our beers and we headed out into the New York night. The lights were all aglow; the traffic was snarled by the increasing volume of snow; People looked annoyed, pissed, at the weather, about the challenge to get home, about the daily stresses of their lives. But Sean and I, we ignored all that, we gave each other as passionate a kiss as we could, one where my toes curled and my cock moved and my heart swelled, and when we parted our smiles lit our faces and our eyes gleamed with the promise of new love.

"I'll call you soon," Sean said.

"I'll call you sooner," I said.

We smiled again, we kissed again, and then Sean walked away, down the street, where he mixed and mingled with an assortment of others who walked the snowy sidewalks of Manhattan. And though they could have swallowed him up, although I could have lost sight of him, they didn't and I didn't, because, frankly, he was all I could see, illuminated by the streetlights and the falling snow and, suddenly, by a new light. And I knew what it was: it was the glow of his cell phone pressed against his ear.

At that point my own phone rang and I picked it up and said, "Hello."

And Sean said, from a visible distance but yet from so nearby, too "I love the way you look at me, too."

And then he was gone, back down into the subway system, ready to head home. As for me, I started walking. Suddenly the snow, the cold, neither bothered me. I was warm from Sean's kisses, from his touch, from his phone call. And as I journeyed home, I watched the snowflakes fall; there were so many, more than you could count, more than eight million.

But only one did I catch on my tongue.

THE DANCE

TIMOTHY J. LAMBERT

ROBERT HOOKED HIS finger in the waist of my jeans and pulled me against him. My hands instinctively grasped his waist and held him close. He put his mouth against my ear and said, "Everybody's watching us. They're wishing they were me right now."

I didn't know him that well, but I knew Robert's statement wasn't true. He was being his usual kind and oblivious self. Everybody was covertly glancing not at me, but at Robert, who was the stuff of wet dreams—a body honed by years of construction work, thick dark hair, Irish eyes that were always smiling, and lips that begged to be kissed.

I was merely a daydream in comparison, a fleeting thought, or a passing fancy. And I was feeling somewhat fancy that night in my favorite Pumas, Diesel jeans, and a worn Def Leppard concert tee. I didn't need a belt or other adornments, since Robert was the perfect accessory. I ignored the envious glares being cast my way and focused on Robert's pelvis as it ground against mine.

"You're feeling kind of solid," he observed. A meaty paw gripped my shoulder and squeezed. "Have you been working out?"

"Is that a line? The Chelsea mating call?" I cocked my

head, flexed, and affected a gruff voice when I said, "What's up? What gym do you work out at? Wanna fuck?"

"You're being mean," he remarked, which I knew was true. But he also laughed, so I knew I hadn't offended him, although several of the guys around us sneered in my direction.

"Push-ups," I said.

"That explains your arms," Robert said, "but I was referring to your ass."

"My what?"

"Your tight little butt," Robert said and planted his palm firmly on my posterior to punctuate his statement.

Before I could think of a witty retort, someone firmly tapped my shoulder. I turned to face a smirking Latino who said, "What's my boyfriend's hand doing on your ass, bitch?"

"Mining for gold?" I guessed and tried to look sheepish.

"He was just keeping me warm until you got back from the bathroom," Robert said. He reached out and pulled Marcos to him, kissing him hard.

"Don't mind me, guys," I said. I tried to slip away, but Marcos and Robert sandwiched me between them as they moved to the throbbing bass line of a Junior Vasquez mix. "I'm having serious déjà vu," I said. "I swear this happened in a dream once."

"Dreams weren't enough? Leave my man alone," Marcos said and bit my neck. I laughed and slapped his head away. "Speaking of men, where's yours?"

I sighed and scanned the club, instinctively looking beyond the dance floor toward the walls or the bar. "I don't know. He's probably up in the lounge or something."

"Why does he come here with you if he hates clubs?" Marcos asked.

"It's not that he hates clubs," I explained, maneuvering so I could face my friends, but remaining close so I didn't have to yell too loudly. "He likes clubs. He just doesn't like to dance."

"Sounds like someone takes that 'never let them see you

sweat' thing a little too seriously," Marcos said. He saw Robert's frown and said, "I'm sorry, but I think David's wound way too tightly. He's obviously afraid to cut loose."

"Maybe he doesn't know how," Robert offered.

"That excuse is tired," Marcos said and waved his hand dismissively. "It's not like we're out here doing the Mashed Potato or the Frug."

Robert laughed and started doing the Bus Stop. Several of the guys around us joined in, as if they were part of a dance sequence in a movie, much to the annoyance of the crowd around them. I chose that moment to check in with David and wandered through the cavernous club looking for him.

I found him exactly where I'd suspected, perched on a plush cube in the upstairs lounge, drink in hand, talking with a man in horn-rimmed eyeglasses. David was wearing muted gray and blue, which complimented his smoky blue eyes; impeccably dressed as always, which made me wonder if Marcos's earlier jibe was on target. I knew David hated the way his clothes smelled of stale cigarette smoke after a night out with my friends and me, so sweating in them probably violated a moral code. My life, unlike David's, had never been dry clean only.

"There you are," I said, sitting next to him. I kissed his temple and the man with the glasses walked away. "I hope I didn't offend him."

"He works for a magazine. An editor," David said.

"Did he offer you work?"

"No." He sipped his drink and stared at me, not offering an explanation. I suddenly felt exposed, like that moment in dreams when you suddenly realize you're naked in your old high school algebra class. "I thought you said you don't know Robert and Marcos that well," David said.

"Not really."

"The three of you looked awfully intimate from up here," David accused.

"That's crazy," I stated. "We were having fun."

"It did look fun being sandwiched between them."

"We were just dancing."

"Baloney," David said.

"Why did you even come here if you don't like to dance?" I growled and stood up, not waiting for an answer.

"And bring on the storm," David said, sounding like a director calling out a cue to a special effects team.

"What are you talking about?" I asked.

"Isn't this the moment in our arguments where you storm out of here in anger?"

I did my best to look appalled and declared, "I don't do that."

Minutes later I was striding down the sidewalk away from the club after telling David that I was going to the bathroom. I stopped in the middle of the block, suddenly dizzy. I took in large gulps of air, which seemed so fresh and clean compared to the recycled cigarette smoke and sweaty staleness inside the club. Once my head cleared and I looked up at the night sky, I saw the buildings towering around me and remembered that I was sharing the air with millions of other people. I leaned against the brick wall of the club, finally sinking to a crouching position. The wall felt solid against my back, supporting me and keeping me from falling. I felt spineless, as if I might ooze across the sidewalk and slide unnoticed into the sewer.

A pair of drag queens walked by. Their strides were long and determined in spite of their impossibly high heels. I was impressed by their multitasking skills. They were walking, chattering back and forth like a pair of squirrels, and repairing their makeup all at the same time. One of them, dressed head to toe in pale green and white chiffon, stepped around me effortlessly while blotting her lipstick and complaining about supply-side economics and high insurance premiums.

A tissue was tossed over a shoulder as they walked away,

and my eyes followed it, watching as it fluttered through the air and met up with a plastic baggie in the gutter. They swirled around each other, propelled by a light breeze. A trashy pas de duex.

I heard a voice calling my name and turned to look, hopeful that it was David, even though I knew he'd never chase after me. It was Robert.

"Where are you going?" he asked.

"I had to get out of there," I said. I wished I'd made up some sort of excuse instead. Unexplained, hasty exits were too dramatic, like a soap opera character. I thought about changing my name to Bolt. "David was driving me nuts," I added.

"Marcos hooked up with two knuckleheads and I'm not in the mood. Do you mind if I hang out with you tonight? I don't want to go home."

This was news. I wasn't aware that Marcos and Robert had an open relationship. I suddenly had a million questions, but I knew it was the wrong time to ask. Robert was a recent friend, so I didn't feel close enough to pry. I'd met him a few months earlier at the bar where I worked. Although we had flirtatiously fun conversations, this was our first night together without a bar between us. Instead I said, "Sure. I'm going to my friend Anne's for breakfast."

"She won't mind if I crash?"

"Of course not. She'll be thrilled to see you."

Most people probably find it difficult at best to be thrilled at four in the morning, but Anne managed to pull it off. She was unfazed to see a stranger at my side when she opened the door to her Chelsea loft. She looked from Robert and me to the bowl in her hands and said, "I guess I'll have to add more eggs. Come in."

I scooped up Anne's Italian greyhound, Hemoglobin, and plopped down on a settee as I introduced Anne and Robert.

"Are you sure I'm not intruding?" Robert asked.

Anne waved her eggbeater in the air dismissively, oblivious to the omelet mixture she was slinging across the kitchen, and said, "Not at all. I know everything there is to know about Andrew. It's good to have fresh blood around." She pointed to an onion sitting on a cutting board and added, "But try not to bleed when you chop that onion. Get to work."

Dr. Anne Landree was my best friend. She was tough, brutally honest, and the most caring person I'd ever encountered. We'd known each other since high school. Back then she was a fun, smart girl with dreams of getting out of rural New Hampshire and becoming a doctor. We lost touch when she went to Cornell, but when she moved to New York City to attend NYU and intern at Beth Israel, I was thrilled to have her back in my life.

Anne was always my trusted confidant. She knew about my rocky upbringing and would always offer a shoulder to cry on when we were teenagers. She was the first person that I told I was gay. I believed she'd keep an open mind and love me for who I was. Luckily I was right. She faltered only briefly—what girl wouldn't need a day or two to sort out the news that her boyfriend was gay? Somehow, our friendship became even stronger. She became more determined to protect me, give me support, and help me laugh to keep from crying.

Robert pointed a knife at me and said, "Why isn't he helping?"

"Andrew?" Anne said with a look of horror. "You are new. Andrew may be good at mixing drinks, but never, ever let him cook. He's the reason I invested in a stomach pump."

"This from the woman whose favorite snack is brie on a Ritz cracker," I said. Hemoglobin rolled over on the settee and begged for a belly rub, then snapped at my hand when I tried to touch him, his favorite game.

"It's an acquired taste," Anne said defensively.

I watched and listened as Robert and Anne sliced, diced, and got to know each other. I learned that Robert played cello, which I thought was sexy. The image of his thick, callused fingers dancing over the strings and creating sweet, hollow music made me feel a little dizzy again. Hemoglobin nipped my elbow, as if he knew what I was thinking.

Robert occasionally stole glances at the colorful décor of Anne's loft, a style easily defined as The Eighties Stopped By And Vomited. With furniture shaped like body parts, shelves covered in toys, neon clocks, Nagel prints, and other pop art. Pee-Wee's Playhouse had nothing on Anne's loft. Whenever Hemoglobin stood still, he looked like a stuffed animal.

Breakfast—omelets, bagels, lox, juice, and several kinds of vitamins—was served on Keith Haring dinnerware. I glared at the figures dancing under my eggs and felt angry. I looked up at Robert and asked, "How long did you date Marcos before you two moved in together?"

Robert swallowed and said, "Four months, maybe? Five. I was in his apartment all the time when I helped him turn his maid's room into a breakfast nook. Moving in together just happened." He turned to Anne and explained: "Marcos is an architect. The architect and the construction worker: a match made in heaven, right?"

"I thought it was made in Midtown," I said.

"Hell's Kitchen, to be precise."

Anne laughed and said, "That's too much. You're lying."

"No joke," Robert insisted. "His firm designed the restaurant. We built it. Anyway, I swore I would never fall in love, and look at the bitch now." Anne and I both looked at each other. "I do love him though, in spite of the bullshit."

"There's bullshit?"

"Don't pry, Andy," Anne said.

"I'm not prying," I said. "And don't call me that."

"He wants an open relationship. I'm not sure I do. At first I went along with it. I thought it was no big deal. Plus the idea sounded kind of hot. We spent a few weeks shopping for a third, going to bars and checking out guys together, trying the idea on to see if it would fit us. Listening to Marcos describe what he wanted to do with me and our potential third really got me worked up. It was like three weeks of foreplay."

"That is hot," Anne admitted.

"It was. The first time we brought a guy home was great. It was exciting, slutty, and a little nerve-wracking too. What if Marcos was more interested in the other guy than getting me off? What if the other guy was a dead fuck? I shouldn't have worried. It was the best sex I'd ever had."

I glanced at Anne and could tell she was restraining herself from asking if they'd used condoms. Anne had recently opened an office in the West Village, and although she was a general practitioner, she focused on Immunology and Internal Medicine. Eighty percent of her patients had HIV.

"A lot of guys have open relationships. It takes a lot of honesty though, from what I've heard," she said.

"Marcos is too honest," Robert said. "For the longest time we only had sex when someone else was in our bed. Then somehow he went from threesomes to solo adventures. He never hesitates to tell me about them. It would be one thing if he told me every detail about his exploits while ripping off my clothes and shoving his cock up my ass, but no. It's all for him." He looked at Anne as if suddenly aware of his surroundings and said, "I'm sorry. This isn't appropriate table talk."

"There's nothing you could say that would shock me. But I hope you're not looking for relationship advice. I've been married four times, and he's commitment phobic."

"I am not," I retorted. "Feel free to have me committed any time you'd like. I'll welcome the sanctuary."

Hemoglobin, who'd been sleeping under the table, jumped up and ran in circles. After a minute he collapsed in a heap. Anne looked at her watch and said, "It's time for his walk, then I have to get changed. A colleague is giving a discussion on low-dose Naltrexone in a few hours. I promised to attend and back him up with my own findings."

"Hasn't that been around for a long time?" Robert asked.

"Yes. But for some reason the lower dosage hasn't received FDA approval. The discussion's about educating other practitioners though. Blah, blah, blah. I could go on for hours. Go. Save yourselves. Live your lives." Anne walked us to the door and said, "Robert, please feel free to accompany Andrew to breakfast again."

"Thank you," he replied.

"And you, Aurora," she said to me. "When are you going to wake up?"

"Someone has to dream," I said.

Robert and I decided to walk home, even though we were both tired from staying up all night. On the way he said, "Anne's great."

I hurried us out of the path of an oncoming taxi and once we were safely across the street said, "Yeah. She's cool. We only ever get to see each other before dawn because of our different schedules. That's why we have 4:00 A.M. breakfasts."

"Has she really been married four times?"

"Yeah, but that's her story to tell." It was a good story though, and one of the reasons I liked Anne so much. I held out until we reached the next red light. "Anne's gotten married to a few of her friends when it became obvious they'd reached the point of needing critical care. So they'd be covered by her health benefits, so she could have power of attorney, and so their wishes would be taken care of after they'd passed away."

"Isn't that above and beyond the duty of a fag hag?"

"Don't ever let her hear you say that. She prefers the moniker One of the Boys." After a few more blocks, I said, "Can I offer you some advice?"

"Sure."

"Marcos is being honest with you. I think you should return the favor."

He nodded and said, "You're probably right. I'll try."

After finally sleeping, I pondered my advice to Robert,

called David, and asked him over for dinner. David was adventurous and accepted my invitation, probably to point and laugh amidst the aftermath. Whatever the reason, I was left wondering what side dish best accompanied a heaping helping of crow.

The last time I'd cooked anything remotely edible was when we had to make blueberry muffins in high school. It was a pass or fail assignment—if the muffins turned blue, you failed. My muffins were a pale aqua, which baffled my teacher. She examined my results with the studied curiosity of a munitions expert and finally broke tradition, awarding my muffins the first *average* in the history of Chadwick High Home Economics.

With visions of aqua muffins and Anne's stomach pump dancing in my head, I ordered takeout and washed the layers of dust from my serving dishes. "If you can't bake it, fake it," I muttered to myself.

Later I surveyed the seduction scene with a sense of triumph. My normally drab rooftop had been transformed into a setting worthy of a Meg Ryan movie romance. With the time saved by not burning down my kitchen, I'd picked up several plants, candles, a new tablecloth, and white Christmas lights. The abandoned café table I'd found was repainted a crisp white and festooned with wine goblets, new china, a basket of rolls, and serving dishes heaped with the best creations the restaurant down the street had to offer. I'd created an urban oasis and was quite proud of myself. However, I was short a few veils and could only do the Dance of the Seven Hanes Beefy-T's.

I went back downstairs to change clothes, then let David into the building when he arrived. He eyed me warily, but acquiesced when I hugged him.

"I'm sorry I ditched you at the club," I said into his shoulder.

"It's OK. I probably would've ditched me too. I wasn't

exactly a barrel of monkeys."

"I hate that phrase. A barrel of monkeys sounds gross," I said as we climbed the stairs. "Maybe just one monkey and a Slinky. That sounds fun." When we reached the landing that led out to the rooftop, I stopped and said, "Get ready for the most romantic and apologetic dinner scene ever. Once you see this, you'll have to forgive me."

"But what if I've already forgiven you?" David asked.

"You're way too easy," I protested. "I thought some terrible things about you after I left the club. You should reconsider."

"OK. You suck."

"That's better," I said and opened the door to the roof with a flourish, anxiously awaiting David's gasp of delighted surprise when he saw the feast I'd ordered and the romantic setting I'd prepared. Instead his gasp was one of appalled horror, which confused me until my eyes adjusted to the light and I saw the hundreds of pigeons who were fighting over our dinner. "No!" I screamed.

"It's so wonderful," David said, pulling me into his arms and laughing. "You're right. I'm hopeless to resist your charms. I forgive you."

I was horrified and embarrassed, but quickly gave in and began laughing when two pigeons clamoring for a dinner roll fell off the table and twisted on their backs like dueling break-dancers. A sudden flurry of wings in the doorway caused me to yelp, and I quickly shut the door.

"I'm sorry," I said meekly.

"It's OK. We'll order a pizza. It's just nice that you wanted to do this for me," David said.

"I wanted to set a scene. Not for seduction, but for honesty." I sat on the steps leading to the roof and leaned against the door. The muffled sound of the Hitchcockian scene on the other side was both frightening and comforting. "It really bothers me when you come out to the clubs with me and my friends."

"Why?"

"Because you don't dance. You sit on the sidelines and get jealous of anyone who dances near me. Why would you want to just sit there and not dance?"

"Why do you like to dance?" he asked.

It always infuriated me when someone answered a question with a question. But I fought the urge to roll my eyes and said, "Because it's one of the few times that I'm really happy."

"It shows." David knelt in front of me, between my knees, and put his hands on my waist. "When you dance, you smile. You're truly beautiful, handsome, and radiant. Why wouldn't I want to watch you?"

I couldn't answer that. I could only sit there and feel like a jerk—until he kissed me.

"I don't dance because I'm somewhat older than you and I don't like to do all those newfangled moves you kids do." David stood and made a big production of wheezing and grunting. Then he offered me his hand. "But I do know how to waltz. May I have this dance?"

I smiled and took my partner's hand.

STROKE OF LUCK

ARTHUR WOOTEN

"DON'T BE SHY, Billy," I whispered. "Bend over sexy and open it up."

He looked back at me with a sly grin. "Should I arch my back?"

"We have to turn this up a notch," I said laughing as I punched in 375 degrees on my computerized Presidential professional oven. "Now I want you to grab hold of my baster and gently squeeze the knob so that my delicious juices squirt all over that chicken."

And a chicken Billy was. Who knew that at age fifty-one I'd be addicted to Wonder Bread and I'd have my pick of the loaf? And Billy, a dancer and wannabe actor, was definitely the favorite amongst my bevy of boys.

He basted the bird and then closed the oven. "I didn't know cooking could be so sexual."

I looked at my watch and then scooped him up into my arms. "I'll show you sexual."

I carried him out of the kitchen, through the dining room and into the bedroom of my New York City apartment. At five feet eight and weighing one hundred and sixty pounds, Billy was the perfect fit for me. I like guys a bit smaller. It keeps me on top of my game, if you know what I mean.

"My God, you are the hunk," Billy said looking up into my eyes blue eyes. "I'd better be careful or I could—"

I cut him off. "Don't say it. We've talked about this before."

"I've just never met anyone like you and I know you have other boys but I—"

I threw him onto my bed, planted my lips onto his, and kissed him quickly to shift his train of thought. I heard him moan as he surrendered to my touch and like any one of my signature dishes, I ate up every morsel of him, from head to toe. I take great pride in satisfying people's hunger, both gastronomically and sexually. I think they go hand in hand.

After our big quickie I checked my watch as Billy jumped into the shower. By the time he was dried off and wearing one of my bathrobes I had dinner plated and wine poured.

Billy sat down at the table and looked at the feast before him. "You feed me too well, Chip Lowell. In more ways than one."

We clinked glasses.

I pondered. "What should we toast to?"

Billy didn't hesitate for a moment. "Here's to *City Cooking, Country Boy*, and an Emmy."

"From your mouth to voter's ears!"

I had recently landed my own television cooking show. The day before we had finished the pilot episode and the buzz in the industry was fantastic. I had come into my own. But trust me, I had paid my dues. After slaving away for years in restaurants, first starting out as a busboy and then a waiter, I got on the job training and eventually worked my way up from sous chef to head chef at one of Manhattan's most prominent French restaurants. After securing my celebrity chefhood, I was courted by other restaurant owners and encouraged to jump ship. Several even offered to open up my own place. But the best offer of all came when the program director of The Eats Network discovered me and thought I had the potential to be their next superstar. We shot an audition tape and considering I live in the Big Apple but grew up on a farm in New England it made perfect sense to call my show, *City Cooking, Country Boy.*

In no time at all, both Billy and I had devoured our simple but tasty dinner.

He winked at me. "What's for dessert?"

"You asked for it, kiddo."

I jumped up from the table and surprisingly he did too. He may have been small, but Billy was fast. I chased him all over the apartment and finally corned him against the back of the oversized leather sofa in front of my west-facing wall of windows. Recently I had purchased this fourteenth floor loft-like dwelling, which was located in an ultra modern building built on the corner of Jane and West Streets.

I tore open the bathrobe and started devouring Billy all over again. How could his skin feel so soft and taste so fresh? Maybe because he was only twenty-two? Honestly, I had never been into young guys before; it's just that after I turned fifty they started flinging themselves at me. My mouth and hands were everywhere.

"Stop, Chip," Billy squealed. "What if someone sees us?"

"Then lucky them," I laughed. "Besides, we're facing the Hudson River. They'd either have to be in a helicopter or have a gigantic telescope aimed at us from Jersey."

I've never been this horny in my life. And once we were both sated, I pulled myself off and he fell asleep on the couch. I looked at my watch, jumped into the shower, and then went into my bedroom.

Eventually Billy walked in and saw his clothes laid out on my bed. "I hate it when you do that."

I was sitting at my computer returning e-mails as I looked up at him. "Would you rather I say please leave now?"

"It's just so obvious."Billy reluctantly put his clothes back on. "Why won't you ever let me spend the night?"

"Because I have to be up at the crack of dawn and I need my sleep. I have an onsite food demo I have to do at the Chelsea Food Market tomorrow for the press to promote the show, and I'm still working on the script."

"It's always career for you."

I stood up and put my arms around him. "It is right now, kiddo."

. . . . .

UP AT 5:30 A.M. the next morning, I jogged to my gym, did a light weight-lifting routine, and climbed the rock wall. I love sports. All sports. In high school I was quarterback for our football team in fall, ran the relay and did the long jump for indoor track in winter, and played shortstop for the baseball team in spring. Once I was in college I enjoyed skiing, both snow and water, mountain climbing, racquetball, and tennis. Hey, I'm an all around jock.

After my workout I opted for a quick thirty-minute massage. I would have allowed the practitioner to go beyond the call of duty and allow him to give me the release I could tell he was aching to offer but time was short and instead I gave him a nice big tip.

I thank my parents for the great genes I've inherited and coupled with my healthy eating and vigorous lifestyle, I must admit, I've preserved myself pretty well. Most guess I'm at least ten years younger than I am. And some may call me cocky, others obnoxious. I'm just self-confident and it's gotten me to where I am today. I love my fucking life.

As I headed out of the gym, the bright sunlight as it always does, triggered off a sneeze. It may sound weird but I enjoy sneezing. I like the sensation of it. And I'm fascinated with the fact that colds don't make me sneeze; allergies don't make me sneeze, just bright light. Go figure.

I hailed a cab and shot up to Fifteenth Street and Ninth

Avenue. I ran my hand over my carefully shaven head and checked to make sure that I had thrown my clean white chef's coat into my garment bag. It was an exceptionally warm September day and although it was still early, the market was teeming with people on my arrival.

The Chelsea Market was once the Nabisco Cookie Factory where the Oreo was invented. But after being left abandoned for years, the warehouse was transformed into an upscale city mall offering more than twenty specialty shops ranging from kitchen supplies to flowers to exotic foods, spices, desserts, and wines. They also offer food tastings, live concerts, and today…moi!

From the moment I signed on the doted line I felt like I was at home with The Eats Network. From the president and CEO to my stage manager and food assistants, I was in heaven. This was one organized organization.

My food station was all set up for the demo. A combination of city and country décor, it reflected the approach to my show. Constructed around my cook station was a semi-round table set for eight people. Included would be food critics from *TV Guide, Gourmet, Bon Apetit, Country Living, Food & Wine, Southern Living,* and *Good Housekeeping*. But in my mind, just as important as the industry bigwigs, so were the shoppers mulling around the market. In truth, they would make up more of my audience than the critics.

After a quick run-through of the three-course meal I was going to prepare and making sure everything was in place, I dashed upstairs to a rented space next to the Oxygen Network offices. I dropped to the floor, did fifty pushups, slipped on my crisp white chef's coat with my name and the show's monogrammed onto it, and then had makeup shine me down. The Eats Network was also filming the event to use for future promos.

Excited, to say the least, I headed back downstairs where my producer Paul Connor rushed to my side.

"Hey, big guy," he said shaking my hand. "This is the beginning of a long and beautiful relationship."

"The feeling's mutual, Paul." I checked out the scores of people gathered around my set. In the back of the crowd I was actually surprised to see Billy. Catching his eye, I threw him a wink. And then it was show time.

Paul introduced me to the crowd, there was a round of applause, and I stepped up to my cook station and into the bright lights.

"Thank you for joining me today. My name is Chip Lowell and welcome to my show *City Cooking, Country Boy.*"

There was more applause and I started in with the concept of the show.

"I'm just a country boy living in the big city. I want to share with you the comfort of good old fashioned home cooking with the speed, ease, and healthiness that today's lifestyle calls for."

There was another round of applause.

"On today's menu we have a three-greens salad with a champagne vinaigrette topped with edible and peppery nasturtium flowers. We also have my grandma's brilliant shepherd's pie with her secret ingredient of cabbage and caraway seeds. And for dessert, well, I'm going to let that be a surprise."

As I started prepping the salad I wanted to warm up the crowd and critics with a personal story.

"In my family, everyone loved to cook. And because I'm an only child and my grandparents and parents have all since passed, cooking for me, especially recipes we shared together, keeps them close to my heart."

I heard a collective emotional sigh from the group and then suddenly an extra bright light overhead popped on. Not surprisingly, I felt a sneeze coming on but not wanting to spray germs all over my food I turned away from the counter and held the sneeze in, making a ridiculously high squeaking sound. I smiled, turned back to the eager crowd, and then felt an odd pressure surge down both my arms.

"Well, that sneeze was not on the menu," I said while quickly washing my hands.

The crowd laughed as I regrouped.

"As I thaw slaying." I stopped, hearing myself. I was thinking the right words, they just didn't come out. I tried again. "Af a vaw fray—" Suddenly, white dots appeared in my vision and then everything went black.

· · · · ·

WHEN I CAME to I saw Paul and a paramedic standing over me. I was being strapped into a gurney and tried to ask what was going on, but my words were all distorted. The crowd made way for them to wheel me out of the market and Paul was allowed to ride in the ambulance with me. The last face I saw as they closed the back of the ambulance door was Billy's. He looked so frightened.

In the ambulance I heard discussion as to whether or not I should be taken right to St. Lucia's Hospital or down to Maxwell Radiology for an MRI. It was obvious that time was of the essence so it was off to St. Lucia's for a CAT scan.

I've never been hospitalized a day in my life and considering the whirlwind of activity I didn't even have time to be frightened or upset. In fact, my brain felt foggy, like everything was on hold. Upon arriving at St. Lucia's I was rushed into the CAT scan room, locked in place under the X-ray tunnel, and they started computerizing my brain as fast as they could. I remember a dye being injected into my arm and then the rest was blank.

I woke up in a hospital room. No one was there. I was connected to an IV and some sort of monitoring system. I could just barely move my right arm and leg. The left side felt dead. I tried to speak and gibberish came out. Just then a zaftig Latino entered the room.

"Hey, Chip, welcome back," he said smiling. "My name is Allie." He pressed a call button and then came over to my side.

I tried to talk but he shook his head no. "Rest. No matter how hard you try right now, it's not going to come out right. Talk about drama. Nothing like having a stroke while on television."

A stroke? I had a stroke? But that's impossible. I'm healthy as a horse. There's no history of it in my family. I'm only fifty-one!

"I know what you're thinking but anybody can have one at anytime. You're going to be okay."

A disheveled looking doctor entered the room.

"Mr. Lowell, I'm Dr. Laytner. How are you feeling?"

I wanted to say that I had to get back to the live demo but what came out was unintelligible.

The doctor touched my arm. "I can see that you're having some trouble speaking."

You bet the hell I am. Give me something and let me get back to work!

He continued while looking at my charts. "The bad news is you had an ischemic stroke. A blood clot blocked a blood vessel in your brain and we're already treating you with a drug called t-PA. It dissolves the clot. The good news is every minute counts when someone is having a stroke and they got you here pretty quickly."

A generic looking nurse entered and fiddled with the IV.

"Chip," Dr. Laytner explained, "although stroke is a disease of the brain, it can affect the entire body. The effects can range from mild to severe and can include paralysis, problems with thinking, speaking, and emotional outbursts. Patients may also experience pain or numbness after a stroke. Time will tell. I'm hoping that with your strong body, determination, and the help of your occupational therapist, Allie, and the rest of our team, we'll keep symptoms to a minimum."

A minimum? I have a fucking television show to do!

"We'll watch you closely and put you through so much testing that you'll want to run out of here." The doctor laughed at his own bad joke. "And hopefully you will. Allie will work with you and help re-teach you how to feed yourself, get dressed, bathe…all the day to day stuff that we take for granted."

Just my luck to get an overweight man who was probably in his late thirties to sponge bathe me everyday.

"Hey buddy," Paul whispered as he walked gingerly into the room.

I tried to smile, I tried to sit up, I tried to talk, but I couldn't.

He could tell I was struggling. "Just relax. All is good. Of course the show will be put on hold but not to worry."

I tried to talk again.

"And financially, insurance is taking care of everything. Hey ,buddy, gotta run. A lot of fires to put out. See you soon?"

And then he started out the door. I wanted to scream at him and order him to stay and help me and tell me more. But he left.

Dr. Laytner looked at his watch. "I'll check in with you later, Chip. You don't have high blood pressure, heart disease, diabetes, or high cholesterol. We even checked to see if there's a hole in your heart. Sometimes a piece of plaque can escape that way but yours is perfect. My suggestion to you is, never ever hold a sneeze in again." He smiled at me. "Hey, you know why you close your eyes instinctually when you sneeze? 'Cause they'll pop out." He laughed and left with the nurse.

Allie looked over at me. "It's true."

What nightmare was I in and how do I get out of it? How long do I lie here? When can I speak? Or walk?

There was a knock at the door and Billy popped his head

in. "Alright if I say hello?"

I tried to smile but sensed my face was lopsided.

Allie got up out of his chair. "Chip's a bit tongue-tied."

Billy walked in and stood next to me, at least an arm's length away from the bed.

"Hey, big guy," he said nervously. "Wow, you gave quite a show."

I tried to tell him with my eyes how grateful I was, not only that he had shown up at the demo but also that he had followed me to the hospital.

"I just had a quick lesson in how life can throw you a curve ball." He laughed nervously.

You did! How about me?

"Listen, I'm going to come back everyday and stay as long as you like and keep you company. I'm sure you'll be out of here in no time and back on the show before you know it." Billy looked at his watch. "I have to head off to a dance class and then I have an audition at 4:00 P.M. I'll drop by after?"

I struggled to nod my head and then weakly waved my right hand. He smiled but didn't touch me. And then he left. Billy never came back.

. . . . .

I WAS IN St. Lucia's for almost a month and in that time my muscles atrophied and I lost fifteen pounds. Paul visited me once more. No one else dropped by. No one. My doctors zoomed in and out and the nurses were pleasant enough, but it was Allie whom I spent most of my days with. I confess that he had really grown on me and as pathetic as it sounds, he was the only friend I had.

When I wasn't being tortured in physical therapy, I wasted way too many hours watching shitty television and tried hopelessly to concentrate on a novel. Everyday Allie read the newspapers to me and I discovered that he had a wicked sense of humor. He also told me that his full name was Alejandro del Valle, and I was impressed to find out that he was actually fifty. Although chunky, he was doing something right.

With rehabilitation therapy I had gained back some use of my left arm and left leg. I was actually capable of walking short distances on my own, but after a few feet I was completely exhausted. And my speech was slow but much improved. Two of my biggest challenges were undressing and bathing.

Allie turned on the shower as I struggled to get my boxers off my left leg.

"Get your ass in here, Lowell."

I sat on the edge of the bed. "These fucking bloomers you have me wearing get caught on my left foot."

He stuck his head out of the bathroom. "I told you, I'm not helping you with that anymore, you can do it on your own. Just lift your left foot with your right hand."

I did and managed to untangle myself.

"Now march yourself in here, private," Allie ordered.

With all my strength I got to a standing position as he watched. "You just want to get a great big look at my dick," I said playing with him.

"Oh, please! I've seen so many of those little things in my day."

I grabbed hold of my walker and made it to the bathroom door. As I struggled to get through the door I unexpectedly brushed against Allie's body with my butt and suddenly I was erect. I was actually stunned at my reaction. Embarrassed, I turned away from him, but the shower water was a little too hot so I twisted back in his direction.

"Mmmm, and I see your private is at attention also."

I turned away feeling like a hormonal teenager and it got harder.

"Hey, Lowell, this will help."

Allie walked toward me with his hand outstretched. I thought he was going to grab it, which in turn made it throb, but instead he shut off the hot water, showering me with cold. I screamed as he left the bathroom laughing.

"I have to run down to administration, Chip. I'll be back in bit," Allie hollered.

I adjusted the temperature and had to quickly jerk-off. After cleaning up I carefully made my way back into the room and laughed so hard when I saw my bed. Allie had laid out my clothing just like I had for Billy. This truly was my biggest challenge, getting dressed. I managed pretty well to get everything on except for my shirt by the time Allie got back.

"I'm sorry I missed you taking care of your little friend," Allie snickered as he walked back in.

I gave him a devilish grin. "You'd better be careful what you ask for."

I lifted my left arm with my right and he slipped my left hand through the sleeve of my shirt.

"You know Allie, upon discharge I need a full time professional to live with me."

He adjusted my shirt and started buttoning it. "Yes, I know."

I felt a bit awkward asking him but I thought I'd give it a shot. "I know they are going to assign someone, but would you be willing or even capable of moving in with me for while, till I get my feet back on the ground?"

Allie smiled. "That was a bad pun. I'd have to get clearance through my boss. But why me?"

"Well, I've gotten used to you?"

He stopped with the buttons, took a step back, and stared at me. "Thanks man," he said sardonically. "It's nice to be used to."

"You know what I mean." I felt bad the way that came out. "You're great at what you do and I like you, but I didn't know if you had someone you were close to that would mind if you were gone at night."

"You're fishing and I'm single."

"Oh, okay. Where do you live?"

He put my loafers in front of me. "After weeks of practically living with me now you want the personal details? The Bronx. I'd tell you what street but I'm sure you've never heard of it."

"I'm sure, too." I slipped the right one on easily.

"Have you ever been to the Bronx?"

Allie wrestled to get my left shoe on my foot.

"Of course."

"You lie!"

"I drive, or I used to drive through the Bronx all the time, very quickly, to get to Westchester."

We both laughed.

. . . . .

ALLIE DEFINITELY FELT the wow factor as he wheeled me into my loft.

"Welcome to my digs," I said as I rolled over to my plants. "I can't believe they're all dead."

He put his suitcase down and went over to a window to let in some fresh air. "These are all cactuses. They shouldn't have died in the time you were gone."

"Uh, well they were dead before then."

Allie gave me a sarcastic look.

I spun around in the chair. "But now what?"

Allie checked out my state of the art kitchen. "Now what?"

I threw my good arm up into the air. "I mean what the fuck do I do now?"

"I think you congratulate yourself."

I wheeled over to him. "What the hell does that mean?"

"In the beginning you were frightened, then you were depressed, and now you're angry. And that's good. Healthy.

137

Progress."

Hell, I was always angry.

Allie picked up his bag and walked down the hallway. "Where's my room?"

I chased him with my chair. "To your left."

He threw his suitcase on the bed and started opening it. "First, I check out your apartment. Then, what we do are daily things. Like vacuuming, washing clothes—"

"I have a freaking housekeeper that does that. I want to go to the gym. I want to run a mile. I want to climb a mountain." I struggled to get up out of the chair and to a standing position. "I want to cook. I want to do my TV show. I want to be me again!"

I was very unsteady and aimed my body for the bed but misjudged, hit the side of it, bounced off it and landed on the hard floor. Shockingly, I of all people, started to cry.

Allie got down on the floor next to me and rolled me onto my back. I couldn't stop the tears. He sat above me and laid my head in his lap.

"Just let it out," he whispered quietly.

"It's all just so…shocking. It's fucking shocking. I mean I know I'm doing well but I still can't believe this has happened to me. My life was all planned out. I was just about to make it big and—"

I slowly quieted down as Allie gently massaged my forehead. A few minutes must have passed by when I looked up at him. His eyes were closed and he seemed to be in a meditative trance.

Suddenly he said very sweetly, "Shit happens."

It sounded so inappropriate yet so perfect that I started to laugh. Then he started to laugh.

"Allie, you know what I want?"

"What's that?"

I rolled myself onto my strong right elbow. "Food. Good food. Any kind of food but hospital food."

. . . . .

FROM MY WHEELCHAIR I tried to hover around Allie once he got back from the store and watched him take items out of the bags. Among many things I could see that he had bought oregano, garlic, cumin, and bay laurel leaves.

"I have most of these ingredients here."

"And you've been away for weeks. I want fresh!" Allie exclaimed.

"This is all wrong. I told you what to get."

He looked me straight in the eye. "No, you ordered me what to get. And considering I'm making dinner, I'll choose the ingredients."

I sat there with my mouth open. "Who's making dinner?"

He looked me up and down. "I don't think you are."

I checked out all the ingredients. "Black beans, jalapeños, jicama? What are you, Puerto Rican?"

"*¡Pido su perdón!*" Allie exclaimed indignantly. "*¡Soy Cubano!*"

"Cuban? But you have sandy blonde hair and green eyes."

"And everyone from Cuba has to look like Ricky Ricardo? Go make yourself useful and mix us up a couple of cocktails."

"So bossy," I said under my breath.

"And thank you for noticing the color of my eyes," Allie said winking at me.

"You're welcome."

"And I bought some mint so you can make us Mojitos." Allie looked over at me. "You do know how to make a Mojito, don't you?"

"Yes," I boasted. "I know how to make a Mojito."

I think. I wheeled into my bedroom and to the computer to quickly look up a recipe for the drink when I heard him holler from the kitchen.

"Save yourself some time. It's three parts rum, one part lime juice, two teaspoons sugar, four mint leaves, dash of soda."

I came out my bedroom with my tail between my legs.

"You're a mind reader."

"I knew you were going to say that."

. . . . .

IT FELT SO odd not to be the one cooking, especially in my own kitchen. But considering how strong I made the Mojitos and it being my first drink in weeks, it actually was enjoyable to let someone else take care of things.

"It's all ready," Allie said as he started to serve the meal.

I wheeled over and lit the candles on the dining room table as he brought over the dishes. "Allie, I'm sorry that I don't have a Cuban wine, but I did open a Chilean Chardonnay."

"Good. Cuban wines suck."

I struggled to get out of the wheelchair and onto the dining room chair. And I like the fact that he could have helped me but sensed I wanted to do it on my own. "This meal really smells delicious."

"My abuela's recipe for spicy mojo chicken with black beans and mandarin oranges."

I went through my broken Spanish. "Grandmother?"

He nodded as we started eating. "I was raised by her. In the early 50s my grandfather died and she immigrated to the States. My mother and father were going to join her but stayed in Cuba a bit too long. Unfortunately, Castro appeared. I was their only child and born with a congenital heart disorder that needed complicated surgery and just by luck of the draw, I was allowed to leave Cuba and was flown to New York."

"Damn, that's tough, being a little kid and all."

"The operation was a success and my family, knowing I would have a better life here, encouraged me to stay on with my abuela in the Bronx. I was really close to her, but she is gone now."

I smiled at him. "You know, the day…it happened…I was preparing my late abuela's recipe. Shepherd's pie."

We held up wine glasses and toasted, "To our abuelas."

. . . . .

IT TASTED SO good and not just because it wasn't hospital food. We gobbled up each and every little bite.

"Allie, you truly are a wonderful cook."

He actually blushed which I found very endearing. "That is a real compliment coming from you."

"Someday you'll make someone a great husband."

"Actually I did, once," he said rather flip. "But he's history."

"Left you for another guy, huh?" I asked, teasing him.

"No, he died." He got up from the table and took our plates into the kitchen.

I was mortifyingly embarrassed. "I'm so sorry."

"Don't worry about it. Like I said, shit happens. I met a great guy, loved him for almost ten years, and then he got cancer." He came back and poured more wine into our glasses. "But that was quite a while ago. Chip, why don't you go over to the sofa and I'll bring the dessert?"

I sensed he wanted to change the subject. I managed very carefully, to stand up, and while walking over there I rested against a chest in front of my large mirror.

"Jesus, the left side of my face still looks like it's melted."

"Maybe if you have an overdose of Botox on the right side, it will even out," Allie shouted from the kitchen.

I smiled as I barely made it to the sofa. Allie brought over two ramekins full of flan, two spoons, and set them down on the coffee table.

"Now these I did not make myself, as you know."

He dashed back to the dining room table, brought over the wine and our glasses, and plopped himself down on the couch.

I studied him. "You have beautiful skin."

I realized this made him uncomfortable as we each took a sip of our wine.

He gently brushed his hand along his forearm. "Don't be silly."

I looked at him seriously. "I really mean it. You have beautiful olive skin."

Allie eventually broke the awkward silence. "And I think you're much more attractive now than when you entered the hospital."

I almost choked on my wine. "I what?"

Allie laughed. "You were all puffed up like a blowfish."

"I wasn't puffed up, I was muscular."

"And insecure."

I frowned at him. I had to think about that one.

"But, Chip, talk about insecure. I'm shocked that your little friend never came back to see you."

"Billy," I said almost under my breath.

"When a crisis like this happens in your life, you realize who your real friends are."

"Or if you had any to begin with." We both sipped our wines in silence. "You seem to be somewhat of a loner, too."

Allie eyed me suspiciously. "I guess I've never looked at it like that before. I have acquaintances but, actually, my work fills up the social void in my life."

"Are your parents still in Cuba?"

It was obvious that I pushed an emotional button. I put my glass down and touched his arm. "I'm sorry, I didn't mean to intrude."

"You're not intruding, I already brought them up. It's just that I haven't talked about them in a long time." He took a deep breath. "My father was an outspoken journalist against Castro and his Communist regime and was eventually imprisoned. I think he must have died in jail sometime in the late 70s, because in 1981 my mother boarded a small boat in an attempt to flee to Miami. Overcrowded and with no life preservers, it capsized during a storm and all were lost at sea. I was so young when I moved up here that I don't remember my parents at all. It's like they never existed."

He looked so sad it broke my heart. "I'm sorry, Allie."

He slowly turned toward me and smiled. I leaned in and our mouths almost touched. I took a chance, kissed him lightly on the lips, and then he pulled away. A moment passed and then he slid his forearm behind my neck, pulled me to him, and kissed me with fiery passion. It's hard to explain, but something clicked inside of me, like that last number you're fumbling for that opens up a lock. As odd as it felt intellectually, my heart knew I had met a kindred soul. I kissed him deeper and we fell into one another.

When we finally parted lips, we looked into each other's eyes and then burst out into laughter. Not laughter like this was such a stupid thing to do, but laughter because it took both of us so long to find this.

Without speaking, Alejandro del Valle stood up and reached out for my hands. With all my might, I made it to a standing position and then without any warning, he scooped me up into his arms. Life had come full circle. I was now the man being swept off my feet.

But Allie made it about three steps, and thank God we were still next to the sofa because he didn't have the strength to carry me and we both fell over onto it.

"¡Dios querido del Oh!" Allie cried. "I think my back went out."

He helped me back to my feet and together we supported each other, arm in arm, back to my bedroom.

Who knew that a chubby middle-aged Cuban with blonde hair, green eyes, and olive skin would turn out to be the sexiest and kindest man I have ever kissed in my life?

CHERRY BLOSSOMS AND REBELLION

MARCUS JAMES

BRACKEN COURT HATED his parents, they never understood him; in fact they could care less about who he truly was; they only kept him around as an ornament for social gatherings, an accessory that helped them to project the image of a perfect family; but a perfect family they were truly not.

He looked at neglected CDs and tattered books resting on mahogany shelves and wrought-iron stands, filed alphabetically and reflecting a life that he tried so much to live; a life made with perfect structure and order; a life so different from his reality. He lay on his large bed, dark bangs curtaining his dark eyes, he had a cherubim face with pouty lips, soft and luscious, and skin as smooth as silk. Dressed in the blue slacks and white polo of his school, he dreamt up ways of escape, solutions to his situation, a way to run away.

He felt trapped in this penthouse on Park Avenue, looking out on the city beneath him and the bay beyond him, each thing moving with its own life. He would never know that life, not as long as he was kept inside this kingdom, this modern citadel in the middle of a metropolis.

He never thought that eighteen would be so hard; he never

imagined that his world would make itself understandable then, and he never knew that he would fall in love—that he would truly know himself in ways never experienced, with thoughts that had been previously undreamt.

And it was all because of Nate Peterson.

Nate had told him who he really was, had shown him what he really wanted, and all of this he did through the poetry of his body, the tempting contours of the muscles, and those solid abs, abs that tasted of salt and sulfur under his tongue, abs that collected with gooseflesh under his hot and teasing breath.

It had all started with lacrosse, and lacrosse turned into something else, something expressive of sex and teenage fantasies, the dreams of another life, a life that traveled across the borders of private school and penthouse apartments, reached past high society parties and mothers with cocktail glasses always in hand, too drunk to remember that they were alive; too lost to understand that they coursed with blood, and the people who flowed with the same blood were in desperate need of a gentle hand.

Parents are fine with not being parents until their kid turns out to be gay, and then suddenly they become determined to be named parent of the year, never really caring to see what was inside themselves.

He was just a project.

. . . . .

THE FIELD HAD glistened with green; and the smell of the bay drifted in the air; scents of salt and fungi laced in the breeze, rolling off the tides and onto the school's field. Gothic towers reached up toward heaven, aged orange bricks forming its solid foundation, reaching out to the brownstones nearby and dominating the skyline—the congestion of cars and people unable to penetrate the school's walls.

They had been playing for hours now, and yet their coach

was not pleased; he wanted winners and winners they were not; in fact he called them faggots and sissies, all of which Bracken took to mean himself, hearing these simple words and realizing that in his case they were no longer so simple.

He stood there lean and sweaty, his fair flesh glistening with a sheen of sweat, the sun lighting his dark hair, his eyes taking in the view around him—namely Nate Peterson.

Nate stood there on that field soaking with perspiration, with a shaved head of brown hair, exquisite olive skin, and strong cheekbones, all of which contoured perfectly with his strong and muscular build. The blue tee was stained dark from a combination of sweat and water, his honey eyes catching the light and reflecting just like the sun. It was enough to drive Bracken crazy, and in fact it did.

He watched as Nate stood there, his legs firm and his calves strong, standing at an angle as he lifted the hem of his tee and wiped his face dry with its fabric, his torso revealed and tempting to Bracken, who could only stare with his mouth hanging open, watching as the sweat made Nate's ridged abs glitter in the sun's clear light.

That thin trail of hair that lingered around his navel and led down under his shorts was unnerving; the gray elastic band of his jockstrap was visible and sat snug over the bones of his pelvis, hinting what waited beneath the concealment of his blue cotton shorts.

He moved his hands in front of his crotch and tried to think of other things than that which was before him, reveling in the glory of the spring air and the comfort that the bustling noise of Manhattan could bring.

Nate looked back at him and smiled, winking for a moment before letting his soaked shirt fall back to its place and returning to the game, leaving Bracken to stand there on the grass stunned, unable to think of his next action.

In the locker room they were all horsing around and slapping one another with towels, though Bracken could take no part in it; the idea of playing this game with the other boys was too alien, too intrusive; besides, he had better things to do.

Undressing was torture, allowing himself to be seen semi-nude by these boys, these boys who were so unlike him, these boys with the sexual eyes and the strong bodies, these boys with the cruel names and the macho charm, these boys who teased him and hounded him, torturing Bracken with their ferocious beauty; all of these boys, that is, except for Nate.

Nate was quiet when not aroused, and he looked at Bracken with gentle eyes, eyes that were like sunshine, eyes that seemed to burn away everything that seemed dark and threatening; in fact all of Nate was sunshine and sometimes that sunshine would even reflect back on him.

"Oh dude, that's sick!" Nate proclaimed, slamming his locker shut and looking from one of the boys who seemed to be making fucking motions and then to Bracken, both boys locking eyes from opposite ends of the locker room; the dreary light shone through dirty bulbs and gave them both a chill.

"Well that's what a faggot like him would do!" The boy said, laughing then stopping when he could not understand why Nate wasn't, oblivious to the fact that Nate did not laugh because he was understanding Bracken Court for the first time and he was now lost within his heart and with his guilt.

Bracken finished in a hurry and gathered his book bag, racing for the door and escaping to the outside, taking a breath for the first time since he and Nate had locked eyes.

That night Bracken dined alone. His parents had gone to another fundraiser, leaving him with the anonymous cook and the five-bedroom apartment feeling so alone in a world that was supposed to grant him everything that he could ever want.

"This fucking sucks—" He said under his breath, the dimmed recessed lights above him casting a minimal glow in the dining room, the dining room with the sparkling skyline and the candy-peach colored walls, the dining room with it's massive French doors, with its twenty windowpanes of glass and polished gold knobs; the chandelier hanging unlit above a long and polished cherry wood table, a table long enough to seat thirty and yet always empty.

The food was gourmet but Bracken would not touch it, unable to eat with these thoughts of Nate spinning in his brain, memories that seemed to ooze from his fleshy membrane and seep out of his ears and nose; pouring out from a startled mouth, these thoughts like poison that reacted to his desires and made his heart skip a beat.

That night in his bedroom, a bedroom with red gossamer walls and another set of French doors with more glass panes, he lay, staring at a ceiling that reached twelve feet, two massive windows that reached from the floor to that ceiling, open and revealing the labyrinth of a world beneath him and beyond him.

He waited for the last hints of pale blue light to fade into black, casting his room into darkness, though a kaleidoscope of multicolored light danced on the windows. He watched them on the ceiling, imagining what it would be like to *be* that light, to be able to travel on everyone's wall and watch them as they slept and dreamed, their faces expressing of what their minds created while lost in slumber.

Bracken rolled over, feeling barren on that massive bed and thinking of the field and the vision that he had seen earlier that day. He smiled as he re-created that vision of Nate's bare torso, focusing on each press of his rib and the hint of chest that he could see, allowing his hands to journey down his green pajama pants and begin to stroke the semi-bulge that was hidden beneath. He focused on the straps of his jock resting on his pelvic bone and found himself removing his shirt and sliding down his pants to his ankles— the goose-flesh covering his naked skin.

With one hand he rubbed his body and twisted his nipples and with the other he began to pump his cock, sliding up and down his eight-inch shaft, his balls rubbing against the fabric of maroon silk sheets. The surge of orgasm raced through his legs, causing him to convulse as it rode up through his cock and out onto his body, shooting jism all over his chest and face. He let it drip into his mouth, sticky and warm, the image of Nate fading from his mind, replaced by the lethargy of sleep.

. . . . .

THE AIR WAS cool as he walked to school, his breath somewhat visible though winter had long passed; and yet he wasn't certain if this was still true. The world seemed different and as he passed the doormen along Park Avenue and he wondered what it was that made this day so strange? Were the people around him acting differently? Were the animals acting up like the dogs in *The Exorcist*? It didn't seem to be the case. No, in fact everything seemed to be normal, the normal cars and the normal sun, hidden behind trees and skyscrapers and casting cool, grey-blue shadows on the streets and buildings; the city was the same as every other morning that he had ever experienced.

"Bracken!" He turned to face the voice behind him, unsure if someone was really calling to him.

"Hey!" It was Nate Peterson, jogging up to him and wearing his blue blazer with a white collard shirt beneath it, tucked into navy blue slacks and a black belt, a matching blue tie hung loosely around his neck, the school's crest stitched into it.

"Who, me?" He asked, pointing to his chest, pressing his finger into his tie lightly, his eyes searching around the perimeter.

"Yeah you, who did you think I meant?" He laughed.

"Yeah, I guess there aren't too many people named Bracken in the world, huh?" Nate smiled and nodded, brushing his shaved head with his hand.

"So what's up?" Bracken asked him, resuming the walk to their school, trying not to sound too interested in Nate's presence.

"Well I just wanted to apologize for those guys at practice, they're assholes—" Bracken shrugged.

"Don't worry about it; it's really not a big deal—" He took a step and was met by the force of Nate's hand.

"What do you mean 'don't worry about it'; how do you not worry about it?" Nate's eyes seemed to burn with eager understanding, wanting so desperately to dissect the situation.

"Look, you don't get it, it kinda works a certain way; I get teased by the big guys and I put up with it, I don't let it get to me; that's the way it has always been; besides the word faggot doesn't scare me as much as those who say it; and I have nothing to worry about from those guys." Nate shook his head and his lips seemed to pout, making Bracken wonder what it would be like to touch those lips, to feel their softness on his mouth and to graze them with his tongue.

"Well if it were me I wouldn't let them get away with it!" Bracken shook his head and smiled.

"Well it isn't you, this isn't your situation it's mine; this is me and this is how it is." They walked the rest of the way in silence. Cars rushed them, eager and impatient parents desperate to drop their children off and get to work. Most of them had offices on Wall Street and Madison Avenue to get to and New York traffic to beat; the rest were students trying to show off their wheels and look cool in front of their peers, not caring if they got to class on time.

Their school was sprawling, a former hotel turned upscale educational prison located on the north side of town, the pride of the city with its gothic presence and ancient history—an old building, one that was stained with its history, much like its grounds were stained with dried gum and paint.

Students bustled and gathered into their posses, unwilling

to acknowledge or welcome another, and yet they all seemed to exist together, matched with their common dread of going to class and falling into the drone of the day.

They had stopped in the quad, standing on flagstone and watching as people went by, all in uniform, all seeming to be the same, as if they lacked identity; and this made Bracken feel all the more the outcast within this fishbowl of student life.

"Well, you should probably get to your friends but thanks for walking with me…" Nate nodded, the sunlight spearing over the sharp gothic towers, glittering in his honey eyes, glistening on the sheen of his moistened lips. It made Bracken fidget with uneasiness.

"Well, um later then," Nate said, watching as Bracken began to pivot on his heel and make his way toward the school; it was now or never. "Wait!" He called out, grabbing Bracken by the arm and making him face him.

"Yeah?" His eyes were large and full of questions.

"You know how you said it's not my situation?" Bracken nodded and took note of the arm that held him; it was shaking. "Well you were wrong—" Nate pulled him close and placed his lips on Bracken's and they tasted the sweet of each other's mouths, delighting in this sense of uninhibited lust that had seemed to take them over.

Their hands traveled down each other's backsides and felt the firmness of one another's bodies, their cocks filling with blood and beginning to drill into one another. It was a moment of complete and utter happiness, not a loss of innocence but a gaining, a new sense of love and realization.

They parted and each boy smiled, unable to contain his joy.

"See, it's my situation too." Bracken laughed and nodded, both boys forgetting the world that they belonged to.

"Oh man, that's sick!" They turned to see one of their teammates staring at them in shock mixed with hidden jealousy, and they were unsure of what to do; the students were staring and there was no turning back.

"C'mon, I know where we can go." Bracken nodded and they ran; they ran away from a world that had tried to control them, to tell them their place in life and what they would be; it was the perfect example of escapism.

As they moved under shady trees and passed aged brownstones and corner stores, they had no thoughts other than what they would know of themselves. This world had opened up and it was paradise, a paradise that would never be forgotten or destroyed, even if the world came to a bloody end at that very moment.

Nate led him to a three story brownstone, Bracken knowing that this was Nate's home and feeling as if he were discovering a forbidden piece of the world.

"Back here—" They moved to the back of the house, a giant wrought iron fence filled with a hidden wood made up of willows and cherry blossoms; their fragrant pink shower rained down upon them and blanketed the earth with its petals. They slipped in and laid their jackets on the manicured ground, allowing for the perfect bed.

"Are you sure you want to do this?" Nate asked him, his eyes large and soulful, and his face searching for reason.

"I'm sure; I've wanted to do this for a long time—" Bracken responded, already placing his lips on Nate's neck and slipping off his tie, unbuttoning the white shirt, and exposing the hard body underneath. He watched his pulse race as he nibbled on Nate's neck and searched his waist for his belt which he removed quickly, tossing it aside and pulling out the rest of his shirt, running his hands over that sculpted body and pinching its dark nipples.

"Bracken—" Nate could manage nothing else as he removed his shirt and Bracken's slacks, both boys now clothed only in white briefs, their cocks long and stiff, brushing against the form of the other.

Bracken trailed his tongue along Jake's abs, smiling as

he tasted his sweet flesh, tasting what seemed to be sulfur resting within the pores, dragging his tongue into the ridges of his muscle and pulling on the elastic band of his underwear, letting go and finding his strong orbs beneath the white fabric, and breathing his hot breath on his sack, desperate to get him inside his eager mouth.

Nate ran his fingers through Bracken's hair, his lids fluttering like the wings of moths and his breath was drawn and heavy; his mind felt as if it were floating and he wouldn't have it any other way. With a grin on his face and hunger in his eyes Bracken slid his fingers under that white band and pulled down those little white briefs, throwing them off Nate's legs and making his way up to that long and eager cock head, trailing his tongue on the thick shaft and rolling it along the mushroom-shaped head, teasing the slit and taking Nate in deep, closing his eyes and going with the rhythm of the moment, glimpsing cherry blossoms in fall, descending from the sky and snowing pink flakes.

Nate was in dreamland, lost in his desire for Bracken; nothing else seemed to exist, certainly not the possible consequences of this day, this day that seemed to be forever. He slid his hand down Bracken's smooth, white backside and found his ass, sliding his fingers in and tracing the space between the cheeks, wanting desperately to have Bracken's cock in his mouth and to be inside of him.

"Fuck!" Nate let out, just as he shot his load in Bracken's hot mouth, watching in stunned silence as this beautiful boy with the angel face took down his hot come, finalizing the loss of virginity.

Bracken felt that sticky heat shoot against the back of his throat and catch on his tongue, it was difficult at first to get that first stream down his throat, but he did, and from that point on he would drink Nate dry, unwilling to accept anyone else but him.

They made love for hours, exploring the maps of their

flesh, learning every flaw and perfection, experiencing sublime ecstasy. Nate fucked him nice and slow, treating his ass with respect, bucking in waves, whispering sweet nothings into Bracken's ears. His eyes closed, his long, black lashes grazed his plump cheeks, his breath reeling against Nate's force, moving with the breeze.

Nate took him in his mouth and sucked Bracken for several minutes, tasting him and teasing him, licking his balls and sucking his dick; it had been exactly what he wanted to do. The day pressed on and morning turned to noon and noon drifted into evening, and they knew that they had to go home.

. . . . .

THEY STOOD OUTSIDE Bracken's building in the midst of teeming Manhattan; bits of grass and pink petals rested in their hair, their eyes looking at one another with uncertainty.

"So which one is your room?" He looked at him and smiled, Bracken pointing to the third floor.

"That's it, that's my prison cell—" He hadn't said this with humor, and in fact Bracken's face grew dark with the prospect of going back home.

"I'm sorry, but you know I'll walk with you tomorrow; though this time we should probably try to sit through one class. Afterward we'll have lunch and I'll take my dad's car—" Bracken nodded and Nate planted a gentle kiss on his cheek, smiling as he walked away, unaware of the events that were about to unfold.

. . . . .

BRACKEN COURT LAY in that room, pissed that the school had called and reported his absence, pissed that a teacher had seen the kiss and divulged that information to the housekeeper, angry with his parents for suddenly deciding to act like parents, and hateful that they sent him to his room and forbade him to see Nate Peterson again.

They were both drunks and never around, and yet they felt that they could dictate his life. None of it seemed real anymore, and he wished so much to waste away, to die, and become just another piece of the city's walks.

There was a tapping at his front window, a tapping that beckoned to Bracken, calling him to his window and forcing him to open the doors and look out on the street below him.

"Bracken!" It was Nate. He seemed flushed from running, and he held a black duffle bag in one hand and tickets in the other.

"My parents will kill you if they see you!" Bracken called out, unable to suppress a laugh as he watched Nate twirl around, a pair of sunglasses on his face and his shirt hanging open except for the last three buttons; his sports coat waving in the oncoming breeze.

"The school called my house and my parents flipped and then I realized something!"

Bracken shook his head. "Oh yeah, and what's that?" He heard footfalls coming down the long hall, making their way towards the study next door, most likely to yell at Nate.

"I'm in love with you! I've been in love with you for the past nine years, ever since the fourth grade; you're all I think about, Bracken, and I want you to be my boy!" Bracken was smiling and all that he had been wishing for since he first laid eyes on Nate Peterson was coming true, and he hadn't the slightest idea of what to do.

"You there, you pervert. Just what in the hell do you think your doing?" Bracken looked to the right of him to see his mother standing on the stone balcony, her hair blond and short, and her body thin and draped in a lilac gown, a string of rhinestones around her neck. Nate flipped her off and turned his attentions back to Bracken who was looking from him to his mother.

"I've got my own place near N.Y.U. that my grandpa left me; we can live there and still go to school, it'll be perfect, please say you'll come with me. I'll die without you."

Bracken looked over at his mother, who shook her head and told Nate that Bracken wouldn't be going anywhere, but he had already made up his mind and he was going.

He shoved clothes into a large suitcase and grabbed all of the birthday money that he had collected over the years; saving it for a day like this, a day when he might have the courage to run away—a day of rebellion. "How do I get down? I can't get out of my room and even if I could they'd stop me!"

Nate searched around and shook his head. "You're eighteen, they can't keep you—"

"Oh this is ridiculous!" Bracken's mother left the study and turned the corner, twisting the knob and opening the doors, her staunch husband behind her, both determined to put an end to all of this.

"Trust me, Bracken, please trust me—" Nate only mouthed the last part but it was enough for Bracken, those large honey eyes watching as Bracken tossed the suitcase and looked back at his parents, shaking his head with tears in his eyes; he couldn't believe what he was about to do.

"Bracken, you can't, this isn't right." He could see their refusal to get out of his way but the truth was evident and they couldn't stop him.

"Mom, I'm going. I can't do this anymore, I just can't." He forced his way past the both of them and walked to the elevator, knowing that everything was changing, that his life would never be the same again.

The door opened and he ran outside, past the doorman and out onto the street, jumping onto Nate.

"Fuck, Nate said as he toppled, looking at one another and grinning. Bracken was sitting on his chest and looking down at him, too stunned to move and not sure if he really wanted to, especially since his legs were shaking.

"See, I told you they couldn't stop you—" Nate said, chuckling to himself.

"Yeah, you did—" Bracken closed his eyes and leaned down, their lips pressing together gently, tasting the sweet of spring; it was heaven.

He looked back at his parents and they watched him, holding Nate's hand as they ran down the block, heading through the thick of the city with their things in hand. The world was finally theirs and nothing could take that away, not their parents or the world's hatred; they would be on their own, carving a new life for themselves in the world, both open to all of life's possibilities.

They would get regular jobs and make their own money, shedding the silver spoons and promises of conditional trust funds. They would be free and they would be happy. They could tell their story of survival and prison, of love conquering all and what it meant to leave the world behind, a story of cherry blossoms and rebellion.

The tale of every American boy.

FOLLOWING TUESDAY

STEWART LEWIS

I AM RUNNING like lightning down Ludlow Street, as fast as I can, with no particular destination. I am sporadically bumping into people, startling them. I am crying. The wind is drying the tears against the skin of my face, leaving a colorless film that hardens and cracks. Nobody notices my desperation, just my speed. I get as far as the Williamsburg Bridge and have to slow, approaching complete exhaustion. I think of jumping (how could anyone resist the thought when looking over such a tempting edge?), but know that I will not. The strength and impulse to actually give myself to the air does not exist inside of me. I feel only a tireless and saturating fear, my feet and legs sinking into the bridge, barely holding me upright.

A guy approaches, swift and light on his feet, his arms waving through the air in a pedestrian dance. His emerald eyes come into focus and his gaze is hard. He breaks the stare by turning to his left profile and sucking in on a cigarette, holding the smoke in long enough so that barely nothing comes out. He takes my hand and lifts it to his heart, does not smile but pulls me with him fast, leads me blocks and blocks into an alley, up a fire escape. He jumps to the fire escape on the next building over, turns around, and puts out his arms. I try to speak but can't find any words.

"Hurry," he says. He has an angular face, jet-black hair, and a thin smile.

I jump over and we crawl through a window, the building long abandoned and eerie. There is a pale-faced teenager crouched in the corner playing a handheld video game. The victorious bleeps suggest that he is winning. As we rise slowly up the dilapidated stairwell, I notice groups of people huddled together on each of the levels, some very still, some with slight animation.

We get to the top floor and he urges me to close my eyes, leads me to the center of the space, and lays me on the floor face-up. His breath shortens.

"Open." The ceiling of the building is a great big dome, with thousands of tiny pinholes, varying slightly in diameter, letting minuscule rays of light leak through, creating the illusion of planets, a solar system.

Poor man's planetarium, I think.

"Perspective," he barely whispers, "is a delicious thing."

My lips slowly open and relax, in awe of the display. I feel weightless, as if the dome above me, the thin wires of light, are suspending me slightly above the floor, creating levitation. He rests his head on the corner of my chest. His skull feels extremely heavy, but there is nothing gained by resisting the weight. The best thing to do is to simply acknowledge and welcome it.

We stay like that for a long time and I have no more tears.

We end up in a small diner on Rivington where he orders us coffee.

"Why were you crying?" he asks, moving a strand of hair from his eyes.

"My father," I tell him. "He's…he's a drunk, an asshole, he broke all of my CDs. I gotta get out of this city. I want to find my mother."

"Where is she?"

"She took off last year, who would blame her. My dad

treated her worse than he does me. She told me she'd give me some sort of sign when she'd settled somewhere, so I could join her. I keep looking for that sign."

He looks at me with his soft green eyes and slowly licks the bottom of his lip. With nothing to lose, I continue.

"When I was a kid, six or seven maybe, she used to sneak me five-dollar bills so I could play the video games. She would always wait up for me to get home, like she couldn't sleep unless she knew I was safe. Kids take that shit for granted so much now, you know? They resent their parents but don't realize when it comes down to it, it's all they have."

"You are sweet," he says, patting at my unruly hair, "you're like an injured animal."

"You are too," I say, and he kisses me under the sting and hiss of the neon light above us. His lips are smooth and his tongue dances subtly, tempting mine. I feel my erection tug underneath my jeans.

We stop and stare at each other, until I ask him his name.

"Tuesday," he says.

"Really?"

"Yep, Tuesday Ross."

"Sounds like a famous person," I say. "My grandmother was famous. She was the first woman to play flute in the New York Symphony Orchestra. She gave me her flute before she died. It's worth a lot of money, but I don't think I could sell it. Unless it was for something she'd want me to have."

"So, why were you crying?" I counter.

"Me?"

"Yeah, a little, when we were in the building."

"Oh. I think I was crying of happiness. Sometimes the beauty of that place hits my heart in the right place."

Another silence fueled by locked eyes, then he asks for my name.

"Oliver. My mom named me after her first pet. A turtle."

"You're named after a turtle." He giggles and I am warmed

by the sound of it. I feel an unspoken kinship, as if I am meant to be here, that I've known him all along. He looks at his watch, throws five dollars on the table, and says, "C'mon, I want to show you something else."

Walking down Avenue A, I wonder what it will be this time. I notice how small his frame is, with hands of a child. His hair is the color of night and gives off a slight sheen. He walks languid and hums.

We climb through a fence and over to the side of a building. He turns over two trash cans and gets on top of one, gestures for me to get on the other one. I climb up. Our chins rest on the windowsill. Inside, there is a rehearsal—ballet dancers. They are tall, lithe, and beautiful. Their bodies move with a seemingly effortless grace.

"She's my favorite," Tuesday says, tapping his tiny finger on the window. He is referring to a girl in red with blond curls, warming up on the side.

"It's amazing how they can hold their legs that high," I say.

A person comes in and starts playing the piano. We turn around and sit on the garbage cans, our backs to the wall. We listen to the muffled classical piano.

"Are you a dancer?"

"Yes," he says, "but only by myself. I freeze up when other people are around."

"You don't strike me as the shy type."

"No, just with dancing."

"Will you dance with me?"

"Not on the first date," he says, jumping off the garbage can and running down the alley. I catch up to him and he says, "Oliver, I like that name."

"I like Tuesday too. Want to go steady?" I have never said that in my life, the words sound strange coming out of my mouth. He smiles, and neatly tucks a piece of hair behind his ear. "Sure. But I have to know one thing. Well, two."

"Yeah?"

"Do you like chocolate?"

"Yes."

"Do you sleep with clothes on?"

"No."

"Both good answers. C'mon."

Once again I am following him across the avenues and we get to his apartment. One room in an old, pre-war building on Ninth Street, the walls painted blood red. Old magazine and newspaper cutouts of his grandmother hang above his bed. He takes out a bottle of white wine and pours some into two plastic cups. We listen to the distant dogs, sirens, and squeaking bus brakes.

"Here's to imperfect strangers," he says.

He shows me his photo album and tells me a few words about each picture and I feel like I was there, that I could have taken each picture.

"Is he your boyfriend?" I ask, pointing to a picture of a man in a white jacket.

"Was. He died."

"I'm sorry."

"Don't be. How old are you?"

"Twenty-one. You?"

"Thirty-one," Tuesday says. "Usually, you don't understand death until you're at least thirty. Unless you're unlucky."

I look at the pureness in his face, the way his expression is exposed, uncovered, real. I touch his cheek and say, "I feel lucky."

"I'll bet you are."

We fall asleep in each other's arms and he snores a little. It is the most delicate, softest snore I've ever heard.

In the morning he's not there, yet somehow I feel at ease, content. I am not thinking about my father, or my mother, or my dead-end job that I'm probably fired from by now. I am simply lying naked in a big bed, the red walls smooth and rich around me. He bursts in the door and hits me in the head with a bag of bagels. They're sesame, my favorite.

"How did you know?" I ask.

"Intuition."

We chew and look at each other, still discovering the shape of our faces, the looks in our eyes. We like what we see.

He pulls out a Tom Waits CD and says, "Here, we're starting your collection over."

"Cool," I say.

He puts it on and we slowly make love. His body is warm and smooth. He kisses me with precision, and I feel delicate, exposed. He spends long minutes on the insides of my legs, slowly traveling to the space between. It is all I can do not to scream. I grab his head and pull it up for a kiss. He enters me slowly and I want time to stop, I want him inside me forever, I want to cry.

After, he gets up and puts bread on the windowsill and we watch pigeons snap their mouths at the pieces. They are curious and happy, like us.

After a while he says, decisively, "I'm going to sell the flute and we're going to find your mother. I'm the sign."

"What?"

"I'm the sign. Where did she grow up?"

"Florida, she has a sister there."

"Perfect, we don't have to pack much." He says.

"Are you serious?"

"Serious as I'll ever be."

"What about your life?"

"This place was my grandmother's, she kept it for me; it's mine, it will always be here."

"Do you have a job?"

"Not right now."

"What about my father?"

"What about him?"

"He barely eats unless I feed him," I say.

Tuesday thinks for a second. "We'll stack the fridge with frozen dinners."

I feel the rush of a life beginning, a door opening, a wonderful unknown. He hands me one hundred dollars.

"Go buy the dinners and I'll sell the flute and we'll meet at Grand Central in two hours."

"Just like that?"

"Just like that."

I follow Tuesday's orders. On the train to Queens, the faces look different. I can see a yearning in people's eyes, as if the train is a cage and everyone wants out. I can see a wish for flight, and I can feel my own body almost weightless, thinking of Tuesday's kiss, the honesty in his eyes, the goodness in his smile.

My dad is asleep while I load all the dinners in. I write him a note.

Dear Dad, Don't forget to drink water. The dinners are easy, 30 minutes on 350. Remember to shut the oven off. I am going to Florida. I want to find Mom. I will call you when I get there.

Love O

I grab an old letter from my aunt with the address in Florida, my favorite jean jacket, a picture of my father and me from happier times, and some clothes. I look at my watch: forty-five minutes. I run to the train and it comes right as I enter the platform. A woman across from me recognizes something in me, a bursting hope, a chance at better things. She smiles.

I know I am probably crazy, but I am beginning to believe in love.

I get off the train and walk with my head high. When I greet him, we don't speak but just embrace. He smells like bread, and a spice I can't pinpoint. He is beautiful.

Grand Central is bustling with so many people but I hardly notice them, just the feel of Tuesday's tiny hand, leading me on to the rest of my life.

NEAR MISS

JACKSON LASSITER

SAID JUAREZ DOESN'T just walk into Uncle's Lounge, he slithers, like an apparition making an appearance at his own funeral. This is a reasonable entry given the circumstances. As the voice inside his head cautions, *If Mama finds out, she will kill me.*

He creeps through the entrance facing Christopher Street. All of Uncle's patrons use this doorway, but compared to their ribald, ass-slapping, hey-everybody-look-at-me entrances, the pallor of Said's appearance is eerie. He doesn't so much make an entrance as simply manifest. Not that anyone notices.

It is 9:30 P.M., Saturday, late October, the Village in New York. These are prime logistics for cruising under any circumstances but the warmth of an Indian summer tilts the rut to full swing. Eager men cram the small space. Their laughter and repartee—the din of which seems tangible, as if it was a sentient being with purpose and need—rushes to greet Said but then parts around him like Biblical water. It is cleaved by the dagger of unease he brandishes, sliced by the switchblade of his fear (a blade honed by the constant harassment of his ever-present internal dialogue, a voice that sounds remarkably like his mother's).

Said carves out standing space near the outermost edge of the frivolity. He wafts near the edge of the scene, just inside the bar's entrance. He tests the waters. If they chill, he will bolt.

More than fifty men carouse in the long, narrow space of the tavern (every single one of them, Said's inner voice reckons, more handsome than he). Should one of the men cease the carnal pursuit long enough to notice Said, he might observe a pronounced tremble, a shimmering of the heavily starched, lemon-colored shirttail that drapes over the intentionally baggy jeans. Said adopted this look to camouflage the hefty humps of his ass. That ass niggles; it gnaws at his nerves and it forms the very foundation of his concept of self.

"You're Puerto Rican," Mama Juarez scolded when an adolescent Said fussed about the dimensions of his burgeoning *culo*. The heavy accent tumbled from the downward-drawn corners of her frown as she continued, "We're known for our *traseros grandes*! Besides, *niño*, boys aren't concerned about those kinds of things."

One eyebrow arched in accusation, and she fired a meaning-riddled glance at Said's father, who eavesdropped from the king's perch of his well-worn Barca-lounger. But Señor Juarez ignored his son's plight. Eight children preceded Said; seven were high-pitched and raven-haired Latinas who refused to be neglected, the one other son was a baseball-playing-skirt-chasing-replace-the-carburetor kind of boy. A father's quota is sometimes limited, and this father's allotment of caring was already depleted; his youngest son's indelible deviancy permanently locked the deadbolt on sympathy. Señor Juarez declined to be bothered with this, his last offspring's sense of identity.

"Don't worry, *miho*," is Mama's final comment on the subject, nonchalant yet delivered with the clear intention of closing this topic for good. There will be no more talk of butts. She turned her attention back to the intricate embroidered panel spread across her lap, a receiving blanket for the most recent grandchild. A new generation beckoned.

Said chafed, anyway, about both his queen-sized rearend and his parent's disengagement. The fretting shaped habits: he concealed his curves beneath layers of fabric (as if he could; the ample mounds humping beneath the flapping tails will have no part of camouflage; there is no hiding that appendage). More efficiently, Said stashed his private thoughts and desires, relegating them to the realm of the voices within—the voices that drove him to Uncle's tonight.

None of the men notice Said, yet, or his quivering. Not even his butt. Notice comes slowly when a boy hides with such diligence. Still, Said carries a certain youthful appeal: an exotic, soft prettiness that fosters fantasies of plump submissiveness and quiet, thick acquiescence. Plus he earns bonus points for being fresh meat in this den of carnivores. He will eventually get noticed. But for now, although he has come on a mission, and swears to get to it soon enough, he needs this time to adjust. His senses are aflutter and before he joins the fray, they must be calmed.

If pressed, Said will lie. He will lay the blame for his shakes on the close call he had crossingthe busy intersection of Christopher and Bleecker Streets on the walk here from the Fourteenth Street subway stop. After fifty minutes of self-psyching on the Seventh Avenue Southbound Express from his conservative block in the Bronx—*your butt isn't* that *big*, the inward-facing voice had repeated, mantra-like—he was promptly distracted at the street-level window of The Village Gym as he walked by. Only he wasn't trying to catch a glimpse of the muscle-heads hoisting grandiose poundage in the free-weight room, like the other passersby. He wrenched his neck backward to judge, via his reflection in the polished glass, how well he had managed to disguise the protrusion of his bottom.

"Not well at all," he mumbled to himself, tugging fruitlessly at the too-short tail of his Oxford.

The weight of Said's fabricated self-image crashed to the ground like a barbell that got away from the shaking arm trying to boost it. At the same moment, he stepped from the sidewalk directly into the path of an oncoming taxi. A horn blared and a small, feminine gasp escaped from his pink lips. Although he leapt backward to the safety of the curb just in the nick of time, it was too late to salvage his self-composure.

Still, his persistent shuddering infers an upheaval that goes deeper than a simple near miss.

His escape to the Village for a tryst induces this quake, the forgoing of his usual Saturday night spent sequestered in the bedroom he still occupies in his parent's home, door shut tight against his mother's overbearing supervision while he watches the latest from Netflix and shares *pastelillos* with Diablo, the family cat. But even an insecure chico has hormones, and tonight Said enters the race. He stumbles blindly toward a life that he can't visualize, knowing only that skin-to-skin man contact will be a first step.

"*Voy al cine,*" he lied to his mother, slipping away from the radar of her guardianship.

"*Voy al* dick," he might have said, had speaking the truth been possible.

But since it isn't, he arrived here in secret, under the dueling influences of testosterone and adrenaline.

Said hovers just inside the barroom until a duo of spit-slathered lovebirds shoves past him, grappling, walking, and kissing all at the same time with such focus that they don't even acknowledge the hard push that sends him careening to his left. He alights on the short end of the long bar where he stays, parked at the periphery of the party with his back to the wall.

All the better to hide what isn't my best asset, justifies the internal dialogue.

The dim green flickering of the exit sign overhead provides a slim measure of comfort to Said; there is no telling when a quick escape may be necessary. Still, in dogged pursuit of both sexual release and socialization—the basal and the higher needs—he assumes a pose.

His right thumb parts the flaps of his shirttails and hooks into the front pocket of his jeans; the rest of his hand hangs provocatively near his crotch. Shoulders press back, chest pops out, eyes rove. He emulates his role models, the naked and narrow-waisted men displayed in the glossy magazines he hides from his mother's inquisition. Every cell of Said— even those comprising his rotund gluteus—is willed to climb toward that pinnacle of studliness. But his impersonation falters: he stands too erect, as though the current of insecurity running through him carries a charge that stiffens his torso. His arms jut outward at an unnaturally stiff angle and his chin rides slightly too high. His eyes dart rather than rove. He strives for virility, but he only achieves a look of tense over-compensation. And he squirms.

"What'll ya' have?" asks the boy behind the bar, a twenty-something artist-cum-bartender with tousled brown hair, tight jeans, and a sleeveless shirt. He speaks more in Said's general direction than at him, focusing instead on the dirty glasses he twists once on the upright, soapy bristle in the below-counter sink before swiping them briefly through the tepid rinse water and placing them on the "clean" rack.

"Vodka tonic," comes the muttered response.

The bartender wipes his brow with the back of his hand, and as he lifts his bare arm Said notices the patch of dark hair sprouting from the guy's pit, the tendrils trailing down his triceps to a moistened point. Said is nearly hairless, not bushy in even the usual places, and he swallows another wave of inadequacy as the bartender's thatch retreats beneath his lowered arm.

"What?" the bartender asks, finally lifting his gaze to his

customer. "Hey, you new here? What's your name?"

"My name is Said, and I'll have a vodka tonic." The words are spoken with precision but the delivery remains timid, and they are lost in the ruckus swirling though the bar. "Please."

"OK, Ted, comin' up."

"SAY-eed. My name is Said."

"You Saudi or what?"

"No," Said responds with a sigh, "close, but no cigar. I'm Puerto Rican."

Said has never grown easy with this line of questioning. His mother chose this name after hearing it on a late night movie. Full-bellied in the ninth month of her ninth pregnancy, she had risen from bed fighting a bout of indigestion stirred into froth by the kicking fetus. She liked the way the word rolled off her tongue, and so tagged her youngest child without thought to the confusion it will cause later in his life. Puerto Rican, Saudi, Indian, Thai: to some, they are indistinguishable.

Said has argued with people about his name.

"Yes you are, you're Middle Eastern," some insist. "It's OK."

But the bartender doesn't argue; he isn't that interested.

"Mmmm," he grunts, instead, turning to mix the drink. But what he finally pushes across the bar to Said is a gin and ginger ale, with a squished maraschino cherry slowly sinking to the bottom. Said pays anyway and tips, and then sips without complaint. He so rarely disobeys his mother's directive to avoid alcohol that the simple act of imbibing connotes sacrilege. Confronting the inattentive barkeep stretches beyond Said's capacity for rebellion. Instead, he accepts what is handed to him, a just punishment for his intentions.

· · · · ·

DETLEF VON STEINLE stands at the waist-high, circular tabletop smack in the center of Uncle's, his right hand casually curled around the green glass of his cold Heineken, his fingertips tapping to the music that blares from the over-head speakers. The beers arrive as if by magic, the empties whisked away and replaced by full bottles without his even asking. Detlef has slept with all of Uncle's bartenders at one time or another; he has slept with most of the men who patronize this dank watering hole. He lives up to a credo of living while the living is good. Even in his relative youth he has more notches on his belt than many, and yet he maintains an easy rapport with most of his conquests. Bartenders included. They remember what he drinks and they keep the Heinies coming.

Detlef stands here because he knows—this is his hangout—that this centermost table offers the best chance for garnering attention from the men who inhabit Uncle's. Not that he needs to worry about such; his blond-Adonis looks imply an all-American diet of grain-fed meat, fresh sweet corn, and whole milk, belying his solid German heritage (he was in truth reared on the handcrafted gnocchi and strudel his mother had delivered from the German deli near Lincoln Center). Whatever the diet, it worked, as the sum total of golden curls framing clear skin, wide-set blue eyes poised above a lantern-jaw, and broad shoulders tapering to a narrow waistline far outscores the other numbers in this bar. Detlef doesn't need to pose. He naturally entices and has never hesitated to take advantage of this lucky draw. Detlef has never wanted for attention.

So it is no surprise when a stranger sidles up to his table.

"'Sup, handsome?" asks the stranger. "I'm Randy. Randy Bartlett."

"Hey man, how's it goin'?" Detlef answers. He auto-replies, more from force of habit than desire. It is a conditioned response, rote pleasantry stemming from a long history of tawdry positive reinforcement. He smiles on cue and the stranger interprets his slight participation as encouragement. Mr. Randy Bartlett embarks on a rapid, blurring monologue;

he will not squander this good fortune with uncomfortable conversational pauses.

Against the backdrop of the numbing ramble of Mr. Bartlett's soliloquy, Detlef's own inner voice rings clear, bell-like: "The guy is not quite butt-ugly," it allows. "In fact, he was probably a stud a hundred years ago."

Randy is taller than the coveted hunk, and beefier, but not with the thick musculature of steak. His girth hints more of potatoes: a dollop of self-abuse spooned over a hefty portion of neglect. No regular sleep, pyramidal meal plans, nor exercise regime; just drink after drink after drink interspersed with fumbled huffing of poppers on the dance floor culminating in too many ambitious sex acts with more men than he can count.

The result? A fleshy triangle, a heavy apical midriff hanging from narrow, slanted shoulders.

"I like a stout man," Detlef's internal dialogue observes, with honesty. Given his preferences, he will pick someone with physical substance. "However," his rumination continues, "this one grew into a pear of a man."

Detlef amuses himself with the witticism of the pear-man's unfortunate but fitting family name until another surreptitious glance reveals a black leather belt cinching the pursuer's significant belly tight across the most bulbous part, overhung by the dimpled mass it strives to contain. No joke in that.

Pear-man blathers on, and in lieu of Detlef's standard modus operandi of taking on the fellow's fantasy purely for the sake of conquest, ending up (no pun intended) naked in the rumpled sheets of the distorted stranger's bed, he pauses. Occasionally even the fortunate, the genetically blessed and sexually experimental, are tugged from beneath the warm blanket of attention and thrust buck-nekkid into the chilly air of reality. As difficult as habits of pleasure are to shake, of late a new hankering colors Detlef's inner pondering; an itch not easily scratched by the luck of good looks and the fixation of strangers. This thirst requires a different drink.

He has his mother to thank.

Flashback to Detlef's thirty-third birthday just last month. Mama Von Steinle hosted a party for him, inviting his innermost circle of man pals to join the family in the flat high above the East River on Beekman Place. They celebrated the prodigal son with champagne, truffles, and song, but Mama struck a lingering chord when, in German-tinged but impeccably enunciated English, she issued a call to arms, an invitation for him to change his priorities. Not that Mama objected to his lifestyle; she and the senior Detlef (an organizational psychiatrist lured into the lucrative service of the United Nations) had immigrated from Amsterdam the year before their only child's birth, and along with the good Lenox china and Waterford crystal they imported a cultural acceptance of the range of human sexualities. Detlef-the-junior's sexual orientation was—*is*—not of concern to her. What is of importance is her son's continued bachelorhood.

"You listen to me, *Bübchen*, it's all fine and dandy that you and your *reisigbündel* friends have had your fun drinking and whoring like a pack of she-wolves, but sooner or later you will need to settle down," she chided as Detlef and the gang prepared to shift the celebration to Uncle's. "You're not getting any younger," she added, swatting the Belgium lace tablecloth in her hands at the American denim stretched across his perky bottom. He just laughed as he moved past her, ushering his friends out the door.

But her words stuck with him, and since then his inner voice increasingly directs him to search at Uncle's not so much for a roll, but a role: that of partner. Husband. Significant other. The plucky boy wants to get lucky for more than the night. He seeks the charm of a lifetime. Trouble is, the men at Uncle's aren't the stay-put sort. They have been around this block more than once and they can't stop circling. They are a hardened lot, jaded by a life spent maneuvering between the thrill of the adventure and the letdown of rejection. They are man-sharks who frenzy feed, yet no number of fleshmeals will satiate their appetites.

"These barracudas don't fit the bill," admits the inward-speaking voice, as Detlef eyes the motley collection. "Especially not pear-man," whose droning, nonstop prattle, the content of which Detlef would be hard-pressed to remember, serves only to further diminish his minimal attractiveness. Pear-man might suffice for an hour's play but Detlef fishes for a different species. His pining requires a special catch: a spawn that has not yet developed the hard shell mandated for survival in these predatory waters.

I need a newbie, says the internal dialogue.

"Like that guy over there," Detlef says, aloud, noticing for the first time the youngster—Said—standing across the dusky room. Detlef surveys the uncomfortable pose, the fidgeting, and the timid sipping of the cocktail: all good signs. And it's just another benefit that he looks to be full-figured. For Detlef, a round ass sets the hook. He has a passion for some junk in the trunk; he's fond of the cushion. This one seems to offer a nicely filled-out résumé.

"What?" asks the pear-shaped man, but without pausing for a reply continues his one-sided dialogue, oblivious to the give-and-take concept of conversation. The syllables fall from his mouth and land, unheard, in the pile of noise in the room. Detlef pays no mind; he sees nothing but the dark-featured curvy boy across the room. His vision narrows and he will not budge, will not waver, until acknowledged. Like one of Central Park's falcons targeting a popcorn-fattened pigeon, contact is inevitable.

. . . . .

ACROSS THE ROOM, Said questions his decision to venture to the Village. His anxiety grows in direct and inverse proportion to the shrinking of his commitment to this undertaking. He may have been better served by sticking (although not literally) to his nudie photo spreads and all-accepting right hand.

Maybe, concludes his internal dialogue, *this was a mistake*.

He studies the men congregated around him. He looks carefully at each specimen, panning from left to right, but he sees no indication of interest in him: not a nod nor a smile. Not even a casual but intentional self-caressing of the carefully positioned bump straining the front of worn jeans.

Until his gaze lands on the striking blond fellow standing toward the back of the room, staring.

Staring at what? asks Said's skittish inner voice.

The blond produces a smile that out-dazzles any tooth-whitening advertisement and imbues more mystique than all of the beefcake spreads tucked out of maternal sight between Said's mattresses. This smile is very nearly a laugh—mischievous, conspiratorial, direct.

Must be someone behind me warns the voice within, growing more critical as it feeds from the plentiful trough of doubt, nagging so loudly that Said has no choice but to listen. With what he intends to be a casual, dismissive move (but in truth, and consistent with his overall presentation, is more a reactive jerk), Said looks back to see who prompts the stranger's mirth.

Only there is no one behind him, just a floor-to-ceiling mirror that perfectly illuminates for all onlookers a larger-than-life reflection of his nether region, its expanse broadened not as much by the convex curvature of the flimsy and inexpertly-hung glass as by the funhouse distortion of Said's self-perception.

"*Ay, dios mio!*" Said says out loud. "He's laughing at my ass."

Said tosses his unfinished cocktail toward the bar top,

sloshing the remains of the bitter concoction over the smudged surface. The lopsided cherry scoots across the counter and disappears over the far edge of the bar. The bored bartender glances up in response to the clatter but makes no move to clean the spill, while Said turns on his heels and scampers through the passage below the green exit sign. Color him gone. He won't look back, he won't pass go. He doesn't even pause to blink after passing from the dark privacy of the tavern to the vigorous, neon- and halogen-lighted perpetual brightness of the street. He trots straight toward the subway, hell-bent on the safety of home (mindful, however, of oncoming taxis). Diablo and warm *pastelillos* wait, and at this juncture he craves that measure of reassurance.

. . . . .

DETLEF WATCHES THE *hinter* of his dreams hustle what could have been the man of his dreams out of the bar. He makes no other move. A different man might run after the boy, but here's the sad truth: the backside of being godlike is that the beautiful become spoiled—why plant a garden when the farmers throw food at your feet? And having never grown a garden, Detlef can't even harness the plow. Watching the ass vanish is all he can muster. Still, his history doesn't include ditching and this quarry's sudden departure unsettles him. He lurches momentarily toward an abyss he has never faced. His golden aura tarnishes.

Fuck me, am I already that old, he questions, but then quickly retreats from this line of thought. The ramifications are beyond him. His equilibrium may have been momentarily upended, but he teeters only briefly on the edge of the gaping pit of self-doubt. He moves quickly to regain his footing.

"So, Randy, right?" he says to pear-man. "You feeling randy?"

Pear-man replies by sliding the tip of his index finger, chilled from clutching his own bottle, along the top of the low-rise denims hugging Detlef's butt. His fingertip disappears into the downy cleft just below the fabric's edge.

"Mr. Bartlett, just like the pear," Detlef quips, "what do you say we make like fruits and peel outta here?"

UNSPOKEN BUT SAID

JAMES ANDREW CLARKE

ORLANDO AND I met at a club on the Lower East Side. It was one of those Monday night parties for the unpretentious, the die-hard house music aficionados. The mere fact that it was held on the Lower East Side was an indication in itself that this was a serious, check your attitude at the door, party. There was nothing pretentious about the Lower East Side, everything was taken seriously, there was nothing half ass about what you were, punk skinhead, starving artist or drag queen, you lived it twenty-four seven. If you weren't sure about what you were then you belonged on the west side. The east side after all was "the hub of counter culture." That was how he had explained it to me while seated around my kitchen counter the next morning sipping coffee. He took house music seriously; all else in his life was incidental.

I was a serious lover of house music; I would travel anywhere to hear some good hard house tracks and dance from start until the last track fades. I wasn't half ass, even though I lived in Sunnyside, Queens. Then again technically I was on the east side, only across the river— I was connected by the Fifty-ninth Street Bridge. I could be taken seriously, I told him. What I really wanted to say was that I took everything I did seriously. More than anything I took love seriously. From his words, I was certain love wasn't something he took seriously. Plus most guys his age, as I can remember when I was his age ten years ago, were nonchalant about love. Sex was the only thing serious about my relationships back then. Everything else was secondary. I guess, because I had learned from very early on that love if real was a scarce commodity and if by chance you find it while stumbling around in the dark then more than likely it was someone else's and not yours. Though I wasn't looking for love when I met him, the thought had however crossed my mind that I could fall in love with him, even if 'love' to him, was just a word in a song.

As I sat there listening to him, I realized that I wasn't just entranced by his chestnut brown eyes; I kept searching them for some possibility that just possibly somehow, there wasn't truth to all the incidental things he had listed in the conversation. Perhaps they weren't just things he could do without but things he was afraid of. But really I couldn't tell. And so I found myself studying him, taking in all of him, as if I was afraid that once he was out of sight, I might forget what he looked like.

His eyes were like cat's eyes with their slight almond shape, as if on closer inspection of his family tree one would find a Japanese guy on one of the branches. His skin, olive, his torso a square frame with sweet swiveling hips, he walked with a gunslinger's gait. His accent was thick, and his command of the English language pretty good, for someone who had only been in the country for fifteen months. He came here for vacation from Peru and decided to stay. The gay life here was more fun and free, he said. Plus here he could be himself more without worrying that his family was around. With his beauty, his sex appeal, not to mention his tongue to nipple play, I thought to myself that he could make a good rent boy or a kept boy for some queen on Central Park West. I don't know why those things came to mind. Maybe I was hoping that he wasn't too materialistic. Usually those types tend to move quickly to the next loaded wallet.

I knew I was getting serious about him because I was thinking these things. Then again, I should have already known since I had made him eggs and pancakes. Normally my overnight guests got coffee and toast. That was if they were good in bed. The ones that weren't were given directions to the donut shop down the block. I caught myself before I reached over and refilled his glass with orange juice.

The fact that it was Tuesday morning and neither of us had to report to work until later that afternoon, him to his waiter job in a small café on Bleecker Street, me to my front desk manager job at a hotel over on Central Park West, gave us some more time to get to know each other and time to jump into the sack for a quick follow up. We were hardly able to pull ourselves away later in the afternoon when time came for us to go to work.

Because of the sex and the mutual attraction, we met a few times after that and would have continued to see each other except I had to go to Jamaica to take care of some family business. My old man was seriously ill and me being the eldest son, I had the responsibility of overseeing his 200 acres of farmland, supermarket, and apartment buildings. My two sisters and their husbands it seemed in my father's eyes were incapable of handling the family affairs. Since I wasn't sure when I'd be back, he decided that it was probably best not to write or call or do any of those stupid things. Being sentimental from a distance, or holding on to something across the miles, wasn't his speed. Should our paths cross again, however, we'd see. And I agreed because I didn't want to seem too desperate to hold on to something that might not really be there, fully well knowing that I was helping him to break my heart.

During all that time away, I thought much about him and the things that made me want to call him. The topics of our conversations, always about life, the big and small things, not the usual gossip about our friends and family. I thought about how he was never impressed by people and what they did or what they had. He didn't even have a favorite actor or pop star, as he cared nothing for those things. We went to see a movie only if the trailer was good or the subject matter of interest to us. He never wanted to see a movie because of a certain actor, director or writer. Afterward we'd discuss the movie; sometimes in disagreement we'd be up for hours until we exhausted our points or felt the need to exhaust ourselves some other way more physical. Because of these things I felt more drawn to him. He was real, he was a person I could talk to and listen to for hours.

After two years in Jamaica I returned to New York. I was back for a year almost before I finally ran into him at a friend's play uptown. This was one of the most unlikely places I'd ever dream of running into Orlando as he was not a big fan of the theater. His fuck buddy at the time was and he had dragged him to this play. I was surprised to find that he liked the play a lot. I thought it was too wordy, most of the dialogue an unnecessary flourish that didn't help in progressing the story. Mostly it was thrown in for shock value. He disagreed. And we were back to where we had left off before I went to Jamaica. We debated through intermission, and his fuck buddy was not amused. I on the other hand was very amused. Throughout our entire conversation we behaved as if we were the only two people standing in the theater foyer. It wasn't until his fuck buddy excused himself to go to the bathroom that we realized we weren't. Orlando took the opportunity of his absence to write down his new telephone number on a napkin and placed it in my pocket.

The next day I was too eager I told myself, but called him anyway. Two hours later we were both naked under the sheets discussing all the movies we had seen separately.

A year and a half later he lost his job. Being an illegal

immigrant he found it difficult to acquire employment so he was without a job for over two months, during which time his savings ran out and he was forced to move out of his apartment. I offered him my spare room, no strings attached. We both decided it would be all right for each of us to see other people. Yet we never did. The spare room has all his stuff, yet he has never slept in there. Today I realized that it has been almost five years since we first met. Five years and we have never said those three words. Yet it felt like we had, each time we kissed.

WITH RELISH

GUYUS MARKS

A FOOT-LONG IS, sometimes, just a hot dog. I was thinking that as I wrapped lips around, sunk teeth into, and bit through the tenderest flesh around. Succulent flavors filled my mouth as eyelids drifted down of their own accord. I acknowledged it, and could barely contain my moan of pleasure as I savored each chew a salvation, and finally swallowed. My mouth wrapped again, eager for the next bite, the next sensation, the next experience.

"Best longs around." The voice was gravely with round tones.

My eyes sprang open. My concentration redirected.

The man before me wore jeans, a wide leather belt, and flannel shirt. The clothes were hard beat, but the man inside was heaven.

"Construction?"

Every muscle on this guy was defined. As if heaven's pencil drew definition to the lines and added flesh for texture.

"Yeah, working the site a couple of blocks down. Seen you come in here a few times. Had to try it out."

"Must admit. I'm impressed by Sparky's."

"Brooklyn's best!"

"Really."

"Twice a week." I leaned toward him and said softly, "It's my big secret."

"So you say. I can think of something -" he chuckled. "Juicier." He rubbed his gut. "I'm a rib guy myself. Adam's Ribs, Carson's, you know, the tenderest in Chicago."

"Where you're from?"

"Yeah, though with the apple, I'm not really sure where to take a bite."

I smiled and put out my hand. "Garrett."

"Jack."

"Solid name."

"Solid everything."

I swallowed. My mouth wetter than it had been a few minutes ago. "Can I buy you a dog?"

Jack leaned in and the smell of mustard and relish rode on the spice of meat. "How about you finish that and let me show you the apartments I'm working?"

It was a heavenly scent. I resisted closing my eyes. "What kind of work?"

"Contract job. Doing detail work. Labor intensive, but exquisite."

"I'll bet."

"Food is getting cold. You don't like it when it's cold."

"How do you know?"

"Told you, seen you a few times. Watched. Hoped you'd notice. But I see you only have eyes for that."

I looked down, could barely resist the sight of the foot-long. I brought it to my mouth, wrapped lips, and bit. Flavors swelled in my mouth as I chewed and swallowed. Then, filled my mouth again.

"If you enjoy me as much as you enjoy that foot long, I'd be a happy man."

Part of the hot dog stuck, and I choked. My hand flew to my throat, but a hand was already pushing hard into my gut, freeing the object.

Air surged into my lungs and I stared at this concrete angel with watery eyes. Of course, my mind mulled, if he hadn't been baiting me, I may not have choked in the first place, but his hand lingered for a minute and there was heat. Such heat.

"Finish. I'll be good."

I nodded and resumed my place. Ate my meal with relish and intent, finished every bite with a little sigh to conclude. It wasn't just a habit, but a reflex, one I could not stop, even for someone watching me.

We stood and tossed the garbage together. The place was getting packed and we had to wind our way out to the exit.

On the street, he started talking. "Been some time since I've been attracted." He slid a glance my way.

"Can't resist you suit types with the three piece set, a short sleek hair cut, and glasses. Too sexy to even think about—taking you out of those clothes, let alone putting you back in them—but I could try."

My mouth dropped open. I couldn't help it. "Me —"

"Yeah, don't go getting all discerning and denying. Probably have every guy in your office after you."

"No, I'm an accountant, and a throwback from the baby-boomers. But one who doesn't want kids, and hasn't figured out what is attractive about the words—settle and down—" I tucked my hands into my pockets, trying to hide away the emphatic gestures and definitive words. Always my hardest and toughest point. I liked being male, gay, and really didn't want kids. Not a popular position to take, but I had to be true to my own sense of self. I bunched my fists and took a breath. Before I could stop myself I forced out, "But I'm still looking for love."

"Love. Really. What does that mean?"

I shrugged. A hand escaped from my pocket and streaked through my fair hair. The short hairs stood up on end as I brushed through and I had to push them back from my face.

The sun struck my forehead, making me wish it wasn't so fair, so wide. "I hope I'll know."

"Okay." Jack's nod was decisive. "Let's try this one, what do you want?"

I stopped at the corner. Watched, waited for the light to turn, to let us pass across the street. When the light finally deemed to change, I bridged the gap, my thoughts finally providing a path. "Passion. Loyalty. Intrigue."

"That's it?"

"Isn't that enough?"

Strides found rhythm and matched pace as they took the curb. Feet ate along the sidewalk, almost singular in their motion.

"Yeah." Jack's voice was steady. His movements exact.

"I like planning. Every detail is important. Expectations known. Results expected. Hard work the taskmaster."

"What if you can't live up to them? What if all the expectations go down the tubes, and all you are left with is anger and hostility?"

"Then change something and see where it goes from there. It's the planning I like more than the outcome anyway. But you have to tackle it. Live it. Because otherwise you are holding your hands out, but because of your fists being closed, you cannot grab onto life."

"Never thought of it that way before." I could feel the click of Yeah! in my head, but didn't want to acknowledge. Not yet, didn't want to anticipate the possibility, but my gut knew— This guy's great!—and already my body was ready, primed and eager for him.

Doubts flooded me, but were chased back into "the Ocean of Overthink" that mind was always in. My lips moved, but nothing else came out.

"You been burned."

"Yes." I couldn't elaborate. Wouldn't allow the feeling to tarnish this moment with a guy who felt so great, so right. It had been too since another.

"Healthy?"

The word hung between them. Could have gone either way. I felt that, but still I had to know. "Would it matter?"

"Now, no. Future planning, maybe. I'm healthy as a horse. It's all about the planning. I like to know."

"But no one knows the future." I felt like an idiot saying the thought aloud. Here I was the accountant who taught everyone how to plan for the future, but I rarely met anyone who agreed. Who is this guy? "Why me?"

"Gut feeling. Been watching you. Something about you is right. I follow my gut."

"Your gut. The only thing my gut knows is good hot dogs."

"Don't knock it. I like 'em too, and I found you there."

"But, that doesn't mean you can -"

"I do, I plan for every eventuality." Jack's tone was even. The words precise. "I leave nothing to chance if I can. Always been that way. But I have to tell you, my pulse is already speeding for you. Just have to know your take on things before we take it further, 'cause we're almost there."

For the second time, I sought definition. My mind stumbled and out came, "How can you know? How can you be that sure?"

"Just am. Just do. It's my way. To say what I mean, and mean what I do."

I nodded. Didn't resist as he steered me in his direction.

The blocks had been made quick work of. A building being remodeled, covered in signs, opened locked doors at Jack's code.

Silence accompanied us inside, and it was comfortable.

Walking up several flights of stairs and through a maze of doorways and halls, Jack stopped in the center of a large room.

"Wow, Jack." Every inch of the ceiling, except for a tiny

corner, was covered in one of the most intricate paintings I had ever seen. "It's breathtaking."

"Thanks. I've got ten more jobs in this building alone."

"Alone, as in, you are alone in here."

He chuckled. The laugh low and gravely like his voice, making me think of warmed butter rum. "I always work alone. Though you never really know who will be working in the building. Of course, here they rarely venture. I don't appreciate being interrupted, unless I invite it."

Those words, the meaning slipped through the doubts in my mind, unraveling my worries and freeing the part that wanted this to be right. Felt it was right.

That we connected.

A hand reached. Daring. Asking. Requesting.

I couldn't stop my body from leaning toward him. Craving the feel of those hands that created such intense beauty, that asked so boldly and sweetly, and was indeed a mirror of the very image he portrayed above. But this was him, in the flesh. He was chiseled, defined, and oh so, real. He wanted me and I wanted him. Could anything be more tangible than this.

I melted. I reached, too.

Lips meshed together, and it was the scratch of dark rough against gently shaved flesh. I should have balked, because I knew it'd leave a burn against my fair skin. But the taste of relish and mustard layered into the spice of meat lapped through my mouth. His tongue a thing of beauty that made me want to grab it with my own, hold it and lave it, until all the flavor was stripped away and he lay bare.

"—best hot dogs," he murmured, voice rubbing on me like spice.

"Mmmmm," I said and captured his lips again with mine.

Taking action, I yanked on his clothes.

He stripped them away, like the peel of an onion.

Followed my lead, then reached back.

I wanted to bite him, flesh darkened by work that obvious

took him in and out of the sun, and was currently dotted with drops and splashes of paint.

"Could I —"

"Mark me."

"Yes." Eagerness must have shown in my eyes, because he smiled and the look added a tenderness to the heat.

He offered an arm to me.

I rubbed, licked, and played my hands and tongue over the muscles until I reached the height of the bicep.

When I trailed my fingers along the inside of his arm, I felt him shiver. My mouth opened wide and he watched as I lay teeth to flesh and bit.

Salt filled my mouth, and flesh tempted me to sink further. I held back, not biting through or tearing a chunk, but leaving a neat mark of teeth, a ring for him to marvel at later. My mouth drew back. Happy. Smiling.

He stared at the mark, touched it, then tumbled me to the ground.

My clothes were removed, one button at a time, and meticulously set aside. "I love the feeling of being undressed. How long since you last -"

"Been a while for me too."

By the time, toe met toe and flesh was prepared to touch flesh, I was trembling with desire.

Crinkles of foil reassured. Protective for both of us. Before desire overcame the last of judgment or thought.

He slid one down me, lingering.

I pushed his hand away. "Your cock is gorgeous."

"It's not a hot dog."

I put the condom in my mouth and rolled it down of the head of his cock, lapped around the top, and smoothed the rest of the way with my hands.

Jack's voice was rough. "Don't bite—"

I swallowed him down in one move and felt his body catch. Like his breath was caught in his muscles instead of his lungs and would stay there forever.

Pulling up, I released the catch and watched his face contort and come back. When I was sure he'd take it. I dove over him again.

His words were lost on a moan as I laid a light edge of teeth to him. In and out, I drew him, only to suck him down, the entire length swallowed into me again.

Whole.

Hands locked to my head holding me, cradling me against his flesh, and I knew that if he wanted he could suffocate me there. But he'd release, and that edge of teeth was back against him.

"Just right. Just the right amount of, fuck, Gar, I'm going to—"

Come spurted against the condom, caught the load, as my throat worked over him dragging and drawing the jets out.

When I drew back, let him fall free from the capture of my mouth, he pulled my face to his and lay me back.

Darkened flesh lay against my own pale as his hands and mouth worked over me. Skin to skin. Flesh to flesh.

"Let's see what I may do?" That gravely voice lapped over me as thickly as his caresses.

My cock felt like it would explode, but I wasn't ready to stop, ready to give in to the temptation.

Hands molded my flesh. I felt like a living sculpture as he teased and tantalized me. My cock hardened past return, and when at last he began to play over it, I resisted the urge to come.

"Playing hard to get."

"Playing hard," I panted.

He stripped off his own safe and replaced it.

Splitting my thighs wide, he said, "Let me show you what else I may do with a foot long." His cock sank deep as my own rode between us. My balls lifted higher as I tried to move, tried to find purchase.

But his arms, those muscled limbs, held me wide, exposed.

"Uh, uh, uh, easy now. Just like that long, one bite at a time."

He moved, and my eyes closed. Sounds escaped from my mouth, unbidden, just as the hot dog did, but these moved, changed octave into something guttural, hard and wild.

My hands found his shoulders and dragged him down to me, closer, and our lips meshed together. Bodies locked into battle, as I fought my own need. I wanted to come. To spew everything, inch by inch, all over him.

But cock was held, covered by his flesh, my flesh and the safety of the condom.

Fingers reached between us as if the thought had been vocalized and ripped the latex from my aching flesh.

They grazed the tip bringing tears weeping from the head. Then flesh laid against flesh, enveloped.

Friction drove, all thought dragged away as his mouth ate at mine. From every point he pushed into me, pierced and invaded me, until I tore my mouth from his, panting for air and came with a fury born of pleasure and driven by passion.

His cry twinned my own. The cycle bringing a second wind to us both with its intensity and a last pitch.

Our bodies shook, yet he rolled us, so we may lay side by side, together. Looking at each other, looking at the ceiling and back again.

"Twice a week."

"Maybe I could—Well, every day is a new day." My heart stuttered. I could really see being with this guy. My gut pushed forward, toward him.

Jack smiled. Hands soothed and stroked. "Yeah."

My hands stripped off his condom, tossed the used safe aside. I admired the length of that gorgeous cock, even as it lay spent. "Sometimes, a foot long really is a foot long."

"What?"

I laughed, the pitch high and joyful. "Just something I was thinking about. Tomorrow—"

"Tonight," He corrected. The look in his eyes as definitive as his words, but there was an edge, a vulnerability there for me to see.

I smiled, nodded. "Dinner, is on me."

Tension eased out his eyes, replaced by a sparkle.

"Remember, hot dogs with mustard and —"

"With relish, of course." I sighed. My hand sought his. "Much better to enjoy together."

GHOST DODGERS

SHANNON L. YARBROUGH

EBBETS FIELD WAS the home of the Brooklyn Dodgers from the day it opened on April 9, 1913, until the park closed in 1957. The park was located near Flatbush Avenue, I think, somewhere in Pigtown. Back then, no one had their own cars, so everyone walked to the games or took a trolley. When the park opened, that whole area was serviced by nine trolley lines that connected to thirty-two others. That's how the team even got its name because all the fans had to dodge trolley cars to get to a game. Not that it matters now, but I hate baseball.

I always did. When I was nine my father forced me away from my comic books and into our upstate backyard so he could throw a few balls and help me work on my swing. He wanted me to try out for Little League that summer. Throw after throw, I could not hit the ball, even if he tossed it under-handed. He became frustrated after our third attempt at this game, but by then I had given up even trying. He would throw his glove at me in frustration, calling me a "sissy" as he walked away. I'd swallow hard, dodging the glove and dropping the bat to my feet, trying hard not to shed a tear until he was out of sight. My father knew what I was even before I did.

But Jake loved baseball. He always had. He told me his father got him started with the same charade my father had tried with me right around the same age. Jake made the Little League team and was team captain in junior high and high school. A scholarship even afforded him the chance to play all through college, but a leg injury his senior year kept the scouts away, and kept Jake away from his dream to go pro after he graduated. Jake's brother took him to his first Dodgers game back in the early eighties. Jake took me to my first game on our second date. I still hated baseball, but I was falling in love with Jake so I attempted to learn the game for his sake.

We met in college, shortly after Jake had broken his leg. He was hobbling around the library on crutches searching for books on the history of baseball for a research paper. I was a library aid at the time and immediately noticed him when he fumbled through the door. He was a sporty-intellect type with short sandy brown hair and big blue eyes accented by wire reading glasses. His crisp blue jeans and neatly pressed polo contoured to the shape of his lean athletic body quite beautifully. And despite his struggle with his bad leg, I found him to be quite charming. I knew that both girls and teachers alike probably crooned at him in the classroom, and his buddies in the locker room probably greeted him with cheers of envy. I was wrong.

I grabbed a cart of books that needed to be shelved and guided it through the stacks spying on Jake at his clumsy research. I could tell he was tired of having to balance himself against the bookshelves on one leg while trying to get books from the upper rows. After a while, I had talked myself into approaching him and offering my assistance. I would like to say that when he glanced up at me from his work that everything went silent when our eyes met. However, we were in a library where the typical sounds were only a pencil rolling across the floor, an unseen student clearing his throat, or that constant hum of a utility unit behind a vent in the wall. But even those sounds couldn't be heard now. Only the quick sound of my beating heart echoed in my ears as I swallowed hard and looked down at Jake's desk at all the books on baseball. I thought of my father and wanted to roll my eyes, but they were too transfixed looking deep into Jake's. My father had long since gone to that baseball diamond in the sky, but I could feel him looking down on me and probably saying, "I told you so." Damn it, I knew I should have played Little League.

Like I said, Jake didn't mind so much that I hated baseball when we first met. He took a chance on me, even though I half expected him to say, "I could never date someone who didn't like baseball," but Jake wasn't like that. Our first kiss was something out of a movie, under the lights of Broadway. With the roar of the subway below, the traffic on the streets, the blinking signs, the people, the noise, it's as if fireworks had lit the sky when we were walking side by side and out of nowhere, Jake pulled me to him under a theater canopy and met my lips with his. It was not the heavy tongued kiss that leads to your neck and ears when you are in bed with a man, but instead it was just a long passionate kiss shared between our warm lips. It was very New York, and it reminded me of why I love this city.

Six months after graduation, Jake and I celebrated our first year anniversary by moving into a small one-bedroom apartment off Fifty-fourth. Although it wasn't the first time we had made love, that night we found ourselves rolling around in sweaty sheets of passion. Jake pinned me to the bed under that gorgeous tan body of his. I massaged his taunt muscles as he explored my body with his tongue. At night, we were each other's perfect lover. By day, Jake was student teaching at a local city high school, hoping to get into coaching, and I had taken a full time librarian job across town at the junior high.

"Do you believe in the afterlife?" Jake asked me one night in bed. He was watching television and I was deep in a book.

"There's got to be something after life," I joked, never lifting my eyes from the pages. "Anything's better than this hell on earth."

"No, I'm serious. Do you believe...in something?" He asked again with that handsome and solemn look on his face that always let me know he was being very serious. I put my book down and looked at him.

"Yeah, I do," I said, "I believe." I was perfectly content to go to a Dodgers game with him whenever he wanted me too, but I secretly hoped I wasn't setting myself up for a trip to church.

"What do you believe in?" Jake asked with a grin. After a long pause and some serious mind searching, I answered him.

"I believe that even in the afterlife, love will find a way," I replied.

"No, seriously. I want to know," Jake said with persistence.

"I believe that we make our own heaven. Wherever you and I go after all of this is done and gone, there will be plenty of books for me—" Jake interrupted me. "—And plenty of innings for me!" He said. We both broke into laughter.

I adored Jake when he made me laugh. He always knew when the mood was getting too serious; and although sometimes I wished it would stay that way just a bit longer, he always offered up an icebreaker to cut the tension he had created. Our love making that night was hard and fervent. He pulled my reading glasses off and tossed them on the nightstand. We fumbled under the sheets to strip each other of our briefs. The bed sheets were flung back and onto the floor. After an hour of sex, we lay exhausted and not even holding each other because our bodies were so wet and sticky. A New York City breeze, filled with the all too familiar sounds of car horns, blew in from the open window and glided over the bed to cool our bodies as we drifted into sleep immune to the city sounds.

Six years passed and we still felt young and were still

passionate without a blink of trouble in our relationship. Jake never missed a Dodgers game. I joined him at a game occasionally, still attempting to take interest in the things that made him happy, and sometimes at home he would even pick up a book to read for me. Things seemed more perfect that way; we had always made the relationship work. Until one night Jake was walking home late from practice at school. I had rushed home with plans for a nice romantic dinner and a hot bath waiting for him when he walked in followed by a long weekend of lovemaking. But two angry students who were mad at the coach were waiting to surprise him in an alley. He had cut them from the team earlier that week due to random drug tests that came back positive. They beat him to death with a pipe.

Again, I thought of my father's spirit probably standing over my shoulder in the cemetery. "I told you so," he whispered, but I ignored him. I was the black sheep, as I stood separate from Jake's family. Like my own, they had never accepted us or him for what we were, who we were. Our efforts at loving one another so avidly had gone unnoticed by everyone except for ourselves. I recalled all the birthdays and holidays we missed out on with our families, but instead we had our own at home and with our close friends that really mattered, our real family. It would have been nice to be recognized as one by our own blood, but our love still grew even without the recognition. Still, it seemed that I was a ghost that someone had chosen not to believe in. Jake and I had believed though, and although he wasn't standing there with me that day, I knew he soon would be. Our love would find a way.

About a year later, six skinheads in orange jumpsuits led me to my own final resting place. I would like to think I died of a broken heart, but it was a stray gunshot instead that I was unable to dodge. That seems to be everyone's destiny in this city. After a busy life of subway rides, skyscrapers towering over you, and nights of dancing on concrete, the city swallows you up and you become part of it. Swept away in an underlying emotion of chaos that overwhelms you, like a rat caught in the water rushing through a sewer drain; the city has consumed you and you drown in it. It has its way with you, and life is hard when you are growing older and lost in New York without your very first love. I had never stepped foot on Broadway again, much less even dreamed of kissing another man. It was too late for me to start over in this city. *I told you so.*

On a humid day like today, the only eulogy those men delivered was the sound of beads of sweat dripping from their forehead onto the wooden box they carried in between them. It's odd that six men usually known for hating fags would now be burying one. These men had no idea who I was though, and didn't care. I was just another John Doe to them, just like all the others they had planted the days and weeks before. My family did know me though; they just chose not to know me for who I really was. They, too, did not care. But with all my family long gone, and Jake, I wrote in my very last words that this island of the dead was the place I needed to be. That, and Jake and I had made a promise long ago on that night we made love after talking about what we believed in after life.

Everyday a ferry called the *Michael Crosgrove* brings prisoners to Hart's Island to bury New York's unknown in a place called Potter's Field. They are paid twenty-five cents an hour to bury lost souls three deep in this mass grave across the middle of the island. In the past, this island has been many things: a POW camp, a women's hospital, a reform school for delinquents, an old man's home, a cemetery, and now it is mine and Jake's final meeting place. When the last bit of dirt is packed over my coffin, my physical body is now laid to rest under ground just a few yards away, and the prisoners are done for the day. They finished early and while waiting for the departing ferry to pick them up and carry them back to the mainland, back to their four by four foot cells, they begin to toss a baseball around. I know that Jake is near.

The first home of the Dodgers, Ebbets Field, was demolished in 1960, three years after it closed. For some odd reason, some of the old bleachers were dumped on this island as well. They lie in a heap of twisted and tarnished metal, torn apart by weather and baseball collectors. Some of them have been turned upright to offer a place to rest for whoever might be visiting the island, besides the prisoners. It is here that I sit, a soul on this old baseball relic, watching the parade of skin and orange headed back to the boat. They left their baseball on the ground nearby, and I turn back to look for it but it is gone. Suddenly, I hear the crack of a bat in the distance, and turn to see the glimpse of the baseball flying high above this catacomb and headed in my direction. I see a jersey running in the distance. It is Jake. I leap from the bleachers to catch the highflying ball. A perfect catch! My father would be so proud. Jake waves at me as he passes by headed for home base. He is safe.

I run toward him waving the ball above my head for him to see. We embrace and greet each other at home base with that Broadway kiss I've missed so much. I hear a roar of a crowd behind us and car horns call out. We're part of this city whether we like it or not, and we fade away together. We are a part of each other again now and forever. *I told you so.*

SCENES FROM WITHIN THE FICUS ENCLOSURE

MICHAEL HUXLEY

With deference to Eugene O'Neill,
Ingmar Bergman,
and most recently, J.M. Coetzee

THEIRS IS NOT a glitzy, an ostentatious love, Oscar's and ER's, but one that abides. Their lives, their life together, forgotten by history, will not negate their having lived passionately. ER would not die, but rather live for Oscar. Asked to expound, ER declines.

. . . . .

IN EARLY SPRING, unbeknownst to ER, Oscar procures theater tickets online for ER's fiftieth birthday, upcoming in August.

ER cries when he opens the premature birthday card Oscar presents to him. Normally privy to such information through his usual media sources, ER, steeped in a challenging edit, had no inkling that director Robert Falls has mounted a revival of Eugene O'Neill's *Long Day's Journey Into Night* at New York's Plymouth Theater. Oscar well knows that

ER worships O'Neill, that *Long Day's Journey* is considered the playwright's masterwork. The clincher is this: Vanessa Redgrave has been cast as Mary Tyrone—to ER's mind the finest role for a veteran actress in the American theater, interpreted by the finest veteran actress of her generation. The entire event is a dream come true for the retired high school humanities instructor and drama coach. It's fate; the tickets coincide his birth date exactly, a Saturday this year.

They make love like the twenty-seven-year life partners they are that afternoon, and—like the twenty-four- and twenty-five-year-old strangers they were the night they met—before sleep that evening. It is a very rare occurrence indeed for them to share sex twice in one day anymore, twice in one week being closer to the monogamous average they have settled into after spending more than half their respective lives together. Who says not finding the perfect gift for the one you love doesn't make all that much difference?

. . . . .

THEY MEET IN a bar at the apex of the pre-Plague disco era. Oscar, a divorced father of two small children, and Elwood Robert, hot off a yearlong affair with a Brazilian concert pianist, sense after two "dates" that their mutual attraction will endure, so proceed to forge a life together, made official when ER moves his stereo equipment into Oscar's apartment. Two weeks later they suffer their first major argument. Oscar explodes without warning; he resents ironing ER's clothes everyday. His thoughtful gesture has not once been reciprocated, Oscar points out, nor has ER thanked him since the first time. ER, appalled, becomes defensive. If someone is going to iron his clothes unsolicited, he is not inclined to protest. It would never occur to him to iron on an everyday basis anyway; smoothing his 100-percent cotton wardrobe hot from the dryer has sufficed just fine for him since college. Truth be known, he prefers an "impeccably rumpled" look. Wounded, loathe to be yelled at, ER broods. French-Canadian Oscar rebounds immediately after the tempest subsides, eager to make up. ER continues to punish him by pouting for several more hours before relenting. They make love. Ironing is never again the issue-du-jour; indeed, Oscar is soon converted to the "impeccably rumpled" look, but twenty-eight years later the same dynamic fuels their frequent upheavals.

. . . . .

ON DIFFICULT DAYS ER, having over the years eschewed alcohol, various recreational drugs, tobacco, and rich foods—in that order—feels that sex remains his sole recourse to bliss, that life is torture enough *with* those forgone compensations. He considers "smart-mouthed" children who, in fits of anger, rail against their indignant parents that they did not ask to be born to be voicing a valid argument. Never one to uphold the sanctity of reproduction, ER, an excellent stepparent, feels he's given his biological children the greatest possible gift by not bringing them into the world, as his nature intended. Oscar pooh-poohs such notions, rolls his eyes, although he has come to corroborate ER's worldview over the years. It is a good case, always laced with bitter irony that ER pleads. For ER, he knows, is an entertainer at heart, a self-described Pagliacci for discriminating tastes, a stand-up tragedian of sorts, and Oscar is the tastiest, the only edible morsel in ER's microcosm.

. . . . .

TWO YEARS INTO their life together, they relocate from suburban Detroit to downtown Denver, where Oscar's upscale day spa becomes quite the forum for the old-moneyed

Democrats in that bourgeoning, vainglorious metropolis. In their early teens, Oscar's two children flee their mother's mental instability and come to live with their two fathers in Colorado. Years pass. The kids raised and on their own, Oscar and ER rashly dissolve the business after two decades and, embarking upon retirement-too-soon, settle in south Florida, where they tend their home and jungle garden and fret about finances. At this juncture, ER has parlayed his passion for literature into freelance editing for a small publishing venue while Oscar oversees their joint rental properties. Long religious about physical fitness, they remain a striking couple, only recently having crossed that dubious line of being considered great-looking men to looking great for their age.

An aside:

Waylaid by the pleasure principle they break from laying fertilizer to pounce upon one another within the ficus enclosure, on the bench beneath the tree ferns. The guava gushing, the delicate Surinam Cherry blushing, the banana stalks fruiting turgid in the heated, Edenic green-shade of summer: the lovers (pri)mate to blinding distraction. Sight restored, semen sown, does that particular love scene deliquesce. Poof!

ER craves men. Seven years into it, his itch for validation outside the relationship reaches a fever pitch. His subsequent ultimatum drives Oscar away. ER has no idea where his spouse has vanished until Oscar calls three days later from a mutual friend's home back in Detroit—only that he'd surely gone insane in the interim: writhing on the floor, keening his greatest loss, for what? Insecurity's sake? Obstinancy's?

"You win, ER; let's hammer out the rules."

Their open relationship lasts eighteen months. Both score their share of attractive lovers, the more approachable Oscar a higher body count, but who's playing tit for tat? Not far into

ER's affair with the truly gorgeous Brent, Oscar unravels.

"I need you to stop seeing Brent."

ER takes umbrage: "Just because you're jealous—"

"You're right! I'm jealous! It's eating me alive!" yells Oscar. "Stop *seeing* him, ER."

ER more than complies by calling off the entire experiment after a humiliating post-Brent fizzle. As if a primary relationship isn't work enough.

Nineteen years later, Elwood Robert still craves men.

They depart for NYC on ER's birthday eve. From LaGuardia they take a taxi to their preferred Hotel, The Essex House on Central Park South. Following the doorman into the lobby, Oscar remembers that scenes from the 1994 Annette Bening/Warren Beatty vehicle, *Love Affair*—an unnecessary remake of *An Affair to Remember*—were shot here, while ER shudders, recalling that singer Donny Hathaway ended his life by leaping from his window on the hotel's fifteenth floor in 1979: a method of suicide ER's increasing acrophobia would adamantly forbid. Despite dissimilar mindsets, the familiar accommodations are much appreciated by the duo, who once again find themselves happily checking in together.

Oscar and ER rise at dawn the following morning. After a brisk run in Central Park, they shower, prepare their getups, and breakfast at the hotel. The remainder of the morning is spent at the Guggenheim, where they check out the *Kasimir Malevich: Suprematism* exhibit (better than expected they admit, quite wonderful in fact), having allowed time for a quick deli stop before heading to the 12:00 P.M. matinee at the Plymouth Theater.

. . . . .

O'NEILL'S AUTOBIOGRAPHICAL *Long Day's Journey* is an aptly named play. After four hours of unrelenting if eloquent domestic tragedy, ER and Oscar emerge from the theater emotionally and intellectually wracked. That Redgrave's being cast as the playwright's mother—a woman miscast in her role of wife and mother, whose shattered dreams are sustained by addiction to morphine—has proven an indelible theatric revelation comes as no surprise to ER. He has admired since *Isadora* the enormously gifted actress whose career was compromised by her vociferous, pro-Palestinian stand at the 1977 Academy Awards, admires her professional tenacity since that seminal moment. To him it is clear that in *Long Day's Journey* she has triumphed over the failure of the American dream by underscoring flaws inherent in human nature, eviscerated hypocrisies such as "love conquers all," the "power of prayer," and "just say no" with a panicked side-glance, by fluttering her fingers along an imagined piano keyboard. Months from now ER will consider it a personal victory when Redgrave wins the 2003 Tony Award for her performance.

How much longer will the arts be allowed to uphold a broader vision in the rising theocracy? fumes ER in silence, in the taxi, as he and Oscar return to the hotel for a respite before evening plans commence.

. . . . .

OVER DINNER IN Chinatown, they don't talk about the play. What is there to say after so cathartic an aesthetic orgasm? Oscar, in many ways ER's adoring pupil, is content to savor his precious sautéed snow pea leaf—a delicacy unavailable in Florida. He is basking in the awareness that, although he has given *His True Love* a flawless birthday gift, the warm NYC night, unlike himself, unlike ER, is still young.

From Chinatown they proceed to Times Square as planned.

. . . . .

THE FLORIDA PENINSULA/ the stage at the Priapus Theatre, like arousal's tongue, extends with longitude into the salivating sea/the audience.

"Max-traordinaire," is next on bill.

Just under six feet, Maximilian superbly rises above his average height by the inspired configuration of his physical specifics. He exudes health, genetic superiority, and gravity: a virility so potent that few homosexual males fail, when in his presence, to be gripped by an urgency they feel his preponderance alone can rein. Unlike the others on display this evening: the NYFD clone, the ersatz pipe fitter, the entire gym-pumped Village Peopled panoply, Max dons no prefabricated persona, flashes no bleached, bedroomy smile, requires no up-tempo bait to thread his hook.

He is not a boy. By any stretch, not a boy, yet he has known since boyhood that he is a marketable commodity that certain...men (in particular) are willing to risk their very security to possess; that he possesses an indefatigable ability to deliver that which, by his very nature, he cannot help but advertise. He has honed his gift for enticement to adamant degree, invested wisely, remained aloof, has never caved to the compromising clichés of his calling. Maximilian, a brilliant piece, does not resent having to pay his taxes.

It is *the way* his jeans fit, *the way* they bunch atop his large sandaled feet, *how* he strips bare his tattooed torso, more than the nipple-glinting perfection of what is revealed by his doing so that matters.

His breathtaking face is blade-scraped to dense shadow, a concession to conventional beauty standards negated/accentuated when he removes his Rasta tam, when Caucasian dreadlocks—a revelation—drop heavily from dark-rooted scalp to flaxen ends that skirt his stalwart, denim-entrusted glutei.

His splendid moves substantiate a magnum opus of erotic entreaty: sleeveless T-shirt, Rasta tam, sandals, and Wranglers divested with seamless choreographic undulation to Ben E. King's *Supernatural Thing"—interplanetarily, extraordinarily—*down to cup-salient, athletic support. But the mid-70s groove, translated, might just as well sing: *You need search no further for I exist to satiate your deepest-seated discontent at your leisure. I am ripe to yield my salten succor in languorous hip rotations of rapture. Such is my involuntary bid for survival, my reason to be, my immortality. Do me.*

He departs the stage. Dumbstruck, Oscar and ER look at one another in agitated disbelief as the lights rise halfway, as the music is lowered to loop at half-volume, as if to ask: in Limbo, how much further can bars raised to the max be elevated?

A brief absence offstage later, when Max reemerges, fluffed for his finale, wearing nothing but petroglyphic tattoo work and nipple rings—his outrageous (and contagious) comeuppance so…*effectively* utilized to punctuate his air copulation—ER and Oscar receive their answer. For the Priapus Theatre's no-alcohol clause permits its performers (though not its patrons, as the omnipresent security attests) to legally expose their genitals, however aroused, given they do not touch or stimulate them further. Alas, all the strippers have likewise returned for their finales erect but, unlike Max, departed the stage otherwise.

Finding the next act pale at best by comparison, ER retires to the refreshment lounge while Oscar holds their seats. He ladles punch into a plastic cup, takes a sip, turns to scan the crowd. Even though the punch is not good, he sips again. Over the cup's rim, across the lounge, back in his jeans but nothing else, stands Max, just ending an exchange with a nondescript older man. Jolted, ER braces himself, places his cup on the serving table. From his wallet he extracts a twenty. He folds it—twice—then transects the smoke-choked conviviality to seize his moment.

. . . . .

"EXCUSE ME…MAX?" ER ventures, undeterred by the man's heart-quaking proximity, his inscrutable scrutiny, his instinctive head-to-toe assessment. The dreadlocks are most definitely not extensions. Max smiles—at last. When he asks, "Where's your friend?" ER is taken aback. Must he always be identified as one half of a couple; has he lost the ability to be recognized as a viable single entity?

"He's saving my seat; how do you know I'm not here alone?"

"I noticed you guys from the stage."

"We're quite a few rows back—"

"I'm sensitive to attractive couples."

ER, discomfited by this offhand compliment, says: "Anyway…I'd like you to have this." He presses the twenty into Max's hand. Without breaking eye contact, Max slips the bill carefully into his key pocket.

"Thank you—"

It takes ER a moment to realize he's being prompted to introduce himself. "It's ER— a pleasure to meet you."

"Emergency Room? Sorry, I couldn't resist."

ER has endured the joke countless times, but delivered by Max, it seems fresh, sparks an amiability that puts him more at ease. "Worse," he frowns. "Elwood Robert. My father's name. Firstborn son, you know."

"I'm named after my father as well."

"Is Max your real name?"

"It's Maximilian, yes."

"Your dreads are amazing—"

"They tend to screen the pedestrian." Max clears his throat, steers the conversation accordingly: "So, I take it you're enjoying the show—?"

"It was fine until you took the stage."

"And then what? It all fell apart?"

"No, it became extraordinary." Normally ER would wait for a reaction to such a declaration but compelled by something larger than himself he blurts: "Forgive my audacity but...I was truly disturbed, watching you. You are hands down the most extreme object of lust I have ever encountered, and Oscar—my lover—corroborates my opinion. To be quite honest, your beauty intimidates me; I realize that's my problem, but there you have it."

To ER's ear, Maximilian's response, "Considering the source, I am humbled," is too spontaneous not to be at least partially sincere.

"Surely you've made films," continues ER, on a roll. "If so, please give me the titles because I intend to own them all." But Max, not from lack of opportunity, has no such titles to offer.

"I've no ambition whatsoever for that level of exposure but am happy to arrange private sessions for...interested parties that interest me."

This provocation is a first for ER, who is experiencing an emotional reaction akin to mild panic, who somehow manages to say: "Sorry, we're flying back home early tomorrow."

"I've not booked anything for this evening...yet."

"I'm flattered—*Maximilian*—but we're monogamous."

"Far be it for me to beat a dead horse but, in my humble opinion, conducting a straightforward business transaction that would avail consenting life partners the opportunity to share their hallowed monogamy with Yours Truly hardly constitutes a rationalization for infidelity, my friend." Max pauses, glances above and beyond ER's right shoulder. "Well," he says as Oscar approaches, "it seems an arbiter has arrived just in the nick of time." ER is quick with the introductions. "I was innocently working the room," says Max to Oscar, "when your handsome boyfriend pounced." His tenor is confidential, intimate, playful. He has sized up the couple's dynamic in a New York heartbeat. "Yes, since he mentioned how much you both enjoyed my little performance—thank you—I've been trying to sell him on the idea of a private session later tonight, but with little success I fear."

"*Really*," Oscar says pointedly, appraising ER. "How much?" Although ER respects his mate's seeming inability to be daunted, he is embarrassed by Oscar's indelicacy.

Max, to the contrary, replies, "Five hundred for a one-hour session with a party of two," without batting an eyelash.

"*Five-O-O for the big five-O—*" ruminates Oscar aloud. Then: "What sort of discount might you consider for ER's special birthday?" After a moment's consideration, Max offers: "Same price for ninety minutes, but I'll need to see his driver's license."

Oscar leans into ER and whispers, "Happy birthday, my darling."

Much to Oscar's (and Maximilian's) surprise, ER graciously declines. Max, with comparable graciousness, excuses himself to resume his circulation about the room after presenting his card "in case you change your mind, birthday boy."

"This is opportunity knocking, babe," Oscar emphasizes once Max is out of earshot. "Don't turn a deaf ear on my account."

"I love you for making the offer, but I can't do it, Oscar. I don't want to."

"I'm not making it entirely for your benefit, you know."

"Of course I realize that; I just can't do it, is all. Please trust my instinct here, and don't ask me to expound right now."

"Then when can I ask: in an hour, tomorrow, next week? Is it the money? Because if that's the reason—"

"Can we go back to the hotel now?"

Back in their room, secure in their bed-away-from-home, the lovers prevail. Sitting up, his back propped by pillows, his body and mind ablaze, noting the still-beauteous lines of Oscar's nudity, ER is being done. Sparks—Maximilian, Brent, Every Man in passing whose eye he has desired to catch—bounce and sputter off the molten weld that his love is so joyously reinforcing. He longs to hold the moment fast, is thrilled beyond words of his own, so defers, as secular pantheists are wont, to yet another god who, in 1971, on the Baltic isle of Färo, wrote:

"—*Come what may, this is happiness. I cannot wish for anything better. Now, for a few minutes, I can experience perfection, and I feel profoundly grateful to my life, which gives me so much.*" *

---

* From Ingmar Bergman's *Viskningar Och Rop Cries and Whispers)* © 1972 A.B. Svensk Filmindustri

BIG CITY PARTICLE

JULIAN J. LOPEZ

I WASN'T EVEN a resident of the grandeur, yet I too was swallowed entirely along with every territorial entity.

The restaurants and corner cafes with panoramic views of the rest of its infinite lights, sky soaring buildings, and indirect traffic of people and cars had taken on a different life. They were night establishments, overruling the corner flower shops, bakeries, and butcher shops that were soon closing. It was all part of the routinely night world, one filled with scents and rushing speeds caused by taxis, subways, and people. And before I knew it, I too had taken on a different life. Already I'd become a tiny parody of its infiniteness at night, as if I had always been a part of it all, ambling through the narrow streets and wasn't just visiting for a week.

Already I had familiarized myself with the parallel routes that led to the renowned vicinities of a Little Italy, fashions throughout Soho and Chinatown, not to mention the central core of Times Square. It had been simple after quickly analyzing the city map that the concierge of my hotel in the Wall Street district provided. I had been there for a business convention, one I was without doubt barely attending.

Even though my feet had already admitted defeat to the city's manner by which the locals journeyed—walking—my eagerness for the city night wasn't ready to surrender. The soreness underneath my feet rendered by a long day of rushing from one end of the city to another for shopping and eating was the first clue that I wasn't a local.

That night, I was unsure of where to go, but that didn't stop me. I had ventured out via the subway followed by more walking into Greenwich Village, assuming the alternative reputation of the charming residence with typical brick homes would be the place to enjoy a night of bar hoping. The uncertainty of what lay ahead, a fresh new page in a different place, ignited my enthusiasm.

For several blocks I followed the lights and enticing hubs where crowds gathered, assuming they were bars or nightclubs. But it was clear that they were either private gatherings or night scenes requesting VIP access.

I looked up into the incoming rush of cars, and just as I raised my arm and thumb in hopes of fetching a cab to serve as my destination advisor, I spotted the place. It was right on a corner facing the wide intersection. I crossed the street where a small park enclosed by a fence to prevent public access faced across the place. For a second I remained still, questioning my assumption, but the statues within the enclosed park of two men sitting intimately close to one another on a park bench informed me that I was exactly where I needed to be.

Inside, men gathered inside, most of them older, with curious eyes setting on me as I squeezed my way inside the island bar surrounded by men. I wondered if it was my tight denim pants I paid too much for on the Upper East Side that caught their attention. Shamefully, I had made the purchase, aware of the effect the jeans promoted over my thick calves and rear end. My coffee brown shoes and matching shirt played their role by increasing my height and exposing the olive skin of my biceps—ones not to large, but certainly with enough mount to reveal my endurance at the gym.

The thump of the music vibrated, as if synchronized with

the moving colorful lights that partly dissuaded by the overall light of the bar. I was finally inside, and all I could think of doing was to find a secluded corner where I could stand and become less visible. Also, I wanted to appear busy so I headed to the bar since purchasing a drink involved action.

I figured it would be a while before I could even order a drink, since layers of bodies tightened against the bar.

To my surprise the bartender grabbed a glass, filling it with ice, his eyes locking with mine before one of them winked. "What will it be cutie?"

"Vodka tonic with lime, please." My hands held out a twenty, but his hand clasped mine with the green between our palms. "On the house, baby."

I smiled, refusing to so much as glimpse at the guys who had been desperately cramming alongside the bar in hopes of flagging the bartender long before I did.

In a matter of seconds I spotted that secluded corner that would allow me to reserve myself from the atmosphere, while keeping the crowd within full-eye's view. Casually, I began merging with the crowd, heading toward the enticing space when the tight grasp of someone's hand halted me. "Must be nice."

I looked up. "Huh?"

"Having your looks must be nice. And your hair so black, it almost looks painted."

I remained still, detecting a tall heavyset guy whose soft pudginess below his chin remained immobile even as he spoke. "Is it always a free first round when visiting a different city?"

My partially open lips gapped wider. "Am I that obvious?"

"It's the outfit. Too trendy for this place, honey."

"Really?"

"Take it as a compliment. It's all sneakers and rugged t-shirts here. And not rugged in a trendy way by any means."

"I thought fashion reigned in the city?"

"Well of course it does." His voice hissed with fingers pulling on the red T-shirt below his neck. "A one of kind that is meant to inspire the inner self into a Marilyn Monroe from Niagara Falls."

"Now that's a flame." I smiled before stretching my hand out to introduce myself.

"The pleasure is mine," he said. "Michael at your service."

"Thanks."

"I think the place you may be looking for is only blocks down. I am actually meeting my friend Shannon there in while. You should come with me. The music is certainly better, not to mention the guys. You and your outfit will fit right in, and even stand out from the rest no doubt."

"That would be nice. If it's okay with your friend Shannon, that is."

"No problem at all. Shannon's great. But we have to have one more drink before we go. It'll be my treat."

When we entered the nightclub, the atmosphere instantly became comparably dimmer and louder with much more space.

"Hey, there's Shannon!" Michael pointed.

My eyes scanned the dance floor, spotting only guys and no females. "I don't see her."

"Hey, Shan!" Michael hollered, his eyes focusing past the dance floor and toward the bar. A guy leaning lazily against the bar with shoulders hunched forward raised his chin in our direction. His arm stretched out, acknowledging our presence.

"Shannon's a real cutie." Michael leaned against me. "A silent one, but handsome no doubt."

I nodded, expressionless, as if his comment meant little, and that I hadn't, all along, concluded Shannon to be a girl.

Casually, he paced towards us, one hand tucked into the front pocket of his dark leather jacket while the other balanced a clear tonic drink.

"Shan!" Michael's right arm curled eagerly around Shannon's shoulder. "I wasn't sure if you would still be here, buddy. We were having these Cosmo shots and...well, you know how it is."

Shannon smiled, his eyes scanning me with undefined motive.

"Oh by the way—" Michael's hand clutched over my wrist, "we have a newbie with us. He's from out of town. Also, I've already loosened him up withalcohol, so he won't be stuck up like some of the L.A. boys."

"Even without the alcohol, I have no reason to be," I nodded, trying to sound funny.

Shannon leaned forward, his hand grabbing mine. "I don't know about that."

It was seconds later that I fully absorbed his comment. I smiled, eyes welcoming him.

"What do you guys say we blow this joint?" Shannon's words vociferated through the loud music.

"What do you mean...we just got here?" Michael demanded.

"I don't know...I was sitting by the bar over there and...I guess I was just done with this place some time ago."

I remained still watching to the two exchange words.

"What other bar do you suggest?"

"Not a bar. I was thinking we could all just chill at some coffeehouse or something. There's this really cool bohemian type coffeehouse—slash—hangout place with cool lounge music. They have international ground beans and herbs from all over the world, chicory, frangelica...you name it, they have it."

Michael looked over at me, lips hissing disappointedly. "Leave it to Shannon to ruin a Saturday night. Ground beans? For fuck sakes, Shan!"

"Common, it'll be cool." He laughed. "Besides, Mr. L.A.

here has to know that our nightlife has different ambiances to offer. I think he'll like it."

I smiled, excited that he had included me in the detour he was presenting. Even more intriguing was that he was eager that I see a place that although it seemed like an abrupt change in ambience, it was a place that he frequented, and which defined him. I was even going to admit the atmosphere to his suggestion when…

"Hell no! We said we were going to hit the clubs tonight."

"And we have—"

"Barely! It's not my fault you're bored out of your ass like always! You can be a real bore. You go to this freaken place on your own! I'm staying here and having another drink."

I looked up at Shannon. The blue in his eyes was revealed when as circling colorful lights swept across his face, and for an instant they froze, eyeing me directly. His golden eyebrows dropped slightly, while his lips pressed together to reveal disappointment. And if I wasn't mistaken, the disappointment was that he and I were going to miss the opportunity of getting to know each other.

"So do what you want. I'm not joining you," said Michael. His nostrils enhanced before allowing himself to catch his breath.

"Very well." Shannon looked down, his tone taking on a sympathetic note before he began walking away. "You guys have a good night."

The red circling Michael's face began to fade as he looked over at me. "I need another shot. You could join me at the bar if you want one."

In that moment I became uncertain of what to tell Michael. The only thing that seemed clear was that I wanted to join Shannon and visit his world. And to my surprise, my words took action without consent from my mind about what would be the right or wrong way to tell Michael I was doing next. "I'm gonna go. I'm not in the mood for more drinking.

Besides, I have to be up early."

"Alright, have a good night then."

"Thanks again for the drink earlier." I began to pace backward. "It was nice meeting you."

"Same here, buddy." Michael began waving, but I turned around too soon to watch him drop his hand. All I wanted was to be outside, and join Shannon, let him know that I was eager to share with him the warm atmosphere he had created. My desperation took got the best of me. Before I knew it, I was running out into the fresh night, where the life continued to rush by.

There was no sign of Shannon. He had already left.

My eyes searched desperately from one end of the street to the other. Only unfamiliar guys stepping out of cabs surrounded me, while other groups of unfamiliar guys rushed past me, heading for the empty cabs.

Without reason the chords of my heart tugged. I knew nothing about the guy. Yet, I felt I knew more about him than his own friend Michael could even know.

I was already near my hotel when I began wishing I had at least returned to the club so that I could have at least given Michael my phone number to pass along to his friend. Inanely, despite my yearning for the complete stranger, I was glad that I hadn't gone back. A part of me was too upset with Michael for disregarding his friend so quickly that I wanted nothing to do with him.

Instead, I decided to simply become lost with the night, and complete it with the same recommendation that Shannon had suggested. I too would sober up with a coffee, one with foreign coffee beans and perhaps chicory, if they had it.

The place was the next one I happened to pass. Not only were its scents nostalgic and welcoming, but also its atmosphere.

Dim lights revealed colorful Indonesian motifs, bamboo plants, and warm large earth color pillows where the locals rested while sipping on their warm drinks. A live duo entertained everyone with the sound of a cello and an intermittent saxophone. The combination was peculiar, yet each instrument complimented the another.

My eyes scanned the display above the counter, realizing the selection was far too extensive for me to decide quickly.

"You should try the Ecuadorian."

"Huh?" I looked up. The voice sounded familiar. And although I was instantly surprised, another part of me wasn't. Perhaps it was that my heart had been yearning for him only moments ago, and had not surrendered to the idea that he was no longer around. But he stood there, tall and confident with the same blue eyes and smile under the dim soft light.

"The Ecuadorian is one of my favorites. You have to let me buy it for you."

I smiled. "What a small city."

"Tell me about it."

"So now that the drama has disappeared," he began, "would you like to join me? I have a table on the balcony right above the stairs. The view is excellent. You can see the night."

"Definitely." I nodded.

. . . . .

AFTER I JOINED him, the only view we focused on was that of each other. Quickly we admitted to one another how much we yearned to be together. And to my surprise, he admitted how his desperation to be around me had become so strong that minutes after he left he had returned to the club, asking his friend Michael if by any chance I gave Michael my phone number, or coudl tell him where I had disappeared to.

"It didn't even matter that I was mad at Michael and didn't want to talk to him. I didn't care. I don't know why I became so desperate." He laughed nervously. "I was afraid the night had swallowed you whole."

"Never," I said, glancing over at the street below for an instant. "It's a small city after all."

"Funny, for the first time, I feel you're right." His hand rested over mine as he leaned forward. Gently, his lips pressed against mine. And this time, it was their soft warmth that swallowed me whole, while the city became smaller—a mere particle that surrounded me and was there to simply support the enchanting night I had yearned for and created.

INTERIORS

CHARLIE VAZQUEZ

REPULSION IS OFTEN a mask for other seemingly unassailable emotions. As an imaginative youth, I'd been embarrassingly unaware as to why certain men repulsed me— I simply believed that certain behaviors or traits disgusted me. The churning feelings were much like being in love, as I would later learn—what appalls us oftentimes has an inverted, Freudian kind of sexual power. Such is the folly of confident youth!

Something about Marco repulsed me, for example.

Whenever I saw him, it was through the muted theater of the huge glass windows of the Athens Restaurant. The Number 2 train rumbled overhead; it mixed with the symphony of clinking dishes and the passionate shouting of the Greek family that owned the diner-slash-donut shop. Marco would appear on the street, miming to his Italian friends like a half-paralyzed dummy without the voice of a ventriloquist. He used his hands to accentuate his point of view and leaned forward when he talked to others. He had a slight limp in his gait. I knew nothing else about him—other than the fact that he scowled at me, when he chose to notice me. And thus I was repulsed by him and his apparent dislike of me—he was a menacing, dirty, and black junkyard dog in my world of trashed landscapes.

Others in my neighborhood did much to fuel my disliking of Marco as well. He was not alone in his category. There were several like him, but Marco would step out of the line to form a line of his own. As soon as my burgeoning sexuality came to a head, my manner of dress changed, as did my attitude, and people in the neighborhood began to suspect that I was an imminent threat to their "civility." I, with the more wicked imagination, did the same back—it created a barrier between me and the "adverse," so that I could navigate through life with less interaction. As I grew into my real skin, I was repulsed by people that hated me before they knew me—and worse, people who'd always liked me and suddenly decided I didn't exist. Repulsion as compensation—for the respect you will never get back.

. . . . .

AND THEN, THERE'S repulsion's twin, obsession. It didn't take a scientist to figure that Tony, one of my neighborhood friends, was a closet case. I simply knew it—I believed my feelings because I wanted him. Tony was a religious pretty-boy with two dangerously handsome older brothers. They were from the simple kind of Italian family whose men were all stunning, even the older swaggering uncles. Their forearms, their chests, their faces—their entire bodies—seemed to be splashed with luscious Mediterranean hair.

The oldest brother, Nick, was the first boy I ever deified to a rank and status once designated to the concept of God—he superseded even that. He had a habit of pinching the head of his dick liberally whenever he wore sweat pants. I remember him catching me admiring his hairy navel once, as he lifted his shirt while flirting with a neighborhood girl. He winked at me and turned away, as if to say *this is what you do to fuck chicks*. Another time, he made it a point to lock the door to their room (all three brothers slept in the same room) and showed me, in private, the hair that was starting to crown his nipples, when he was sixteen, and I was about ten. Now Nick, dear reader, *did not repulse me!*

Nick rode me to the supermarket on his Vespa with his shirt off—on a sultry, New York summer day. I clearly remember the realization of feeling him close to me; my skinny arms wrapped around his belly; the feeling of teenage hair blossoming around his belly button like long, spiraled moss. His skin was a perfection I had never believed in. Whenever he would gradually hit the brakes, my face would come to rest between his shoulder blades. There was no explaining my vibrant euphoria—I just knew what I liked. I often went to find him for more "rides" and he was more than happy to oblige, if he had the time.

And though those erotic memories were wonderful to consider from time to time, as any queer young man in his early twenties, I wanted to fall in love. I longed to relish those physical exchanges as often as I wanted—with someone that wanted them as much as I did. My idealized fantasy world of romance would be crushed, of course—that is, once the complex world of man-on-man "dating" would reshape my outlook.

But romance was real at that time—there was no talking me out of it. Little had I known that it would not be as it was when I closed my eyes to imagine it—but that it would arrive as a possession of my body by an exterior force I had never before encountered. I would be injected with romantic dimension by an invisible, mischievous, and foul-smelling Cupid: A Cupid perspiring in the humidity of Gotham summer nights and mumbling the profanity splattered dialect of the city's warriors.

Let me explain:

I wanted Tony for lots of reasons. He seemed like the next best thing in a lot of ways—my unrealistic longing for his older brother would need to live in my inner spheres of pleasure. My archaic predator, the hunter denied, had matured and was speaking behind the mask of my sincerity. Tony was meat—however I chose to consume it—a temple dedicated to the complex "beauty" of man, in which I wanted to "meditate." Tony and his older brother Nick looked exactly alike—and though Tony didn't ride around shirtless on motorbikes or play basketball in sweaty shorts, he was more available. "Taboo" always seems a more thrilling beast for the hunt, but at one time or another we need to feast on whatever falls in our crosshairs.

I visited with Tony at his twelfth-floor apartment, years later, after the rest of his family had moved to another neighborhood. Tony lived in a two-bedroom, by himself—it was a pigsty, and as much as I thought it repulsed me, I found the stench of the apartment rather tantalizing after we shared our trademark six-pack of beer. I hinted at my queerness and he said he was all right about that. Expecting that he would reciprocate, I was disappointed to find out that he had a pregnant girlfriend in Brooklyn. I suddenly felt "ill" and excused myself—with a lack of protest on his part. My "gaydar" needed a service technician, apparently.

I left his apartment and headed for the elevator. I wanted to run into Nick so badly that my mind fooled me into hearing his voice ascending in the metal box—as the elevator shaft illuminated.

No Nick.

The noisy machine stopped and I slid in. After descending a few stories, it stopped abruptly and made a whining sound—a power failure had possessed it. I rang the emergency call-bell and stood back to see if anyone could hear it. Some moments later, a man appeared through the small portion of glass I could see through. His untied, brown leather boots were visible and his steps were heavy, as a mythical giant's.

"Anybody in there? Hullo?" He banged on the glass so

hard that I jumped back, fearing it would shatter on my face.

I thought to myself *Well who do you think rang the bell dumb-shit, of course there's someone in here!* I actually said, "Yeah, just one person in here, I'm all right though. How do I get out?" The beer I'd had at Tony's was working its way through me. Strangely, I felt safe.

The voice went on, "I'll go get a crowbar." The mammoth stomped away; his heavy, New York-Italian accent full of compassion and power. I wondered what he looked like.

A few moments later, I heard him and, quite suddenly, the elevator moved. It jerked and went up a half-story. I had the feeling that it fixed itself, that power returned to it. It went up to the flight where I'd seen the man's boots—the door rattled open and there he was. Mean old Marco: the dirty junkyard dog, glistening with summer sweat and scowling in a dirty black tank top. "You okay, kid? Good God, you coulda been here for days." It seemed to me that he didn't recognize me in the darkness of the blackout that surrounded us. I had demonized him for years and he was thus radiant to me, in the dark—in his element.

"Thanks again, man." I said.

"You going down?" He stood crooked before me.

"That's the way out, isn't it?" My knees got tight.

As the balmy elevator descended, I tried to understand why Marco had always repulsed me. He was usually filthy; he was perpetually pessimistic and just plain nasty. Marco had never struck me as the kind of man one could spill one's heart to. Society and hard work had hardened him to a repulsive state of masculine coldness. I'd assumed he was an old school, factory-working, homophobic, hypocritical, borderline racist—a brute with a big chest and walnut-sized brain. In those harrowing seconds, next to him in the elevator, I wondered if he critiqued me in his private world as I did to him.

At about the second or third floor, the elevator stopped

again. Marco punched the thin metal wall. "Ah, shit!" As soon as he did, the generated "backup" lights went out. My lips turned salty with the taste of fear—I could hear my pulse in my ears. It beat loudly, like a shaman's quickening drum. I could hear two heartbeats. At times they would synchronize and fall off rhythm again. I feared that he could hear them as well—one of the pulses was faster than the other and it was obviously mine—the pulse of one terrified.

"You all right?" I heard him ask, from three feet away.

"Oh, I'm—" I never finished answering him because he put his hand around my wrist and pulled me close to him. I should've melted but my nausea exceeded that possibility. My disgust, however, was suddenly eclipsed by a helpless feeling: I couldn't help myself. I pulled away from him and coughed, just to do something.

His right hand found the back of my head and pulled my face into his. I allowed myself to be pulled into his power. How revulsion is surely a passion! He pushed me away and cursed in Italian, something Catholic sounding. I assumed it was the voice of the fault line splitting his homophobia and homoeroticism. I had heard of queers that sought that "vibe" in men and not lived to brag about it. I froze and wanted to run, I wanted to be somewhere else. I feared he would strangle me with his iron hands, wilt me to death in the New York summer—in a stuffy elevator car that was heating up from our body heat coupled with failed air-conditioning.

Marco embraced me—again—and I shook in his arms.

The elevator showed no sign of moving up or down, though it squeaked from the movement of our awkward waltz of confusion. He took a lighter out of his pocket, lit it up, and examined the ceiling of the elevator; he was as Goya's *Colossus* in profile. I anticipated a sexual exchange, but interestingly, Marco climbed up through the escape hole of the elevator and lifted me out after him. As we stood atop the stalled mechanical cubicle, I could only say, "Thanks."

"Come here." My hero tried to kiss me passionately amidst gears, cables, and electrical elements!

I again pulled back and away. "Let's pry that door opens before this elevator starts moving."

Marco worked the door out of its resting place with a strong twist of his arm on the small crowbar. We spilled into the hallway where people were stirring with candles in hand. I thanked Marco and told him I had to go home and check in with the family.

Bullshit. He squeezed my hand, pulled me toward him fearlessly, and whispered, "Can I make you dinner or something, kid?"

"I would love that. By the way, my name's Israel."

"I knew that. I'm Marco." His hand was clammy as we officially met. I could still smell his pits in the humid air around us. I felt an unreasonable desire for him once we were safe and out of danger's way. And since he already knew my name, I figured he also knew what the others in the neighborhood were most likely saying about me—I was a suspected "faggot." So I followed him up the stairs to his apartment.

The apartment was what I'd expected from a sloppy Italian bachelor—the sparse environment of an urban warrior in decline. The sports channel chimed in the background—a stadium's worth of people cheered for me. There were small holographic photos of Catholic saints pinned to the corners of family portraits—the saints watching over loved ones. Marco had transcended the category of "unpleasant" man to erotic hero to pagan priest.

As he shuffled things around the kitchen, I excused myself to go piss and wash my hands. And as I contemplated my hero, while washing my filthy hands (in his even dirtier bathroom sink), he stormed in, disrobed—and proceeded to do the same to me! I realized that neither of us could wait any longer. We trembled and crawled awkwardly into his shower stall and cleaned up together. We experienced our first fits of passion under the cascading water of his showerhead, nearly swallowing too much water in our frenzy, and then had dinner. Marco and I continued to see each other—but only in the confines of his apartment. It was made clear to me that our "romance" could not speak its name on the streets outside and below.

Our infatuation was short, but I learned a lot in that very little time. And though the world outside was not open to our "secret"—it would've even been hostile—that only caused our passion to swell like wildfire whenever we had the chance to express it. And much like a wildfire, our flames went out quickly, after spreading outward without a plan or design—a jagged and multi-armed haphazard zigzag.

I gradually receded from the closeted world of Marco's apartment as I began making newer friends in Manhattan, where I could be more open. I didn't feel like hiding any longer and Marco was not as courageous as me. He turned into the scowling, bitter old man I had always thought him to be. I supposed that Marco decided to detest me in order to make sense of things in his inner universe. I, however, could not hate him, but he did become repulsive to me,again. Part of me even denied that we ever "fell in love." I lost respect for him, since he could not surmount quite a courageous thing as "coming out." Never married, no children—I had to wonder what the rest of his life had been like.

The last time I saw him he passed me on the street and ignored me. I never saw mean old Marco again, but a rumor arose in the neighborhood that he'd been killed during a dispute involving a woman in a Brooklyn nightclub. Sometimes—when I'm swallowing my greasy lunch and wiping my oily lips with a cheap paper napkin at the Athens Restaurant—I think I see him, but it's always someone else.

LA FONDA DEL SOL

A REMINISCENCE OF NEW YORK
BEFORE AIDS, OR THE FALL
OF OLD PENN STATION

STEVE DUNHAM

TEDDY'S FIRST BRUSH with unrequited love, involving another male, happened soon after he turned twenty-one, during the spring of 1962. Before that he'd been seduced into a few animalistic couplings with schoolmates, but it hadn't yet dawned on him that there might be more to it. Not until the giddy surge that tackled him, one Saturday afternoon, in the midst of basic training at an army fort in New Jersey. Still confined to post with the other fledglings, Teddy was glumly sipping a soda at the Main PX snack bar, listening to "Soldier Boy" and "Palisades Park" on the jukebox, when a godlike, dark-haired, dark-eyed young corporal in crotch-hugging tailored fatigues crossed the room and asked to join him at his little round table.

"Hi, guy—My name's Harvey. Harvey Malitz from New Yawk," the good-looking soldier said. "You look like you could use some company."

Not only luscious but also lovable—in the sense of until death do us part—the stricken Teddy thought. Moments

229

after they began getting acquainted, he realized that his new companion's knee was softly, fearlessly pressing his. Teddy gamely nudged back and Harvey suggested that they stroll out onto the empty parade ground.

Talking there, out of earshot of anyone, he led them to lie down on the newly mown grass, almost touching but not noticeably so from afar. Harvey proposed that he and, he laughingly emphasized, a straight buddy were planning to drive into Philadelphia that evening for a movie and would Ted, pretty please, come along? Aware of the controversial lesbian theme of the film, *The Children's Hour*, Ted indeed agreed to go—as long as no training cadre were on hand to see him leave post. Harvey and his friend were senior members of a weekend reserve unit who could enter and exit as they wished. Tucked in the rear jump seat of the buddy's MG, Teddy had only to duck down when they passed the sentry box, and he was free for the night. So off the trio sped to Philadelphia to engross themselves in the drama on the screen, while in the dark Harvey grasped his mesmerized new comrade's hand. After a beer, they headed homeward.

Kneeling close to the back of Harvey's bucket seat, Teddy first allowed Harvey to massage the front of his pants for a while by casually reaching around behind, out of view of the driver. Then he let him feel all the way inside and jack him off. Teddy couldn't reciprocate, except to rub Harvey's thigh a little and lick the back of his neck. For both, it was an especially thrilling ride and far too short. Meanwhile, ever since they had met that afternoon, Harvey told Teddy all about himself, that he was Jewish but not very religious, that he had graduated from high school with OK grades and currently worked as a Wall Street runner, and that he lived with his parents in Queens. Conspiratorially, he also whispered that he and a couple of gay pals in the city had just leased a "crash pad" in Greenwich Village, a great place to party and take tricks. Then he implored

Teddy to spend the very next weekend with him there. The training company was to be awarded its first and only three-day pass that particular weekend, so Teddy accepted with delirious pleasure, jotting down his host's two addresses and the Queens phone number. Next morning Harvey and his friend were released from reserve duty, but before taking off, drove over to Teddy's company, "To make sure you didn't get into trouble for going out last night." In a deserted upstairs squad leader's room, Harvey grabbed Teddy and devoured him with a soulful french kiss that refused to wear off the whole rest of the week. Would Friday afternoon ever come? Butterflies cavorting lightly in his stomach, Teddy donned some corduroys, a blue Brooks Brothers shirt, and one of his preppy tweed jackets. Feeling like Holden Caulfield's twin, he boarded the train in Trenton with his small overnight kit. Heading for the cushy club car, he found himself the youngest person occupying it and felt terrifically sophisticated. He lit up a Kent and ordered a very dry Martini, then another, as the train jounced through Princeton, Somerset, Rahway, closer and closer to the object of his new affection.

A smartly dressed, fortyish woman across the aisle began chatting with Teddy as if she were his own Auntie Mame, and he almost pictured himself going off with her in a Bentley once they arrived in New York...To her pied a terre?...To the St. Regis?...To the Hamptons? But no—red-faced at even thinking about why he was coming to the city—he bade the beautiful, slightly sad stranger good-bye as they stepped out into the cavernous cathedral of Pennsylvania Station, smelling of taxi fumes and old suitcases, and were engulfed.

He gave the cabbie the number of Harvey's pad on Sullivan Street and leaned back. Teddy was no novice to Manhattan, having visited several times with chums from his expensive college back in Ohio—even if he had dropped out. Their venue was the limousine-choked avenues of the Upper East

Side, with occasional forays into Midtown to catch some jazz or the latest Edward Albee.

He loved the glossy, towering ziggurats of this world... their fragrant, opulently appointed lobbies and dusky nocturnal wallscapes of softly glinting windows shielding the secrets of myriad unknown, no doubt fascinating inhabitants. Hurtling down raucous Seventh Avenue, through the sun-dappled brick-and-stone maze of Chelsea, and veering suddenly into the dank, shadowy Sullivan Street was a new adventure. Arriving at exactly the time Harvey had specified, Teddy found him there on the front stoop, fresh from work in his striped Oxford shirt, cute bow tie, skintight Levis, and sneakers. "From his belt up a runner's gotta look businesslike," Harvey mugged, "and from his ass down he's gotta rock an' roll!" Leaping up the sagging stairway and along the dingy hallway reeking of pee, Harvey proudly ushered his guest into his home away from home. It was undergoing a frenzied, disorganized spate of redecoration, knee-deep in as many beer cans as paint cans. Amenities were few: bare red lightbulb, scuzzy old refrigerator, battered portable stereo, spunk-stained king-size mattress, and an air-shaft view. Dropping the sackful of paintbrushes he had brought, Teddy's host engulfed him with the tenacity of a boa constrictor, and the beguiled one ceased to care about their surroundings. Before things got too sloppy, Harvey backed off abruptly and announced—surprise!—they weren't going to stay there after all, because that morning his parents had hopped a plane for a week in Miami. So, arm-in-arm, the two compadres descended into what was Teddy's first rocketing subway ride, out to the Malitz family apartment. Emerging on Queens Boulevard and turning down a side street, Teddy was all the more captivated by the vastness and variety of New York. Here was yet another facet to absorb...endless blocks of undulating Georgian and Tudor facades, their pleasant curved bays and diamond-paned casements warming the twilight. Legions of lollipop-like trees, ringed with spiky little iron fences, guarded the sidewalks and entrances as staunchly as the occasional uniformed doormen. Why, Queens was almost swanky! The vestibule was claustrophobic and redolent of fried knishes, but once up the elevator, inside the shag-carpeted, luxurious if overstuffed apartment filled with huge fat lamps, there was plenty of room for two hot new lovers to romp around.

First Harvey mixed drinks from his father's bar, then flicked on the hi-fi console to blast his fondest new acquisition, the soundtrack of *West Side Story*. Finally, engorged in atmosphere, the two could peel out of their clothes and have all the acrobatic sex they wanted, in Mr. and Mrs. Malitz's elephantine waterbed. Teddy was enthralled with Harvey's dancing eyes, amorous growling, and suave body, hairless except for his tousled mop and the silky thatches near his underarms and cock.

Famished after a soapy reprise in the shower, the pair wandered out to a garish, brassy coffee shop on the Boulevard, where Harvey knew every sexy guy in every booth. Arm-in-arm, they sprinted back home for a night of unfettered, unprotected carnality, but this time it seemed to Teddy less spontaneous. Saturday morning Harvey fixed an elaborate breakfast, leaving the dishes in the sink, and they set out for a place called Bergen Beach down in Brooklyn—more strange new vistas for Teddy. Harvey declared that there were probably more queer or bisexual men in Brooklyn and Queens than in all of Manhattan, but that most of them stayed right there close to Mama.

The two went horseback riding over the coarse brown dunes, and through junkyards full of demolished cars and rusty, hulking machinery looking like a giant's discarded toys. Gray, faintly ominous waves swiped at the breakwater, yet the whole took on a curious bleak beauty—an Ashcan School painting come to life.

Packs of cute, tough boys they encountered along the way all were acquaintances of Harvey—current or former tricks, he gleefully bragged. Any or all would be willing to make out with Teddy, Harvey teased, maybe even for free. Part of Teddy wanted to, but a more addled part ignored the possibility that fun-loving Harvey, sated with his new conquest, was willing to casually pass him off to others. He devotedly clung to Harvey's arm, and Harvey shrugged.

That evening was the zenith, and also the nadir, of the visit.

The fellows jumped onto a subway for Manhattan, to meet more friends at a sensational new restaurant, La Fonda Del Sol. The cuisine was Mexican, or at least a highly designer version of it. Anything remotely Latin, back then, was an exotic novelty in an urbane East Coast setting.

Sixth Avenue had recently been renamed "Avenue of the Americas" and La Fonda Del Sol, a kind of showcase of the city's intent, had just opened in a soaring, dramatically glassy corner of the street's most prestigious new office tower. The restaurant's svelte, all-white modern decor, sensual lighting, dazzling mariachi music, and artfully presented food conjured up by frisky, lithe young waiters attracted a glamorous clientele dressed in anything from black tie to Harvey and his gang's version of the Sharks and the Jets. The place seemed light-years away from the Plaza's stuffy Oak Room or Schrafft's.

Not only that, it was incredibly cheap! Eating and drinking in this flamboyant setting, with this uninhibited gaggle of guys around the large oval table they had commandeered, was one of the best—if short-lived—times Teddy had ever had.

Except that Harvey, goaded by the others, brayed endlessly about his own charm and prowess, recounting that every day, on his runner's rounds, he was having the most terrific sex in executive washrooms and freight elevators or with the boss's hunky protégé on the boss's couch. Looking back, Teddy cannot believe how immature he must have been to be so wounded by Harvey's blunt but utterly honest portrayal of himself.

After dinner the pack introduced Teddy to the rancorous, sordid milieu of Eighth Avenue and Forty-second Street... a weird circus where anything was possible, with little vice-squad interference. Part of Teddy loved it—but again he was crushed to see that Harvey knew everybody there, too. He made dates for the next night, and the next, and tried to convince Teddy to pair off right then with one or two of his lusty companions. Finally very drunk, dizzy, and repulsed by the crudely groping, drug-sniffing denizens of a West Side tenement-flat party they had ended up at, Teddy pleaded with Harvey that they call it a night. They rode home to Queens in silence and slept apart in Harvey's room on his twin beds.

After a perfunctory cup of stale coffee next morning, Harvey quietly stated that he had plans, which kept him from spending the rest of the day with Teddy. Guiding him down to the subway and to the correct line that would get him back to Penn Station, he bade his weekend fling an affable but very pat, "So long, it was fun." Before bounding back up the stairs, Harvey indifferently suggested that maybe they could get together again sometime, perhaps in the summer.

Before long Teddy graduated from his basic training and boarded a train for army communications school up in Massachusetts. Months later, in August, he was invited by some barracks mates to share a ride down to New York. Morosely longing for, but vaguely dreading, a reunion with Harvey, he accepted in a flash—then thrust a handful of quarters into the PX pay phone.

"Hello— Mrs. Malitz?"

"Yeah, who's this?"

"It's Ted Chase, an army friend of Harvey's. Is he at home?"

"Nah, Harvey's at the beach with some of his cronies, so he says."

"Would you please give him a message...that I can come down to New York on Saturday and see him at his apartment?"

"His what?"

"Harvey's place in Greenwich Village—" blurted Teddy, discerning as he said it that Pandora's box had flown open. Apparently Harvey's folks were in the dark about their son's alternative accommodations. "Well—" Teddy continued queasily, "please tell him I'm coming."

"Ohhh—I'll tell him all right! He don't pay me no room and board like we ask, and he's got another a-paht-ment?" Bam! Mrs. Malitz hung up. Well, mused Teddy, how could I know?

Feeling even more skittish than before that other trip to be with Harvey, Teddy embarked with his fellows on the hectic drive from north of Boston to a sultry, grid-locked Manhattan. The buddies all planned to stay at the Thirty-fourth Street YMCA (a sleazy place that even boy-crazy Harvey avoided), but Teddy jocularly told them good-bye, without passing on the warning, and hailed a taxi for "his girlfriend's" in the Village.

The driver wasn't buying it. He smirked when Teddy gave him the address as, come to think of it, had the other cabbie on that happier day last spring. "Girlfriend, eh?" he chuckled.

Teddy didn't care. It was oppressively humid, and he felt more and more disquieted as the vehicle crawled toward what would surely be his denouement. A few clogged blocks from the apartment, he could stand it no more. He paid, scrambled out, and ran with his little kit, sweating, until he reached a totally transformed Sullivan Street.

In the gathering dusk, Italian lights twinkled in great arcs over the thoroughfare. Accordionists and trumpeters blared, cherry bombs burst, and frenzied mobs hollered, shoved, sang, and boozed their heads off, oblivious to the god-awful heat. It was some kind of carnival.

Looking up at Harvey's building, he saw half-naked guys hanging out of all the windows, laughing and motioning the randy world inside.

"Harvey here?" inquired Teddy of an insouciant, lipsticked young man he recognized from the night at La Fonda.

"Oh yeah, but he ain't gonna be thrilled to see youse," was the answer. Teddy's heart sank and the butterflies fairly pummeled his stomach walls. His foolish optimism, what little was left, vanished, overcome though he was, still, by his desire for Harvey.

"Waddya say to my mother, you dumb fuck?" was his beloved's greeting at the door of the now fully, if bizarrely, furnished flat. "My old man kicked me out, thanks to you! I can hardly afford my piece of the rent for this dump, where I now gotta live!" Harvey was really angry. "And you're not staying here—I got a hot blond number coming down from Riverdale any minute now."

"Harv— I'm awful, awful... sorry! I didn't know—"

When Harvey fully comprehended the penitent's flood of tears and uncontrollable shaking, he softened a little, but determinedly led Teddy back down to the street, giving him a brief hug and the hint of a kiss. "It's not gonna work out, guy. It was nice knowin' ya, have a great life! Here comes my little blond—"

With that, Teddy found himself alone amid the carnival's chaos, with a billfold full of cash and a free weekend in the world's most vibrant city. Red-eyed, all he wanted to do was to get out, so he trudged all the way uptown to the Port Authority bus terminal (another hellhole Harvey had cautioned him about). He bought a ticket back to Boston and fought off an army of rapacious creeps, one of whom threatened to forcibly abduct him. Dozing fitfully through the all-night bus ride, he found himself enjoying a late Sunday breakfast in the elegant deserted dining room of the Ritz-Carlton, resplendent with blue stemware and shimmering views of the sunny Public Garden—far from grungy Sullivan Street.

In fact, the farther he got from Harvey the better Teddy was beginning to feel. That afternoon at a student hangout in Cambridge, he met a godlike, fair-haired, blue-eyed varsity coxswain whom he would, a few weeks later, guiltlessly treat just as Harvey had treated him.

Still, it took Teddy awhile to get over his virgin infatuation. He even wrote a rambling poem, set in a cadence remarkably like today's rap, rich in Gotham's sights and sounds... the lollipop trees, the wan slap of the surf along junkyard beaches, and lurid hints of what he and his idol did with each other. Maybe it was New York itself he was in love with. He showed his doggerel to his closest, most intellectual army school friend, who thrust it back... "Tear that up, it could get you kicked out!"

Despite countless sojourns in New York over the years, Teddy never laid eyes on his handsome, smooth-talking weekend lover again. Moreover, he never quite realized what a fabled landmark among restaurants La Fonda Del Sol would become until fading away, its choice corner site handed on to how many bank branches, travel agencies, and Chinese buffets.

But he clearly remembers, with a pang, the single hour spent there around that festive oval table—the laugh and silky smell of young Corporal Malitz.

THE STORY OF EAU

LAWRENCE SCHIMEL

OUR KITCHEN TABLE is a once-elegant claw-foot porcelain bathtub nearly as old as the building, with an inch-and-a-half thick slab of oak laid on top of it. The tub is wonderfully deep; in my last apartment, up in Hell's Kitchen, I had a normal tub: which is to say, both too short and too shallow. While my current tub in the East Village apartment I shared with my lover, Tim, was still on the short side for someone like myself who stood on the far side of six foot, it compensated by being deep enough that my knees didn't stick out into the cool air when I sat in it, as they had in almost all my previous tubs. It was perfect for sitting in for long stretches of time, relaxing and reading—provided one wasn't fussy about maybe getting the pages wet. But ever since my doctor had ordered me to take two or three sitz baths each day to cure my hemorrhoids, I've had better things to do in the tub than read.

You might not think that getting hemorrhoids could improve the sex life of a balding thirty-something-year-old gay man living in Manhattan, but then you don't know my lover, Tim. (If you're one of his ex-lovers, then you're lucky enough to know what I mean. But I'm the luckiest of all, since I'm the one who has him now. Knock wood.)

In order to encourage me to follow doctor's orders and take all of the prescribed daily baths, Tim has undertaken it upon himself to create a little bathing ritual to pamper me. I tease him sometimes that his tender ministrations are really motivated by self-interest, since the sooner I'm healed, the sooner it'll be that he can fuck me again. But I have a feeling that even after I'm well, we'll continue our little bathing rituals (although probably NOT two to three times per day)!

We didn't normally take baths, and not just because the bathtub was in the kitchen and was also used as our kitchen table, which meant it was always covered in stuff, from dirty dishes to piles of bills that needed to be paid. Admittedly, it required a concerted effort to decide to take a bath, since one had to first clean off the kitchen table, then remove the heavy tabletop. But even the effort and time lag of running the bathwater took far too long and was too much trouble for the pace of life in New York City, let alone the extra hassle we'd have to go through with dismantling the kitchen table bits. It was a luxury we never seemed to have time for, or didn't often allow ourselves to take even when we did have the time. We had a shower in a tiny closet, and a toilet in a closet of its own right next to it, both of which also stood in the large kitchen that the apartment's front door entered into. East Village apartments are like that, sort of hobbled together after the fact, instead of having been designed to be a living space. But they were cheaper than just about anywhere else in New York City, and necessity made a lot of things worth putting up with.

Our little bathing rituals developed because one of the first times I took one of my post-doctor's-visit baths, Tim was home watching me. You'd think that after all the trouble of running a bath, I'd sit in it for a while. But I felt foolish, especially when I thought about why I was doing what I was doing and thinking it would never really work. Of course, negative thinking is the worst thing one can do in one of these alternative therapies, but that's what I was thinking, and that sort of thinking is what made me stand up after about four minutes.

Tim would have none of that, though. "Where do you think you're going?" he asked me. "I'm done with my bath," I said lamely. "Not yet, you're not," Tim said. "Now sit down," and I did, and he disappeared into the bedroom. He came back a moment later with something behind his back. He stood behind me and I leaned my head back against the rim of the tub to look up at him. He smiled down at me and ran one hand along my torso and neck, leaning forward so he could kiss me. His other hand was still behind his back and I wondered what he held there, but then closed my eyes and thought only of our tongues and our mouths until we paused to catch our breath. I let my arms dangle over the sides, my head resting against the lip of the tub, my eyes still closed as I soaked in the warm water, and I thought this is nice, and felt my body suddenly lose its tenseness, everything opening up, even my anus, which felt almost like a fist unclosing, that sense of relief you feel after you let go of the anger.

It was at that moment that I learned what Tim had been holding behind his back: handcuffs, which at the same moment clicked around my wrist and one clawed foot. "You fink!" I cried at Tim, although I didn't open my eyes. I didn't want to move from the warm place I was in, both the bath and the afterglow of our kiss, which had kickstarted my arousal; maybe that was part of the warmth, I thought, the flush of blood rushing through my body to fill my cock. With my eyes still shut, I felt the cold metal loop around my wrist, and said to Tim, "I want another kiss."

He didn't answer, but a moment later I felt his presence behind me again, his body close, and then his fingers were touching my chest and neck, caressing my throat as they moved to float lightly over my lips. His breath followed next, warm and fragrant of the vanilla-pear tea he'd been drinking after dinner, his lips hesitating a hair's breadth away from mine. My tongue poked out to lick at him real quick and I said, "Ribbit," and we both laughed. And then we were breathing the same breath again, our mouths sealed tightly to one another as he held my chin in his hands, and our tongues tried to wrap themselves around each other. One of the first things that made me fall in love with Tim is how well he kisses, how it makes you feel there's nothing in the world he wants to do more in that moment except kiss you, that he hasn't another thought in his head; so many men I've kissed not only lack the talent or the natural advantage of Tim's thick pliant lips, but you can tell their mind's not in it, they're worrying about whether they left the oven still on or what bills need to be paid before next week or whether your kiss will turn out to be the beginning of an ongoing romance or a one-night stand or perhaps just a kiss. Tim's kisses could make me forget the worst of days at work and think only of him and our romance, and his agile tongue sent waves of sexual energy coursing through me.

"I thought I was supposed to relax," I complained, when we broke apart and I'd caught my breath. I lifted my hips so that my erection poked out of the tub like the periscope of a submarine that was surfacing, its blind eye looking at Tim.

I looked up at him, waiting for his reaction, wondering if he would just leave me like this. I was at his mercy, after all; even aside from the bath, I was still cuffed to the tub, with the keys still in the bedroom, for all I knew.

Tim smiled and slid a hand into the warm water to slide up and down my inner thighs. I relaxed my hips and sunk back to the bottom of the tub. Tim's fingers kept stroking and poking along my legs and crotch and balls, before dropping down to hover near my tender asshole. "You're supposed to relax here," he said gently, his poking fingers as soft in their touch as the tone of his voice. His other hand plunged into the water and grabbed my cock, as he said, "But that doesn't mean we can't get a little excited elsewhere."

My entire body tensed as his second hand splashed into the water and he grabbed my cock in his fist. He just held onto it, as his first hand poked at my asshole again. "Relax," he commanded, and I let my breath go and tried to follow his command, imagining my asshole opening like an unclenching fist again. "Much better," Tim said, and started gently stroking my cock with his other hand. The motion created small waves that made my balls bounce and felt like warm mouths sucking at all the skin of my groin at once.

"Much better," I agreed, and closed my eyes again as I leaned back and purred while one of Tim's hands moved on my cock, the other gently probing my ass. I could feel a bed of precome building and I squeezed once to send it shooting out, wondering whether it would float to the surface or just sit at the tip of my cock.

Tim's hands stopped moving. "What?" I asked, opening my eyes.

He looked directly into my eyes, as he explained, "If you don't stay relaxed here," and his fingers swirled along the crack between my cheeks for emphasis, "I stop moving here," and again his fingers danced for emphasis, this time swirling around the underside of the crown where he knew I was most sensitive. My back arched instinctively as his fingers rubbed along there, and I knew I was starting to clench my asshole again but I stopped myself and breathed out and focused on keeping my asshole as open as possible as the pleasure in my cock kept building as his hand swirled around the glans.

"That's my boy," Tim said, and after a moment more he let me relax, sliding his hand down onto the shaft and beginning to pump, the change in stroke allowing me to catch my breath and adjust to the new, differently pleasurable sensation. Tim knew my body well, and knew how to work me, turning me on so strongly until I was about to crest over into orgasm and then changing his grip to delay things, over and over again, until at last I couldn't hold back any longer.

"I'm going to come," I warned him. "I'm going to clench, and don't you dare stop!"

Tim didn't stop and a few seconds later my hips were bucking as I came, my dick spewing above the rippling water like a whale's blowhole spray.

My orgasm had splashed water all over the place. I looked over Tim, who stood by the tub, his shirt and pants clinging to him. With my free hand, I reached across myself and started rubbing his hard cock where its outline showed through the wet fabric of his pants. I hooked my fingers behind his belt buckle and pulled him toward me, since my reach wasn't very good given the awkward position I was in.

"I think my bath is done for tonight, don't you agree?" I said, tugging on my anchored arm until the cuffs clanked against the porcelain tub. "I think this'll feel much better for both of us if you let me loose again." Tim looked down at me with a gleam in his eye as if he was thinking of leaving me chained there for good. My fingers squeezed his cock tight, and then I let go of him, settling back in the tub as if I were completely unaware of his presence. Tim hesitated a moment longer, looking down at me in the tub as I tried my best not to look up at him or crack up laughing, before heading into the bedroom without a word. He let me stew a good while, wondering if he planned to spring me after all, if he'd gone to bed, if he'd lost the keys. But eventually he returned, sans his wet clothes, but with the key to the handcuffs.

His cock had begun to soften from the state it had been under his wet clothes, but it was still half-hard. It throbbed slightly as the blood pumped through it as he stood beside the tub. He held the key up and my eyes shifted from his genitals to his hands. "You want out," he said, but then his dick gave a jump as he flexed that muscle in the perineum that I was supposed to be relaxing, calling my attention to his crotch again. I didn't need any further encouragement, and eagerly opened my mouth to earn my release—and his.

And thus began the bathing rituals.

The rituals vary, depending on the time of day. Nighttime baths are more elaborate, which isn't any great surprise since both of us have more time then and less pressures from the world outside our little apartment. But there are certain other intrinsic factors that lend themselves to this sort of extra elaboration at night, like lighting. By day, there's really not much you can do, one way or the other, to create a mood or atmosphere with lighting, but for our nightly baths, Tim has bought these enormous three-wick scented candles which he'll place on the windowsill or the stovetop or the floor. They cast a soft, flickering light and perfume the air with their aromatic essences—vanilla, lavender, jasmine—all of which help cast a quiet, romantic overtone to what we're about to enact, the perfect ambiance in which to relax into each other's love and caring and our mutual desire. Sometimes, when Tim's feeling playful, he'll make shadow animals with his hands and cast them against the far wall, the tub, my flesh beneath the water's ripples. His favorite is to cast a wolf's head and have it stalk across my body until the image snaps at my cock beneath the water; depending on Tim's mood the Shadow Wolf either tries to bite it off or perform fellatio.

If we're eating at home, the night ritual starts with dinner. But even if we're dining out, our repast plays a healthy part in the healing, since I've had to cut back on certain foods that can irritate the hemorrhoids. Thai is pretty much verboten for now, since all my favorite foods are either spicy or have nuts, and Indian and Korean have likewise proven too rough on my sensitive system. Also forbidden are my after-work Snickers bar snacks while waiting for the subway. But one of the advantages of living in New York City is the abundance of different types of cuisine, at all price ranges, so we've still got plenty of savory options. But most of the time we eat at home, anyway, not just because it saves money but also because both Tim and I love to cook.

It doesn't matter whether Tim or I is preparing dinner, it's all part of the ritual. We're beyond the score-keeping stage of the relationship, and simply relish in the nourishing of feeding and our pleasure in eating—and the other pleasures that are to come.

Sometimes, while we're cooking, Tim will slide the tabletop a few inches and begin running a bath. The wood lid serves to keep the water hot, and as we eat, the tub will radiate warmth to our legs. It's a delicious feeling that starts the relaxation as tension begins to drain from our legs and drip away through the soles of the feet. Because New York is such a pedestrian town, we're all of us on our feet all day long, dealing with the hassles of commuting and crowds and worrying about being late and in general just pounding the pavement.

And once the food starts to hit the stomach, satisfying both hunger and taste buds, it's so much easier to just let go of all that stored up tension and worry from the day. Which is what made the rituals as important as the baths themselves; they removed, or at least dealt with, some of the possible causes of the hemorrhoids in the first place. They were an attention to the details of daily pleasures in our lives, all those small sensory moments of joy that we so often overlook or don't consider significant. And the most important part of the rituals, the togetherness, is the truest panacea that exists.

All of those small details, more than the sex we had before, during, or after I slid into the warm water, was what came to matter most to us; sex was just one of the ways we expressed our delight in each other, that giving of pleasure and the receiving of it in return.

Mind you, we liked the sex a lot, too, wet and messy as it often became. Nighttime baths always began slow and gentle, with Tim and I taking turns using a sponge across each other's bodies. We began buying water toys for each other: rubber duckies and funny soaps and wind-up plastic frogs that kicked their legs and swam. I bought a little catnip mouse the day after Tim bought me a small boat, and we played Stuart Little for a while until our playing with each other knocked the mouse and boat out of the tub. Sometimes Tim would join me in the tub; sometimes he'd stand outside it, standing naked by my side. Either way, we'd usually wind up splashing water all over the linoleum by the time we were done for the night and moved into the bedroom to drift into sleep or the living room for some mindless television viewing while we cuddled.

The daytime baths have their rituals, as well, although neither of us can really afford to take as much time with them because of our jobs. But the whole act of this enforced daily relaxation has made both of us aware of how much daily stress we had in our life, from jobs to socializing to just getting through the day, and how much of it was self-imposed. Taking time out to interrupt our hectic schedules has been proof positive that we can stop to smell the roses, as it were, and calm down and still accomplish everything important that we need to.

Often, when we were on tight schedules at work and couldn't afford to run overtime, Tim would come home on his lunch break a half hour before me. He'd cook something for us to eat and begin to draw a bath for me. By the time I got home, he'd have eaten already. As soon as I got home, I was ordered right into the tub, and it was only when Tim had to head back to work and I was allowed to get up and dry off and get dressed again, that I was also permitted to eat whatever Tim had cooked up for me

It was hard, sometimes, to relax when we were as rushed for time as these lunchtime trysts were. But at the same time, they were invigorating. There was something both romantic and illicit about having a "nooner"—quick sex in the after-noon before going back to work, and I think both of us tackled our afternoon's tasks with more pep as a result.

For daytime baths, Tim didn't fill the tub entirely. I'd

already showered in the morning, and the important part of my anatomy, as far as these baths were concerned, was my ass; with only a few inches of water in the tub, my sore ass was sure to stay covered no matter at what angle I sat in the tub.

Of course, before any bathing—night or day—there is the undressing. No matter how pressured we were to get back to work, undressing me was one thing Tim never rushed. Often, during the day, I was not allowed to undress Tim in turn, since we didn't have the time for sex or we had to be careful to keep him from getting wet. Sometimes I'd unzip his fly despite his protests, and suck his cock while I soaked my rear. We didn't always climax during these daytime baths, that wasn't the point. And Tim never seemed to tire of making me feel like he truly cared that I was healing, that he was an active part of the cure. I'm sure that if anything helped me get better, his love was the medicine that did it as much as the baths, that focus and attention he paid my body as he slowly pulled a sock from my foot, holding my leg with his other hand to support it as the sock came free and lowering my leg gently back to the ground until I could put weight on it and support myself again.

At night, we had the time to peel each other from our clothes, and it was like pulling away all the cares and worries of the outside world, until only the two of us remained, stripped down to the essence of our being and our relationship, our skin raw with desire for one another other. And we'd kiss and embrace, and caress one another, and our movements sent candle-lit shadows flickering, and whirls of steam rose from the porcelain claw-foot tub in our kitchen.

And to think that when I was a kid, I used to live in terror of one of my parents saying those two most-feared words, "Bath Time!" Oh, what a world of difference being in love makes!

I REMEMBER YOU WELL
IN THE CHELSEA HOTEL

SIMON SHEPPARD

"AND THAT WAS New York—" the song goes.

Only I do remember you well, in the Chelsea Hotel, a fucking long time ago. We met, remember, in the room of a mutual friend, and though I wasn't sure you even liked me, we walked out together and took the elevator down, and in that same elevator car was one of the two guys who wrote *Hair*, remember?

And it turned out we both lived on the Lower East Side, back before it got gussied up, when the instant you left St. Mark's Place it was just one bleak battlefield, all crumbling crap tenements crawling with junkies and old Russians and penniless would-be bohemians, like you.

And me.

Remember?

And we ended up back at my place, walking a long walk through the leafless gray winter. As soon as I turned on the light, the roaches made a halfhearted stab at running away, and I said something, but you just squeezed my hand and laughed, and that was the first time you touched me. You hadn't even shaken hands back at the Chelsea. Fred had been sitting between us, so I doubt our hands had even brushed when we'd passed the joint.

I switched on the reel-to-reel tape recorder, and it was probably the Velvet Underground—as much as I'd liked them back in Ohio, once I got to New York, I played them damn near incessantly. Or it might have been Leonard Cohen, I don't know. And I wish I could remember what we said to each other, but it was such a damn long time ago, long before Times Square got cleaned up and Disneyfied, before the neighborhood south of Houston Street became a magnet for the art-acquiring bridge-and-tunnel crowd, even, I think, before John and Yoko were hanging out at that bar on the Bowery. A long time. Back before AIDS and the George Bushes and the death of hope (or at least hope's demotion to just another postmodern irony). Oh, and back before I'd ever fallen in love, anything like love, with anyone. Until you.

It started with sex, of course. The mattress on the floor was just about the only furniture, and the incense almost made the place smell good, or at least less bad. Afterward, we took baths in the big kitchen sink that doubled as a tub. We shivered while we got dressed, then decided to go to Yonah Schimmel's for knishes, two happy boys in navy pea coats, breathing postcoital steam into the frosty air. I swear, I remember we did that, though at this point, who's to say otherwise? Even if you're still alive, I doubt you'd argue the point. Not that we didn't argue, that winter of slush and love and inexpert anal sex, but it was over Mao and Godard and a lot of things that seemed so damn important back then. Who'd ever have thought that…oh, well.

The rest of the winter? Hmm. Well, I had a straight job, which was odd because you were straighter-seeming than me, looked for all the world like the 22-year-old preppie you probably had been before New York, though you never confessed about that. So we met at night and on weekends, mostly at my place, since you had a roommate. As we fell further into what we both must have thought, or believed, or known was love, you'd spend more and more time with me on East 11th. Sometimes we'd just stand together in the dark, hand in hand, looking out the grimy window at, mostly, an airshaft, and listening to sirens, my reel-to-reel tapes, and the neighbors screaming in at least four languages.

My job was shitty, and I never had enough money back then, so I can't remember us doing much of anything that cost more than a few bucks. I suspect, at this remove, that you had some money you weren't telling me about—who else but a trust-fund baby could live without working, unless he was a hustler or a drug dealer? And though you *might* have peddled your ass or sold smack, I somehow doubt that. Seems more likely that Daddy was rich. But if that was the case, you kept it quiet. And, given the ethos of slum bohemia, that would have made sense. So it was mostly walks through Tompkins Square Park, rather than uptown culture. And that was all right with me. There was that time that Fred took us both to the premiere of some movie—he was better connected than we were, and he definitely came from money. We spotted Candy Darling in line, being squired by that writer who'd been the boyfriend of the cult Russian painter, remember? Remember how gorgeous she looked? Fred knew her, of course, but then, he seemed to know everyone worth knowing in the downtown scene. Good old Fred. I suppose he's definitely gone, now—he was a lot older than us.

That was the night, I think, when we slung our jackets over our laps and gave each other hand jobs while the movie was playing. I didn't come, but you did, which made for some messiness around getting home. It's surprising, really, how vivid that moment seems to me now, even though it's tough for me to reconstruct the details of your face, except in little cubist glimpses: an eye, the curve of your nose, your smile. But God, you had a nice dick. That I remember. And you knew how to kiss, or at least, back then it seemed to me you did. That was before a lot of kisses in my life, and I'm hoping the same goes for you. Wherever you are. Or nowhere.

Spring came, which was a fucking blessing, and fitful flowers bloomed amongst the dog shit and used glassine envelopes. It was about then that I came home from work to discover that junkies had broken into my one-room apartment. Okay, maybe they weren't junkies. Maybe they were just music lovers with a yen for my reel-to-reel recorder and my collection of tapes. Who the hell can know for sure? I went down to the corner to call you—you had a telephone, but I didn't. I, half-hysterically, told you that someone had ripped off my best clothes, some of my books, and all of my tapes, except the Velvet Underground one, which wasn't on the recorder as usual, but had been fortuitously shoved under a rickety secondhand table. The thieves had come up the fire escape and in through the grimy, now-broken, window, and I was afraid they would do it again, come back for what little they'd left, I said, so you told me to pack what was left in my suitcase and move in with you. But they'd taken my suitcase, too, so I bought some big garbage bags at the corner bodega and, after you arrived, we schlepped all my worldly goods back to your place on Avenue B.

Your roommate had never liked me, but you assured me on the way over that you paid the lion's share of the rent, so he'd just have to accept my presence. I think that I never loved you more than I did at that moment, my rescuer whisking me through the Lower Manhattan twilight, off to his shabby fourth-floor walk-up castle. I bet that that was the night you first fucked me, instead of the other way around.

Your roommate, whose name I've conveniently forgotten, soon became so fed up with me sharing your bed that he moved out, and so I took over his room and his rent, paying less than I had on Eleventh Street. The room was nicer, too— at least the walls weren't painted black.

We began dropping acid together. We'd done it once or twice before, but now we tripped together every weekend or two. And if it was sometimes unpleasant, almost unbearably grueling to deal with each other's theoretically naked selves while negotiating the squalor of the Lower East Side, there were also times of incredible wonder, of feeling utterly connected to one another. Remember?

Fred began to get sick. Back then it wasn't you-know-what. It was just cancer, and eventually he decided to give up his rooms at the Chelsea and move back in with his ex-wife down south somewhere. Before he did, he threw himself a going-away party, and just about anyone who was interesting in the New York scene at the time packed into his place—Charles Ludlam, the Factory crowd, I think Patti Smith might have been there but I'm not too sure. Back then, it was possible to live cheaply in some loft somewhere and be an artist—or at least artistic—and be fascinating. Now lofts cost a fortune and New Yorkers are either interesting and desperate, or comfortable and boring. But, you know, that's progress.

Do I sound bitter? I don't mean to. I guess I'm one of the comfortable, boring people now, too. For years, I've lived in Park Slope, not in the East Village. And most of the time I don't think too much about it, where my life has gone. What's the use? Honestly, I don't think much about you, either. It's just that I was going over some stuff I kept from those days: yellowed copies of the *East Village Other*, a program from when the Living Theater appeared at the Brooklyn Academy of Music, things like that. I didn't find any photos of you, unfortunately. I wasn't much into taking pictures back then; I think in some stupid way I thought photography represented a failure to Be Here Now. Nowadays I wish I had more souvenirs: photos of the guys I fucked, the men I loved—chiefly you, I guess—and of myself, when I had hair and hope.

God, I'm getting maudlin.

So we were at Fred's party. I was talking to somebody or other—I'd like it to have been Little Joe D'Allessandro, though I'm not at all confident it was—when I noticed you talking to someone, across the room. Someone gorgeous. He was quite unlike either of us, not really like anyone else at the party. He looked healthy, vibrant, and utterly innocent. Well-built, too—all muscles and tight clothing. I confess: I wanted him; I lusted after his non-bohemian ass. But you had, apparently, gotten there first. So I hung out some more at Fred's place, drinking and smoking dope, trying not to notice what you were up to, until you turned up at my side. You asked if I was ready to go, and I was.

A couple of weeks later, there was a big antiwar demonstration in Central Park. I probably wore my Chairman Mao button—Jesus, that was one thing you were absolutely right about. Anyway, there we were, somewhere in the vicinity of the Bethesda Fountain, which was later made famous by *Angels in America*, but back then just a fountain. We were stoned, and despite the righteous anger of the occasion and the fact my job was going to shit, I looked at you in the sunlight and just felt the most overwhelming affection for you, and an unreasonable, oceanic sensation of joy. I remember that, I do. That moment. Better than things that happened last week.

And then you said you'd be right back. I watched to see where you were going. And then there you were, with the handsome guy from Fred's party. I guess I must have felt jealous. I know I did. Which was stupid, I suppose, since we already had decided we'd have an open relationship, that we were just boyfriends, buddies who fucked around on the side. I mean, those nights you spent at the baths, I usually felt good about having the apartment to myself. But when I saw the way that you two looked at each other—not that it was easy to see among those throngs of demonstrators—it felt different somehow. I just walked the other way and took the subway home.

"So who was that?" I asked when you finally walked through the door.

"Who?"

I found it hard to believe you didn't know whom I was talking about. "The handsome guy from Fred's party. The one you walked off to see."

"Oh, Noel."

"Yes, him."

"He's an actor. From Hollywood, actually. He has a part in a new off-Broadway show. A musical, I think."

I didn't say anything.

"Hey, what's wrong? You jealous? You don't have to be, he's just a friend."

I don't know, something just kind of snapped. Maybe it was time. "Fuck you," I said. "Fuck you."

"God, you fucking asshole. It's not like we're monogamous or anything. But then, that's just like you. So damn possessive. Like you give a damn about me. You don't even know fucking anything about me."

It wasn't the time to say *I love you*. And anyway, at that moment, I had my doubts. The argument spiraled out of control, and ended up with one of us stomping out, I don't remember which. Things were pretty chilly between us after that, like you'd never really loved me at all. Or maybe vice versa. Or both.

A few days after the argument, I called Fred, who was still trying to get himself out of New York, and asked him for Noel's phone number. It turned out that Noel's dick wasn't near as nice as yours, and that he wasn't as good a kisser. Actually, it turned out that he really was almost as clean-cut as he seemed, except for wanting to spank his sex partners. He ended up getting good reviews, but the show didn't, and I guess he moved back to L.A., because a few years later I saw him on TV every once in a while, playing smallish parts in cop dramas and things, until one lucky break in an action film turned him into a star of sorts. I don't know, did we all want to be stars back then? Or legends?

A week or two after I fucked Noel—I hadn't let him spank

me, because I was afraid the marks would show—you told me to move out. I never was sure whether Noel told you what happened, or if Fred had, or if you just figured it was time to finish things; lives do have their shapes, natural arcs, even if it took me a few more years to find that out. It was upsetting and inconvenient having to find a new place to live, but I figured I would survive, and I did. I found another boyfriend, and then another, and I managed to make it through the 1980s alive. I'm hoping you did, too. Both things.

And now it's lots of years later. Lots and lots. I have a boxed set of Velvet Underground CDs, with a peel-off banana on the cover, just like on the jacket of their first LP. I tried doing a Web search for your name, but it's a common name, and I don't remember all that much about biographical details, so I got nowhere.

I'm looking out at spring in Park Slope and listening to Nico singing, and thinking, yes, I did love you. Maybe in that stupid way young guys usually love each other, but I did. I hope you know that. I hope you know that for sure. Wherever you are. Or nowhere.

And sometimes I end up on the Lower East Side, furniture shopping, or something, and I do. I think of you. And those days.

And that was New York.

And I wonder: Do you remember me?

Because I sure as hell remember you.

ABOUT THE
CONTRIBUTORS

SHANE ALLISON has had poems, stories, and interviews published in *Outsider Ink.com* , *Velvet Mafia, Suspect Thoughts, Mississippi Review, Mc Sweeney's, zafusy, juked a New Delta Review, Best Black Gay Erotica, Ultimate Gay Erotica 2006, Cowboys: Gay Erotic Tales, Hustlers, Truckers: True Gay Erotica, Muscle Worshippers, Love in a Lock Up* and has work forthcoming in *Best Gay Erotica 2007*. His chapbook *I Want to Fuck a Redneck* is forthcoming from Scintillating Publications.

JAMES ANDREW CLARKE was born in Jamaica. Presently he lives in New York.

TED CORNWELL's stories have previously appeared in a couple of Alyson anthologies as well as in one from Arsenal Pulp Press. His poetry has appeared in several journals as well.

STEVE DUNHAM's work has won the 2001 Maggie Award for Best Fiction, and his work has been published by Alyson Books, Haworth Press, and Genre Magazine. His well-reviewed novellas, *Tales of Teddy* and *Afternoon in the Balcony*, are available via www.authorhouse.com.

Author/editor **MICHAEL HUXLEY**'s most recent writing

appears in the poetry collections, *Van Gogh's Ear, 2, 3 & 4; Chiron Review; Best Gay Love Stories 2005; Best Gay Erotica 2005; My First Time 4; Ultimate Gay Erotica 2006; I Do/I Don't: Queers on Marriage; Walking Higher: Gay Men Write About the Deaths of their Mothers; Wet Nightmares, Wet Dreams;* and the upcoming *Travelrotica for Gay Men.*

Twenty-one-year-old **MARCUS JAMES** is the author of *Following the Kaehees and Blackmoore* and is a contributor to *Ultimate Undies: Erotic Stories about Lingerie and Underwear* from Alyson Books. He can be reached at: www.myspace.com/marcus_james and www.marcusjamesbooks.com.

TIMOTHY J. LAMBERT coauthored *Three Fortunes in One Cookie* and *The Deal* with Becky Cochrane, and is one-fourth of the Timothy James Beck writing team. His short story "The End of the Show" was in *Best Gay Love Stories 2005*, and he has recently selected stories for Richard Labonte's *Best Gay Erotica 2007*. Timothy currently lives and dances in Houston. Visit him at www.timothyjlambert.com

JACKSON LASSITER's work can be found in various venues, including *Big Tex[t], Jerry Jazz Musician, Harrington Gay Men's Literary Quarterly, South Loop Review, Heartland Review, Bylines, Ink & Ashes,* and *The Binnacle.* He lives and writes in the San Francisco Bay area, in a home he shares with his partner and a snappy Shih Tzu named Mona. Contact him at LuckyJRL@hotmail.com.

STEWART LEWIS's first novel, *Rockstarlet*, is now available from Alyson Books. He is living in New York City where he is finishing his second novel. For more information, please visit www.stewartlewis.com.

JULIAN J LOPEZ, who was born in Guadalajara, Mexico, in 1974, and arrived in Los Angeles at the age of four, now lives in Long Beach, California. He devotes his spare time to writing fiction and non-fiction. His previous published work has consisted of a short story entitled "Alonso's Modesty" in the anthology, *My First Time, Vol. 3,* from Alyson Books. Julian has also published various articles in local Long Beach newspapers and cover stories in an animal welfare magazine, (*Friends for Life Magazine,* a publication by the spcaLA/Society for the Prevention of Cruelty to Animals Los Angeles), which he managed as magazine editor. The journalism major from California State University Long Beach has also served in various public relations capacities, including advertising, which he now commits to during the day. Julian is currently completing his first novel and various alternative short stories. He serves on the Board of the Long Beach Gay and Lesbian Center and lives with his dog, Milly.

MICHAEL T. LUONGO is a New York City—based free-lance travel writer, editor, and photographer who rarely writes about New York. Instead he concentrates on the Middle East, Latin America, and more than eighty countries where his travels take him. His work has appeared in *National Geographic Traveler, the New York Times, the Advocate, The Chicago Tribune, Bloomberg News, Out Traveler, Passport, PlanetOut,* and many other publications. He co-edited Continuum Press's *Gay Tourism: Culture, Identity and Sex,* the first academic book on the gay travel industry. He edited Haworth's travel erotica collection *Between the Palms,* and edits Haworth's Out in the World GLBT travel literature collection. He wrote the 2005 *Frommer's First Edition Buenos Aires,* the top-selling U.S. guide-book to Buenos Aires, bought by 1 in 10 Americans traveling there. His novel *The Voyeu,* based loosely on his previous experiences as a sex researcher, will be published by Alyson Books in Spring of 2007. Visit him at www.michaelluongo.com.

GUYUS MARKS, writer, was educated on the East Coast. With several degrees and too much energy, he learned the hard way that love is a rare treasure. "Live life before it lives you." E-mail Guyus at writerguyusmarks@yahoo.com and keep uncovering that gleam.

TOM MENDICINO is making his third appearance in the Best Gay Love Stories series. He'd like to thank Nick Ifft and Sharon Sorokin, both thoughtful readers.

BRAD NICHOLS is the editor of Tales of Travelrotica for Gay Men series. He's thrilled to be the new series editor for Best Gay Love Stories. He lives in New York, but likes to travel a lot.

GREGORY L. NORRIS is a full-time professional writer whose work can be found monthly in a number of national magazines. He dreamed the idea for "Goombah" pretty much the way the story is told, then wrote the majority of it by candlelight on the night of February 10, 2006, after a violent winter windstorm knocked down power lines across the state of New Hampshire where he lives with his longtime partner, Bruce (who hails from English and German, not Italian, lineage).

NEIL PLAKCY is the author of the gay mystery novel *Mahu* and its forthcoming sequel, *Mahu Surfer*. He is also co-editor of *Paws and Reflect: Exploring the Bond Between Gay Men and Their Dogs*.

ROB ROSEN lives his Best Gay Love Story each and every day with his partner Kenny. He is the author of the critically acclaimed novel *Sparkle: The Queerest Book You'll Ever Love* and short-story collection *Culture Pop*. His work has appeared around the globe in numerous anthologies, journals, magazines, and online literary Web sites. Please visit him at his Web site www.therobrosen.com or e-mail him at robrosen@therobrosen.com.

LAWRENCE SCHIMEL is an award-winning anthologist who has published over seventy books in a wide variety of genres, including fiction, cooking, gender studies, sports, poetry, and more. His short stories, poems, and essays have appeared in over 190 anthologies. He divides his time between New York and Spain.

SIMON SHEPPARD is the author of the short-fiction collections *In Deep and Hotter Than Hell*, as well as *Sex Parties 101* and *Kinkorama: Dispatches from the Front Lines of Perversion*. His work has also appeared in over 175 anthologies, including many editions of *The Best American Erotica, Best Gay Erotica,* and *Ultimate Gay Erotica,* and he writes the columns "Sex Talk" and "Perv." His next project is a historically based antho of queer porn. He went to Morocco a long time ago, but these days he's more likely to be found at www.simonsheppard.com.

From Vancouver, BC, **JAY STARRE** has written for gay men's magazines including *Men, Freshmen, Honcho, Torso,* and *American Bear.* Jay has also written for over 28 gay anthologies including the Friction series for Alyson, *Hard Drive, Bad Boys, Just the Sex, Ultimate Gay Erotic 2005, Bear Lust,* and *Full Body Contact.*

CHARLIE VAZQUEZ is the famed collector of old leather and poisonous lizards. Check out his Web site: www.firekingpress.com. He lives in New York City, and likes e-mails from sexy clowns and horny magicians.

ARTHUR WOOTEN has written for theater, film, and television. Along with *Best Gay Love Stories: NYC*, Alyson Books is publishing Mr. Wooten's novel *On Picking Fruit* and it's upcoming sequel. Originally from Andover, Massachusetts, he currently resides in New York City.

Although originally from west Tennessee, **SHANNON L. YARBROUGH** now calls Saint Louis, Missouri, home. He lives with his partner John and their two cats and two dogs. Shannon is the author of the book, *The Other Side of What,* published in 2003, and an autobiographical book of poetry entitled *A Monkey Sonnet—and other poems that taught me a little about life* which was published in early 2006. His short stories have also been featured on Amazon.com as part of the "Amazon Shorts" program. Besides writing, Shannon enjoys watching movies, painting, reading, surfing the Web, and traveling. He is currently at work on his second novel.